VELOCITY BLUES

VELOCITY BLUES

CLIFFORD ROYAL JOHNS

VELOCITY BLUES

Cover art and design © 2020 by Sean Leddy Creative

Design and interior by ElfElm Publishing

Available as a trade paperback, hardcover, and eBook from Vernacular Books.

ISBN (TPB) 978-1-952283-12-3
ISBN (eBook) 978-1-952283-13-0

Visit us online at VernacularBooks.com

To my wife, Barb, who is my greatest supporter, my first reader, and who keeps me writing by demanding to know what happens next.

And to the faculty, staff, and students at the Stonecoast MFA program. This book grew from a story idea into a novel during the program, helped along by critique, instruction, and enthusiasm from this wonderful crew.

CHAPTER 1

At one thirty in the morning, my boss called me in to work. I ran across the rooftops toward his office, leaping across alleys, tumbling, sprinting, and dodging around ventilation plenums and standpipes as I usually did, hoping he had a job for me but suspecting that he had called me in to fire me because I was such an unreliable courier.

All around me, delivery drones flew out of their holes, buzzing like cicadas, bobbing around obstructions, dodging each other, darting low above the roofs, then floating down among the buildings to leave packages in secure drop boxes. That was usually my job too—delivery drone. Except I was human, more or less, and I couldn't fly.

I worked for Cagle doing odd jobs that required lots of energy but not much focus or concentration. Cagle was a low-end hoodlum with delusions of mediocrity who got lucky a few times and built up a small business. He had a tilt to his head and a swagger that made him look like he was trying to look tough—someone's little brother trying to play a part. He paid me enough to cover my rent but not quite enough for sufficient food. Admittedly, I ate a lot.

I passed security on the first floor of Cagle's building then danced backward up the stairs. I danced not because I was happy but just to expend energy. Ratchet, Cagle's guard and all-around torpedo who was Energy like me, let me in the door. Cagle's office was well lit and glossy but had too many chairs to have much room to fidget.

Instead of firing me, Cagle handed me a box about the size of a pound of butter. The box felt cool and a little moist with condensation. It was light brown on one side, fading to green on the other, and speckled with dark spots—like a slab of dead trout.

Cagle talked while I danced, wiggled, and played finger games. He was used to his Energy employees constantly fidgeting, but he sighed with disgusted irritation anyway. I was young, frenetic, and unfocused, even for an Energy.

"Go to the Castle Wheel," he said. "Find an E-woman dressed in green, wearing a stainless-steel bolt through the top of each ear and a brass-colored tattoo of a Phillips-head screw on each side of her neck. Give her the box, then return immediately." He paused. "Take it directly to the Castle Wheel, Zip. Give it to Bolt. Don't mess around, don't get distracted, don't take the long way. Directly there and directly back. Understand?"

I had trouble listening to such long sentences spoken by a regular person—a Slug as we called them, as in sluggish and slow. The slack time between his words seemed long enough for a whole conversation for an E like me. So, while he talked, I thought about trout-flavored ice cream. About how a fudge-coated ice cream sandwich—maybe not trout-flavored—would taste mighty fine right then. About fishing with my mother. I caught three lake trout in one day when I was ten—back when I was Zane, back when I was Gifted. By the time I had fully transitioned to E at sixteen, I had chosen to call myself Zip. The name fit me.

Before that night—before Cagle gave me that package—all I wanted was to be normal, to be able to stand still or even sit down for a moment, to be able to focus on one thing for more than a few seconds at a time. I wanted to be useful as more than just a courier. I wanted to be as I had been before I changed. But like Wilde said, "When the gods wish to punish us, they answer our prayers."

Nodding vigorously to show I understood Cagle's directions, I imagined stopping by to see Bang on my way to the Castle Wheel. Her place wasn't really on the way, but I figured I had time. Grilled trout tasted good, but I hadn't had the bank for that kind of food in a while. All the food I paid for had to be high calorie, vitamin enriched, and cheap. I was an E. Energy, that is. Running and eating were my life.

When Cagle appeared to be done talking, I strapped the package to my back, dashed past Ratchet, sped down the stairs and out of the building. Running full speed was love and cheeseburgers. When I got to the Gogo Cleaners, I leapt onto a moving Boxwheel delivery van making its slow autonomous way through the alley, reached a ledge, and swung up to the roof, then raced on, keeping my mind occupied with timing my cross-alley leaps while avoiding smog filters, air conditioning units, roof gardens, and solar panels.

Some thoughtless workman had left an empty brown Derpal bottle on the roof path, so I slowed long enough to place it safely out of the way in a corner. There were only about a thousand E in Chicago, but we spent a lot of time running roofs.

At the end of the block, the circle mark on the roof left by the RoRuCo showed clear and bright, and there were no delivery bugs in the air, so I dove a sweet rotating gainer toward the roof across the alley. The alley spun beneath me, displaying the blurred green and blue from the Forget What store-front awnings as they reflected the brilliant white streetlamps. The Dopplered thump of two ground cars echoed from the buildings, and their combustion engines made the greasy, thick, usually delicious odor of donuts hanging over the alley smell like smog. On the flipside, the man in the moon looked back at me with one eye covered by a cloud as though he were winking.

When I landed roof-top on the other side of the alley, I automatically turned toward Bang's but angled back after a few blocks.

Castle Wheel, Zip. Castle Wheel.

I repeated my destination every time I landed after a flip. Castle Wheel. I didn't need to flip as I jumped, but it soothed me to fly through the air, seeing the world whirl, tasting the air, hearing the echoes come and go with the rotation.

Woman dressed in green. Bolts. Brass screws. Castle Wheel.

The Castle Wheel was a gathering place for Energy, people like me who could no longer stand still long enough to hold a real conversation or a real job. We weren't born that way. We were mistakes, a genetic experiment gone wrong. Our parents paid lots of money for genetic modifications to their test-tube babies to make their children brilliant and calm, energetic and strong—the "Gifted Kid" program. But the designers hadn't tested the modifications long enough; they didn't want to wait twenty years to see how adulthood would play out. When the first Energy started having problems, the designers stopped the program, but by then there were many thousands of Gifted Kids spread across fifteen years. And we needed to be among our own at times, like at the Castle Wheel, just to stay sane, just to spend some time in a place where time moved at our pace.

After a bit of rain, running the roofs at night tasted of pennies, spring, smog-grit, and independence, although the independence part was invariably short lived.

There were no street names on the rooftops, and being easily distracted, I often got lost on my high-speed journeys. There were obsessively dutiful E, members of the Roof Runners' Collective who kept up the RoRuCo symbols at the roof edges to guide an E's speed, warning of dangers like damaged roofs, E-traps placed to purposefully trip, hurt, or even kill Energy, and other full-speed worries. As I ran, I watched for the symbols while I scanned for the glow of the Castle Wheel.

Finally, the neon wheel appeared on the street below, glowing like embers. I was a minute or so late, but within what I considered acceptable parameters for a courier job. I swatted away a tube-carrying delivery bug, then flipped the two stories to the ground, landing with an easy give in my ankles, knees, and hips, softly as a falling mouse hair. The street was wet and reflective from the earlier rain. There were no peds. I stepped into the glow and steadied my vibration long enough for the gatekeeper to recognize me.

A gaudy neon model of the door hung over the entrance of the Castle Wheel, announcing the club's presence. It cast a sepia wash on the wood door and on the gatekeeper, making them both appear antiquated. The sign buzzed like a short circuit and smelled faintly of ozone. A square hole to the right of the sign produced a hollow whistle as the fans inside sucked cool night air into the club. The wooden door to the Castle Wheel was round and half again as tall as I was. It was held together with eight wide steel bands secured with one hundred and twenty-nine bolts, each head about the diameter of a walnut. I'd counted them thirty-four times before on past visits. There wasn't anything else to do while waiting for the door.

When the door finally rolled open enough for me to squeeze through, the confused noise and shifting mass of color flowed out onto the sidewalk like a swirling eddy and drew me in.

Energy lived at a higher speed than Slugs, which is why Slugs often referred to us as Fleas, as in skittish, jumpy, annoying.

Where Energy gathered, though, our world felt smooth, graceful, natural, like a Slug's world does to them. So, when I bounced through the doorway and into the allegro filthstep music and the colorful blur of Energy dancing, the scene was comfortable and calming.

A strobe flashed every second revealing everyone in their apparent quiescent state and leaving behind an afterimage of the dancers in mid-twirl or skim. First glance didn't show my woman in green with the bolts, but a lot of Energy were crowded onto the dance floor, and a fair percentage wore green.

There were forty-seven screens arrayed around the room, each showing a different subtitled channel, and since none of the programs were geared for E, the programs were slow enough to watch all forty-seven and not miss anything if you worked at it. Dancing a complicated gymnastic E-TwistSamba while watching a Bollywood comedy and a news program could keep an E's mind at a pleasure point of sensory, physical, and mental satisfaction.

I thought about the smoothness and flavor that ghee added to biryani and masala sauce, and about the California subduction quake.

An enormous exhaust fan mounted above the dancers seemed to draw people and attention into the dance. It pulled cool air in through small ducts all over the round building, creating a wild whirl of wind that cooled the E on the floor while they expended themselves just for the joy of it. Every so often the Wheel sprayed water into the air intakes, sending a chilling mist gusting through the room to prevent us from overheating as we danced.

Package, woman in green, brass-screw tattoos. Bolt.

I didn't want to forget that I was there to deliver the package. I pulled the dead trout around to my chest so I wouldn't lose it. About half the people in the room were willing to steal something if they thought it was worth the effort, and while a degree of honor existed among Energy—most wouldn't steal from another E—I wasn't about to take any chances.

I wiggled between an E-woman wearing a utility SkinSuit like the one I wore and a Slug who stood at the bar loitering through a double something and watching the Energy blur in the bar mirror. I punched in my order for a PowerBurst drink, then palmed the reader and turned around, waiting for the next strobe flash. A second is a long time. A man to my left hopped into the air and started a spin; another grabbed a swing bar and began a reverse flip up to one of the dancing platforms. The entry door finally finished rolling closed, sealing in the noise and flickering light.

Two E conversed next to me about SpeedShoes. After spending time with Cagle, I appreciated being able to understand the conversation without having to concentrate while waiting for each syllable of the word "metatarsal."

The flash popped again and there she was, dressed in a green dance outfit with stainless bolts, just as Cagle had said. Bolt flashed loose and relaxed, her arms flung up and her fingertips touching like a ballet dancer's. She looked as if she might be entranced. Her loose skirt bunched up on her legs and flared out a bit. She was long and tall and put together nicely for an E. She appeared to be falling.

I suddenly recognized her. She was a friend of Carrot's who had been happy, friendly, and enthusiastically welcoming of the nervous, newly transformed sixteen-year-old E I had been just a few months earlier. I hadn't caught her name at Carrot's party, but Cagle had said her name was Bolt, which seemed to fit her very well.

My PowerBurst rose up through the bar. I grabbed it and gulped it down, then strolled nonchalantly—at least as nonchalantly as an E can stroll—over toward where I'd last seen her. I danced a short regression to a stop, then looked down. The next flash freeze-framed several people who were staring at her. Even in the crowded shadows, shaded from most of the flashing, fluctuating light, Bolt's body glowed green. She lay on the floor, not moving at all, completely still. E are never still if they're awake—and alive.

Bolt had short hair, like most Energy, and her ear-bolts were glinting, polished, a very pretty accent. The stunning emerald of her embossed dancing outfit, however, was marred by a two-centimeter glossy black circle under her left breast. In the lingering light from the flash, eight legs from the small, round FleaSapper blossomed out, spider-like, then stabbed into her chest. She spasmed once, arched her back as though shocked with defibrillator paddles, then relaxed again. She was Energy when she hit the floor, but she'd be a Slug if she ever stood up again.

I should have dashed for the door, but like everyone else who saw her fall, I stood transfixed, astonished by the simple, intimate brutality of the FleaSapper. The person who sapped her couldn't be far away, but I stared at her motionless body until the next flash came and showed the spider pattern of the FleaSapper more clearly. The flash also delineated a man with a gun kneeling beside her. He was short and square and had a shaved head, but he was Energy like me. He wore a brown jacket, and his white shoes glowed with the after-image of the last flash. His gun was pointed at my chest.

CHAPTER 2

An explosion of stillness spread across the dance floor carrying with it an echo of the word "sapper."

Even now, I hold onto that moment in the Castle Wheel, thinking that I might have done something. I might have reached down and pulled the FleaSapper off her chest before it sunk its piercing legs into her flesh. The base of the sapper carried a knockout, but that would have worn off eventually.

A storm of wild thoughts raced through my mind while I looked down at her lying on the dance floor, but helping her wasn't one of those thoughts. The music played on. The voices drained away into silence for the briefest moment. The man with the gun looked directly at me.

I'm not a big fan of guns. I never carried one, because if I did, someone might take it from me and shoot me with it. I doubted I could shoot someone else even if I were in danger. I didn't think I had that kind of violence in me. Some Energy were stable enough to carry guns, stable enough to actually think a situation through, at least a little, and decide when to use a weapon. But that wasn't me. I was on the erratic side of the spectrum. Attention problems and guns don't mix very well. Even at the time, I knew that much.

E had a fundamental law when it appeared there was going to be a fight—run away. Run away because in a fight of any sort, the E always lost in the end, especially if the police got involved. Run away, because we were fast and usually the other person was not. Run away, because even a broken toe could slow us down enough that we couldn't burn off excess energy. Run away, because sitting still for medical attention was nearly impossible and most doctors weren't trained to deal with us.

He might not have been the one who sapped Bolt; he might not have known why I was there, but I wasn't interested in staying around long enough to find out. The Energy who had danced close to Bolt sprung into the air like gazelles finding a lion in their midst. I sliced through the stunned crowd and out the emergency door before the gunman could decide to pull the trigger.

I launched myself around the corner, bounded off an old refrigerator, used my momentum to swing from a creaking awning bracket, somersaulted onto the roof, sprinted the length of a warehouse, dove across the street onto the top of a converted school bus that had "Scream" graffitied on the side in fat black-and-blue letters, then jumped to the concrete and tried to slow down.

Who was that guy? Did he sap Bolt? Or was the sapper someone else who watched the gunman and I face off?

No one followed me, but the man with the gun might know who I was, or at least be able to find out who I was.

Think, Zip. Think. But I couldn't.

Since I didn't deliver the box as directed, Cagle wouldn't pay me. If Cagle found out I was more than a minute late, he'd fire me and I'd be starving in a couple of days. What if I'd delivered the box just before she was sapped? Would I have been paid then?

Rainwater pooled over a clogged street drain—smelled of oil and rot, reflected clouds draped across the moon.

Food.

Too hot. I speed-walked west for a while to cool off, but I couldn't stand the slow pace, so I dashed four more blocks, then jogged south to Ohio Street.

Yes, I went home. My one-room efficiency was a coop that allowed me six steps in each direction. It had a fridge and a kitchen countertop that stuck out into the room. Energy don't have a use for furniture. The apartment didn't even have a stove. Cooking is slow, like waiting for a restroom when you're desperate. I needed to pay the rent. The box. Bolts. Brass screws.

I unstrapped the package, placed it on the counter, and eyed it as though it might explode at any moment. It was likely that Bolt had been sapped for this box. I bounced around the room, viewing the box from every angle, then reached out and flipped it over, half expecting it to talk or flop around. It didn't.

The box had no seams. It appeared to be lacking any latch or hinge. A solid, dead chunk of trout that someone had been sapped for. A picture left by the flash of Bolt lying there sapped on the dance floor lingered in my mind. Cagle had given me the box to give to Bolt. If I hadn't been a bit late, maybe I could have done something. Probably gotten myself sapped instead of her, but maybe it wouldn't have happened like that. Maybe she was sapped because she didn't have the box when she was supposed to. Maybe it was my fault she would become a Slug.

Being sapped, changed into a Slug, may seem like the answer to an E's prayers, but it wasn't like that. BetroCo developed the sapper as a fix for Energy. They called it Slow, but the street name was FleaSapper or just sapper. The drug was intended to repair us. But Energy who were sapped usually took months to recover from the initial medical shock, then the slowness of every day got to them psychologically, so they killed themselves or started random, self-destructive behaviors. Toad began picking at his hair until he pulled it all out one day, then he ran full speed into the front of an oncoming train.

We all wanted to be able to focus, to think clearly, to live with hope for a future, to live with more than our immediate needs in mind, but we didn't want to be changed into a Slug either—at least not that way.

Only a few E who were sapped were able to recross the psychological gulf back to Slug life, and only one that I knew of retained her full mental faculties. But even she could not be around other people. She worked alone solving obscure mathematical problems in a specially built house to avoid seeing the rest of the world, to avoid the suffocating feeling that she was moving underwater.

The Velocity vaccine that protected an E from a FleaSapper was also made by BetroCo, the same company who made the FleaSappers in the first place. They made bank off both products, selling to both sides. They called it a "vaccine," even though it was really an antitoxin, so their duplicity wouldn't be obvious to the public, but it was still obvious to us. Velocity would protect us, but it cost far more than most of us were ever likely to ever see at one time.

Because Bolt hadn't had Velocity's protection, all someone had to do was punch the FleaSapper into her skin like a tack to destroy her. Not murder exactly, but close enough. If Bolt had already been protected by a dose of Velocity, she could have smacked her assailant to the ground so the whole of the Castle Wheel could dance a fandango on him.

I bounced a purple racquetball around my room, racing after it, following its trajectory. What to do? Cagle wouldn't know for a while if I'd given the box to Bolt or not. If I opened it, and it contained something of value, then maybe I could say I delivered it on time. I couldn't be blamed for its loss, could I?

Drawing in a shuddering breath, I grabbed the package. It felt cool and moist. There was still no obvious way to open it, no latch or hinge, and no button I could find. It wouldn't twist apart either. No luck.

I did a handstand and hopped around the room upside down, leaving additional SpeedShoe prints on the once-white ceiling, then refocused on opening the box for a moment, then squeezed out the window, climbed to the roof, and ran a few laps, then worked at the box some more. I sucked down a tube of peanut butter and drank a quart of orange juice. I used the bathroom. Three minutes with the box, examining, prodding, and twisting, but it finally hissed, then expanded open when I pressed on all eight corners at the same time.

The inside was icy cold and contained another box. Damn.

I slapped out a progression on the counter, hopped around, then vaulted the counter back and forth a few times.

Shaking and nervous, I was such a frantic, spastic mess by then that if I'd spent the time to try to figure out how to open the inside box, I would have completely lost what control I had. The box was of no use to me. I quickly reclosed the outer box, secured the package back into my carrying strap, and tried to calm myself.

Trout would be a good name for a cat; at least I spent some time thinking about that while I bounced a basketball around the room and thought about Bang and her lavender perfume, and about Gar and his ability to slow down and focus sometimes long enough to talk to his parents, and about Punt who was likely robbing a house right at that moment and stealing all the food in the pantry and the fridge while leaving everything else. Punt had once explained that for some reason Slugs didn't seem to mind theft quite so much if you left all the useless crap they have lying around but ran off with the edibles. "You have to leave the frozen wedding cakes, though," he'd said.

Cagle wouldn't be happy that I'd taken so long. By now he would probably know about the sapping of his client, at least I thought he might. When I had started trying to open the box, I thought I had plenty of time, but an extra four minutes and forty-three is forever to Energy, and while Cagle wasn't an E himself, he had plenty of Energy who worked for him, so he'd know how long four minutes and forty-three was to us.

I strapped the box onto my back again, grabbed my last NutroStick, and dashed for Cagle's place. "The sapper shook me," I'd say. I would say I was worried and hid for a while, then made my way quietly to his place. Yes, that's what happened.

CHAPTER 3

A **light drizzle cooled me as I traveled by roof toward Cagle's** building. The bakery next to his building smelled of fresh bread and sweet frosting. I dropped to the ground and swiped a couple bags of ChewyBacon from the back of an automated Boxwheel that two Slugs were unloading at an S-Mart and ate the treats before I arrived at Cagle's front door.

Cagle lived and worked in a flat-roofed white box—a five-story professional office building, with equally spaced black windows, ten offices, and two bathrooms per floor. He had the whole fourth floor, he and his Energy girls.

The entry guard knew me and let me in. I nodded to the two other guards who wore dark Spyder glasses that obscured their eyes. Spyders looked like large, black-framed sunglasses with black lenses when in operation. They could be programmed for a variety of video feeds and for virtual scenario overlay in dangerous situations. The guards might have been watching me, or surveying the roof and the other exits, or they might have been reading the news, but they were probably watching porn. My wet shoes squished along the carpet as I crossed the foyer, then I trotted up the stairs backward with a skip-step. Elevators made me run in circles.

I knocked on Cagle's door and waited, pacing ten feet in each direction and counting the one hundred and thirty-seven stripes in the Aztec design on the floor and working out Recamán's sequence and the topology it creates in four-dimensional space. Four steps, turn, four steps.

Ratchet opened the door. "What the hell took you so long, Zip, come back via Arkansas?" Ratchet was Energy, but he could slow down just enough to take orders and generally interact with Slugs. That interaction was difficult for him, but he was a good deal better at it than I was. It was a valuable talent I fervently wished I had. Life would be so much easier if I could just talk to Slugs—keep my concentration on anything for more than a half-second. I figured Ratchet was able to talk to Cagle and work a semi-regular job for him because Ratchet wasn't too bright, but he was also a bit older than me. He'd been Energy longer and had likely learned a few more tricks to control his liveliness.

"Arkansas? No, I found a stick and played some bug baseball. I kept hitting grounders, but they weren't delivering anything interesting." I grinned to show I wasn't really smacking down drones and stealing their deliveries, but Ratchet didn't have a sense of humor. I think he actually thought that was what I'd been doing. He continued to glare at me.

"You were told to go straight there," Ratchet said while I ran eights around the office furniture. "He's in the game room. He'll be out in a few minutes."

I hoped the Energy girls would finish him off quickly.

The next three minutes I spent trying to avoid Ratchet's

stare while walking triangular patterns through the abundance of chairs as slowly as I could so as not to get overheated. Ratchet was aggravated, though I didn't really know why. The delivery obviously hadn't happened because the box was still strapped to my back, but it wasn't like it was my fault. Ratchet fiddled with an Aligner, twisting the E-pacifier around and around, sliding tabs over notches, flipping levers, pushing buttons, and compressing the roll, then stretching it out to start all over again. All the while he watched me, but he didn't ask what happened. Ratchet seemed to have expected more of me, like I'd failed him rather than Cagle, which caught in my throat.

Everything at Cagle's place was white or black or polished chrome. His desk and credenza were black lacquer, and even his fixed screen was chrome and shiny. The floor consisted of black and white squares set diagonally, like an old-fashioned bathroom. Ratchet wore black, from neck to tips of toes.

I was hungry. The ChewyBacon was used up.

The window reflected the room. Ratchet wore chrome Spyder glasses, but they were turned off—I could see his eyes still focused on me.

I found some ice water in a steel pitcher, poured myself a glass, and guzzled it down. The ice melted under my tongue as I paced. Finally, Cagle wandered out, looking drained, his blonde hair, cut about an inch long all around, sticking straight out, making his small nose and eyes look even smaller. I fished the box off my back and held it out to him, assuming he'd know the explanation.

Cagle nodded to Ratchet who strode over and took the box. Cagle looked at me, so I tried to hold still. He said, "What happened, Zip? Talk slow."

"Bolt got sapped just as I saw her. A guy was checking her over. He had a gun, and he pointed it at me, so I took off. I laid low for a while, then figured I'd better bring it back here." I paused, then added, "Good thing I didn't get there earlier, or that guy would have taken the package from her when she got sapped."

Cagle sighed, and his shoulders sank. He watched me run twice around the room, then when I stopped and tried to hold still, he studied me for at least five seconds. "You open it?"

I am a very bad liar, so I told the truth very slowly. I said, "It wasn't obvious how." Which was the truth without answering the question. I was good at that.

"Check it, Ratchet," Cagle said. I don't think he trusted me.

Cagle turned back to me. "This delivery was important to me. You were slow."

I wanted to run around the office a few more times to ease my anxiety. Talking to Slugs was a traffic jam. "Couldn't be faster, and like I said, you'd have lost the box."

Cagle didn't seem impressed with my remarkable success at saving his package.

Ratchet nodded an OK, and Cagle pulled a tray of food out of the fridge. I ate a banana, two oranges, a plate of cheese, and some juice with ice, then I started in on the chicken. Cagle watched me. Maybe he thought I wouldn't be able to eat if I was lying, but nothing could take away constant hunger. Not even eating could do that.

"I have another job for you, Zip."

"Don't know," I said, after swallowing the last of a piece of a chicken thigh. It was easier to talk slowly now that I had eaten. "Guns are scary." Fact was, though, I couldn't turn down jobs from Cagle. Without money and food from him, I'd be stealing more than usual, mooching off friends, or else I'd starve to death in a couple days. And Cagle was dangerous. He was erratic and he overlooked consequences, like an E, but he was a Slug, which I couldn't really make sense of. He might make it in the crime business, but he needed to stop wasting his money on E-girls and lavish accommodations and spend more on getting and training a better class of employee.

Ratchet stepped forward. "Did you get a look at the guy who sapped her, the guy with the gun?"

Cagle suddenly turned and glared at Ratchet for interrupting the conversation. I was startled too. Ratchet usually stayed in the background and seldom spoke. I said, "I saw him, but it was only one flash. You know, just a still. He was E though."

Was the gunman really the one who had sapped her? I didn't actually see the assault. Still, I wanted to find out. I hadn't known Bolt well, but at Carrot's party she was the one who gave me the feeling that the Energy community was there with me, that I wasn't alone. Her understanding smile and her clear belief that I'd be fine helped me through the first difficult months after graduating from SlowDown, the special school where my family had exiled me. I had desperately needed Bolt's affirmation then, when my friendless anxiety was starting to feel permanent. I had only talked to her that once, but now I mourned her like she was family. The worst part was knowing that the gov wouldn't care, and being Energy, I didn't have the attention span to investigate who sapped her.

Cagle held up his hand, and Ratchet stepped back and

shut his mouth with an audible click, although he kept furiously working his Aligner. The food tray was empty except for some stripped bones. Cagle said, "Think you would recognize the guy with the gun if you saw him again?"

I thought about that. Not about if I could recognize him; I sure could. His face was burned into my memory. No, the question was whether I should admit it or not. I didn't see anything in it for me. Just dead, maybe.

I was about to say no when Cagle said, "There's money in it if you can."

Ratchet grunted.

"Yes," I said. "I can recognize him."

Strangely, Cagle didn't seem happy about that.

CHAPTER 4

Cagle said it would take fifteen minutes for him to make a few calls, find another buyer, then he could tell me when the second attempt at a delivery would happen. A Slug would have waited there to find out when to come back for the box, but I couldn't jog in place for that long, I'd go mad. Since Ratchet wasn't into two-person E-games, I decided to go for a tour of the neighborhood.

It occurred to me as I spun and double-stepped down the stairs that if I got a good look at the gunman, then the gunman got a good look at me. When I told Cagle I could recognize the guy, I'd expected him to be happy, but he'd seemed annoyed. He didn't say whether or not he knew who sapped Bolt, and he didn't like questions, at least not from me, so I couldn't find out.

Cagle planned to have me deliver the box again. Though the idea of carrying that package frightened me, I didn't have an option—I needed the money now, and I needed the money future employment from Cagle would provide. By the time I pushed through the outside door of Cagle's building, I was worried that I might be considered a witness who would need silencing.

At the bakery where I'd found the ChewyBacon, two Slugs were loading Hoppers into an automated Boxwheel. I slipped up behind the truck, then grabbed a box on my way past. One of the workmen yelled, "Goddamn Fleas," but there was no way he was going to catch me. And they didn't carry guns. I'd checked first.

Hoppers are a tasty combination of sugar and lard mixed with a bit of flour and salt, colored green and shaped like an insect, or perhaps a frog. Quick food, high fat and sugar, ideal for an E-snack. I leapt to an electrical conduit and swung myself up onto a single-story, bounced off a solid-looking metal air conditioner box, and flipped up to a three-story section of an adjacent building. I gulped a few more Hoppers as I ran, then smelled Bang's sweet lavender perfume and hound-dogged the scent to the edge.

Back down at street level, I swallowed my last Hopper and caught up to Bang as she shot out of a jewelry store's rear exit. The alarm clanged, I paused, she saw me, and we bounded up and over and north two streets and through a roof hole into a condemned building, landing on a creaking floor.

We circled each other. She was dressed in loose gray overalls that had vertical black wobbly lines effectively hiding her E build. She wore a matching bandana to keep her blonde hair from flashing around, but her Scandinavian face reflected light even in the relative darkness at the base of the hole in the roof.

"Hey," I said. "Got a customer?" I was asking if her theft

was on spec or if someone had paid for it in advance. Bang was mostly an independent.

"Yeah, I got her ear clamp, it's Movine Pearl with stainless, and a few other things I can find a home for. You?"

"Delivery for Cagle soon, just a little box. I delivered once already, but it didn't take." I wanted to tell her the whole story about the sapping and the gunman and Cagle's odd behavior, but I wasn't going to burden her with too much info. "I got another twelve," I said.

Twelve minutes felt like long enough for us to have a relationship. The whole fall-in-love, make-love, get-over-it sequence, but she said, "Gotta run."

I said, "Bye," and she hopped back up through the hole and was gone. I could have followed her scent, but she'd said not to. "Gotta run" signified the meeting was over. Bang was a good friend. Actually, I was in love with her, but I'm not sure I would have admitted it at the time. I did want to spend more time with her—any time with her. Good friend or not, though, she wouldn't let our friendship interfere with making money. Money was food. Bang was all business when she had business and friendly when she didn't. Regrettably, she had business.

I speed-walked a zigzag to Banko and Booleret's Books, which was really more of a newsstand. Energy could read extraordinarily fast compared to a Slug, which was why screens and Wonky phones were just too slow for most Energy and especially me. If I tried to scroll fast enough to focus on the text, the refresh was too slow, and the text blurred. It took forever to use menus to navigate to the screen I wanted, and the electronics didn't register three out of every four button touches, thinking my quick actions were a detection mistake or a key-bounce. Electronics were designed to interact with Slugs, not Energy. If I wanted to read, I would read paper. I could read at my own speed. If I wanted to talk to someone, I could just run there. Some E had Wonkys, but few actually carried them around.

A magazine near the door had a cover article on Energy, but it was written by a Slug, of course. This writer thought Energy were connected to criminal activity through some kind of genetic link, that Energy would always be a drain on society, that we should be exterminated. He didn't say it exactly in those words, of course, but that's what he meant. Slugs mostly thought that Energy were all criminals and thus dangerous. It wasn't like an E could write a rebuttal. What E could concentrate long enough to do that? And what was worse, there was a snag of truth in the accusation. Hunger and anxiety are powerful influences.

Next to the magazine was a tabloid with a cover story about a once-in-a-thousand-years monsoon storm in Bangalore. The thirty original Energy, the first human experiments and the oldest of our kind, all came from poor families in Bangalore. The city's name rang of home to Energy, of origins, even though no one I knew had ever been there. I didn't read the whole article, I'd bounced in place too long already, but I scanned the first paragraph. Bangalore had been flooded, and not just a small section, but the whole city, and the debris-flow of trees, floating cars, chunks of houses, and other building materials, moved like a bulldozer, slowly toppling buildings and returning the whole city to nature. Purify Humanity had already claimed it was God's wrath.

Either Banko or Booleret came charging out from behind

the counter, red-faced, and tried to whack me with a rolled-up newspaper. "Get the hell out of my store, Flea!"

I worried about the thirty originals and the others who lived there, but I had to run.

I hopped around the corner and entered a grocery, ate three apples and a bag of cheese cubes, then slowed down enough to buy a NutroBar, hoping to make the man think I wasn't stealing.

It was hard to keep a good reputation for Energy. Waiting to pay took an interminably long time even though the person in front of me was getting her change just as I arrived at the checkout. By the time I finished paying and was back on the street, I was hungry again.

I went to KO's. I'd heard the place was fun, but it had already evolved into a mud joint, a mixture of E and Slugs that felt more like a tourist dive than an E-bar. When Slugs found out about an E gathering place, they sometimes went there to see how the Energy lived. I had a Slam drink and watched two Energy girls take a young Slug boy into a back room. It was the same everywhere. Still, it was a shame. An older Slug woman tried to dance with one of the girls for a few seconds, but I couldn't stand to watch, and I squeezed out. In some ways, Energy were a genetic accomplishment, a new revision of humanity, but we were so dependent on Slugs that we might as well have been pets.

I still had a few minutes, so I trotted at street level over to the Long Ochre Mile. Long Ochre was a long thin room, not a mile long, but it was one of only two places in town where there was room to run-dance. The place got its name from its length, and from the wavering color of the walls reflecting the ring of gas jets high in the center of the ceiling. The gas jets generated enough heat to create a chimney effect and pull in cooler air through a variety of oddly shaped and placed windows. I had a Gulp, used the bathroom, and talked to the bartender, Quip, for a few seconds while he danced, kept four half-full wine bottles in the air, and made special drinks for the other patrons.

That's when I saw the gunman again.

He stalled while a waitress scurried past in front of him. Last time I'd seen him, he'd been kneeling beside the sapped Bolt. He was taller than I expected, but he still wore the same brown jacket and white shoes.

Some Energy didn't wear SkinSuits because it marked them as Energy as though by dressing like a Slug they could somehow pass. We couldn't pass, of course. We appeared too obviously different with our wide thighs and arm muscles and long limbs. We looked a bit like Popeye if he were a long-distance runner instead of a sailor. Still, the Slugs liked the idea that some Energy were making the effort to look normal. It made the Slugs feel more comfortable with their invention.

I wore a SkinSuit. I saw no reason to make the Slugs more comfortable.

"Gotta run," I said to Quip, and slipped out the top window, hoping the gunman didn't see me. Running the long way back to Cagle's, I made sure I wasn't followed, though I suspected that the gunman knew who I worked for because he apparently had known Bolt was supposed to receive the package.

CHAPTER 5

Ratchet opened the door. I tried to flash through, but he stopped me. "Slow, remember. So Mr. Cagle can see and hear you, Zip."

I tried to meditate, to ease down. Ratchet finally stepped aside, and I ambled into Cagle's office. Cagle sat behind his desk and stared at his screen, a peaceful scene of boats reflected in the glass front of the bookcase behind him.

"I saw the gunman at Long Ochre a quick run ago. I don't think he saw me."

Ratchet was suddenly next to me, hand on my elbow. "What was he doing?"

"I don't know. Having a drink, I guess. I didn't stick around long enough to spy on him. I got away clean."

Cagle held out his palm to Ratchet in a stop gesture. Ratchet relaxed his grip. Cagle said, "What were you two saying?"

Ratchet took a deep breath. "Sorry, Mr. Cagle," he said slowly and distinctly. "He says he saw the gunman at the Long

Ochre Mile a minute ago, but claims he wasn't followed."

Cagle nodded. Ratchet stutter-stepped back to hover near the door. Seconds ticked by while Cagle thought. I started pacing, saw a few muffins sitting on a tray and ate them. They were probably Ratchet's, but I didn't mind.

"All right, Zip. Here's a hundred," he said, handing me folding. "The client can't take delivery until two. Come back here then. Don't go running around and getting lost or distracted in the meantime. I want you to stay at home and wait, and I want you back here on time.

"That box," he continued, relaxing back in his chair and nodding toward the trout which squatted ominously on his desk, "contains a Velocity vaccine."

Why did he have to tell me that? Just to make him feel important? Why would he try to impress me? I ran a quick loop around the room and did a few jacks-and-toes.

I'd been carrying around a Velocity and didn't know it. What would I have done if I'd known? How on earth did Cagle get his hands on a Velocity vaccine? And he was going to give it to me to deliver again! I wished he hadn't told me what it was. Why did he have to tell me what it was? I read all of Wilde when I was still a kid, back when I could sit and read all day, and like Wilde, I could resist anything except temptation.

Cagle was still talking. "Velocity is expensive. You lose it, I take your life as payment. Do you understand?" He used his tough-guy head tilt. It seemed unlikely he would actually kill me, but I got the idea.

"Yes," I said. His was a rhetorical question, of course, but his statement made me feel guilty anyway, as though I'd already stolen it and used it on myself to protect me from being sapped like Bolt had been.

Cagle went back to looking at boats on his screen. I tried to walk slowly on my trip to the door, but I shuddered and shook all the way.

Ratchet stopped me at the door with a hand on my chest, then handed me a piece of light-blue paper with an address written in pencil. He leaned in close and spoke fast. "Listen, Zip. This is the most likely place he's going to send the package. I know there's no way you're going to stay at home until two, so if you have to get out and run, run there." He pointed at the paper. "Make sure you know the way, so you can go directly there when the time comes. Got it?" Ratchet looked worried. I thought he might be worried about me, but that seemed unlikely.

"Yeah, sure, Ratch. But he said to stay home."

"Good luck with that," he said. Then he pushed me out the door.

So, I went home like Cagle asked. He'd paid me a hundred, and I felt like I owed him that. On the way, I stopped by the KulfiKlatch, an all-night Energy buffet that's fully automated and fast enough, though expensive, and bought some things to hold me over. It was only a few miles out of the way, close enough to a straight line home.

At home, I took off my wet shoes and paced the one small room of my apartment, playing finger games while sucking down a peanut-butter-and-chocolate Swizzie to help me focus my thoughts. The peanut butter had a calming effect, but it didn't help me figure out what to do.

Cagle had said to stay in my apartment until two, but I

figured he knew that was unlikely. Clearly, Ratchet knew that. I decided to go back to Long Ochre and talk to Quip some more. While the Long Ochre wasn't actually in my apartment, it was close. I put my shoes back on, wishing I had a pair of dry ones, and tumbled to the door.

Just as I landed on my feet and reached for the knob, it moved. On tiptoes, I looked into the peep hole. I saw a woman standing to the left, a man with a gun on the right, then noticed a large E push off from the far wall. I leapt away just before a bullet hole opened up where the handle had been. The door flew open with a whump. I guess I screamed or yelled or something, but they caught me before I could turn and run to the window, which was closed anyway. What I was thinking, I don't know.

There were two E-guys and a Slug woman. She was medium height with dark skin and black hair, Pakistani perhaps, or North Indian, wearing a charcoal form-fitting suit with a cream-colored Oxford shirt under her floor-length red coat. She stood still while the men put a clear plastic hobble around my legs and strapped my arms behind my back. One of the men held me still with a hand on the wristband, while the woman closed the door then turned and inspected me. She seemed unimpressed and a bit bored, although to Energy, Slugs almost always look bored. Their faces move so slowly that they appear to lack any animation in their features unless you really watch for it.

"You're Zip?" she asked.

I briefly considered denying it. She was just asking questions she thought I would answer honestly because, why wouldn't I? I'd read a book on police-style interrogation when I was seven, and she was using the right technique. She wanted to start me talking, get me in the mood to answer questions, make me think that if I could give her just a little, I wouldn't get hurt.

I nodded but didn't speak. I didn't want to answer her directly. I didn't want her to feel as though she had power over me.

The E who held my hands twisted the plastic band, tightening it and forcing me to lean to the left to ease the pain. I glanced back. He was smiling at me. He'd probably seen a movie where people in his position smiled to look tougher than they really were, but this guy didn't need to. He was huge for an E. He must have had to eat constantly to keep up all that mass. I probably could have outrun him, but I would never have been able to break free in the first place. The other guy watched from near the door, calmly swaying while rolling three large washers around in his left hand and over his knuckles. He must have been doing mathematical meditation games in his head to stay so otherwise still. He was probably the professional killer, her torpedo. The guy doing the twisting was just muscle. A great deal of muscle.

The Muscle said, "Give Damini her due. Answer her, and slowly. We don't want to hurt you."

It was nice to hear that they didn't want to hurt me, but I had wanted to deprive her of the satisfaction of having me answer. Seemed to me she didn't deserve it. I sighed, slowly enough for her to hear, then answered her question. "Yes." I wasn't sure how much of our sped-up conversation she caught, but she seemed satisfied anyway.

Damn.

She walked to the window. Must have taken six whole seconds. I tried to play finger games to keep from frothing at the mouth, but the Muscle grabbed my two middle fingers and held them together, so I couldn't. I would have played toe games, but the shoes I wore for roof travel were too tight. This was an interrogation method the cops used. Force us to stay still until we'd sell our souls and our friends' souls.

I tried to focus on the woman and suddenly realized that he'd said her name was Damini. I'd been roughed up a few times before, but Energy usually go easy on other Energy. It just wasn't that hard to convince us to talk, so nobody needed to go overboard. Damini, though, had a reputation for having her interrogators go overboard anyway, breaking bones and sometimes even using sappers. I didn't know anyone who worked for her, but friends of mine knew people who did, and they all said not to ever work for her, or even let her become aware of you. Once in her circle, you couldn't ever get out.

Damini was the archetype Cagle aspired to be. She had made a lot of money off E-crime, especially by training Energy to steal, intimidate, and even kill.

I tried to bob up and down to calm my body, to expend some energy, but the E held me down with firm pressure. I tried to meditate but couldn't remember how. Back when the reality of Energy was just coming to light, and psychologists and doctors still had hope that the symptoms were just a temporary effect, they devised mathematical games and tantric tricks that were supposed to calm us, tricks we could employ daily to calm our overactive bodies and imaginations, but more importantly, tricks we could use whenever our worries built to the point of explosive terror, when we were in danger of self-annihilation. I'd learned all those methods at SlowDown, the institution my parents sent me to when I started showing symptoms of transition, of becoming an E. Yet, whenever I needed these techniques most, I suddenly couldn't remember how the games and tricks worked, or I would convince myself they wouldn't work, or I didn't even think to use the techniques at all. It was bank-loan logic. If you were whacked enough to need meditation, you wouldn't be able to summon the concentration to use it.

Damini finally walked back and stared into my eyes. At least I think she did. I was so wild by then I couldn't focus very well. Damini's E, the Muscle, held me decisively in place with his grip on the plastic strap around my wrists. All I could do was breathe rapidly, flop my head around, and blink a lot. Any further movement caused excruciating pain in my wrists.

I didn't deal with stress well. It was one of the reasons I was not a good liar.

"What were you carrying for Cagle, Mr. Zip?"

Was Cagle a competitor, or was he running a part of her business and just working outside her instructions? Maybe Cagle didn't work for Damini, but I still thought she knew as much about what I had carried as I did.

I didn't want the wristband any tighter, so I said, very slowly, "A box." I said it like I was talking to an idiot, but she seemed satisfied with that answer too.

Damn.

The red of Damini's coat reminded me of the poinsettias my parents bought every Christmas. The coat had a smudge on the hip shaped like a duck, a diving duck.

"Mr. Zip, here's what I want you to do. When he gives the box to you again, deliver it instead to this address." She shoved a piece of paper very slowly and needlessly far into a

SkinSuit pocket near my crotch. I would have jumped to the ceiling if I hadn't been held down. Even so, I started bouncing around until the Muscle bent my middle fingers backward and held me down by the wrist strap with even more force.

I grunted. "Cagle's giving me six hundred." A Velocity vaccine was valuable, so I thought I should get a delivery fee, and since I was delivering it to her chosen address instead of to wherever Cagle wanted me to deliver it, I should get a better fee than Cagle had offered, which was actually four hundred, but she wouldn't know that.

She lifted the right side of her lips in what might have been a smile or a smirk, but either way, it scared me. "Your life, Mr. Zip. That's what is in it for you. Your life. I admit it's a lower payment than what Cagle is offering, but it will have to do." She smiled again. She didn't have fangs, but I could feel the arbitrary drip of malevolence, or, perhaps worse, indifference.

I considered telling her that my life was part of Cagle's offer too and that she had a smudge that looked like a diving duck on her coat, but there are times when I am able to hold my wit in check. When I'm terrified is one of those times. Usually.

She nodded to the Muscle, and he released me.

I started furiously playing fingers as best I could with my arms still banded together and remembered for a moment how to meditate, did a few numeric sequences, silently sang a nonsense ditty, did some squats, and shook my head like I was emphatically saying no over and over, all the while resisting the unrelenting urge to slam my face onto the counter.

When I'd settled just enough to look around, Damini's pro had the door open. Damini walked out first, her steps slow as a grocery line on Friday afternoon. The Muscle followed her, doing a happy little toe-heel-toe dance. The Pro went out the door last, closing it slowly while watching me through the decreasing opening.

No smile from him.

was in straps and hobbles, and desperately hungry and anxious, but I still had the focus to realize that, while she could have found me easily enough, I couldn't imagine how she knew Cagle would give me the package again or even how she knew about the package at all.

I hopped around the room twice before it occurred to me to hop over to the cabinet beside the sink, wiggle a serrated knife halfway out of the drawer, and jam its handle by leaning against the drawer so I could saw at the restraints.

Perhaps Ratchet was playing the other side. Maybe that's how Damini knew about the package and found out where I lived so quickly. There was obviously money in it, so I couldn't really blame him.

Well, OK, so I could blame him.

When I'd finally cut myself free, I shoved a precious Erg pill down my throat to calm my hunger and resolved to hear Ratchet's side of the story, then kick him in the head for about three seconds.

I tumbled around my apartment, picking up E-gadgets and putting them down, bouncing balls but not chasing them, drumming on surfaces, thinking about Damini, cheese soup, my broken door, programming stacks and hash tables, ducks, that Fret would be a good name for a cat.

My door hadn't been bolted when Damini's toughs shot the lock and muscled through, so that part of the frame wasn't blown out. I locked myself in, hoping that would secure my room for the few minutes I needed to sleep.

For Energy, sleeping felt like dying. We didn't just fall asleep. We had to shut down at a deep level. It had to be a complete mental release, and it had to be instantaneous, or anxiety and restlessness took over, and we'd start pacing and chewing on our problems again.

Often, when I tried to sleep, I would begin to analyze, dread, and, most of all, worry. I would worry about paying the rent, worry about the pain in my foot, worry about my friends, the police, the guy next door who didn't like Energy and blamed all the problems in the building and even the neighborhood on me because I was the odd one, because I was the one who wasn't like everyone else.

There were E-centric apartment buildings in Chicago, but they were expensive, and I had to eat. Most Energy had rich parents. Normally, only the wealthy could afford the genetic alteration that produced an E, so an E's parents would often pay for an apartment, leaving everything else up to the ridiculous parody of a teenager they had made their kid into. There were also many E who didn't need to work at all, living entirely off their parents' guilt money. But I was an aberration among aberrations. My mother had worked for BetroCo on the Gifted Kids project, so she'd received a deep discount, a special deal. Her Gifted Kid was cheap, but by the time she'd paid the medical expenses, psychiatric bills, and institution costs, all I could do was leave and hope I could survive on my own. There was no trust fund. My parents couldn't help me after I left the SlowDown school.

For the most part, once our parents realized we weren't going to change back into the world-class, focused geniuses we'd been before adolescence, they were willing to see us out the door. No Slug could live happily with an E.

At times, there were E who couldn't, or perhaps wouldn't, settle their minds even for that one micro-moment needed to fall asleep. They couldn't sleep at all. They just kept pacing, their minds running at full speed until they broke down. Usually this happened to E who were first transitioning, but sometimes an E who had been E for a while would crash this way. If I allowed myself, I could keep running long enough that I too would lurch over that precipice. I sometimes wondered if there were E who did it on purpose, who just kept running until it all fell apart and they didn't have to worry anymore. At times that sounded peaceful to me.

I dreamt when I slept. Or, more precisely, I remembered. My dreams were invariably replays of scenes from my childhood.

When I was a child, I was someone else. In my dreams I watched that child who had my old name, Zane, as though I were watching a hidden camera movie that could record the actions and feelings of the protagonist.

Calming my mind with images of Norwegian architecture and log-cabin quilt patterns, I trotted once around the bare room, then leaned against the wall. Corners of my apartment became crisp and defined, the empty NutButter tube on the sink stood out, three-dimensionally bold, vivid in every crease and bit of green-and-red logo, the smell of the E-toughs and of the Slug woman's perfume and her leather coat sharpened, pungent and acrid. The neighbor across the hall was cooking curry, Madras curry. I could hear a clear, clean tone from a violin. and also the diminishing taper of a G chord from a strangled electric guitar played on a radio somewhere. The room was cool. I'd opened the window. I imagined a Mandelbrot picture, drawing the lines and coloring the fields in my mind, disassociating my fears with the momentary tantric trick.

Then I let it all go.

CHAPTER 7

Zane is wearing the cowboy shirt his Aunt Maria gave him for his birthday in February of the year he turned five. He is reading at the kitchen table because his text from the library is too heavy to hold on his lap and the download is too expensive.

His father calls out: "Zane, come into the garage. I have a surprise for you."

The voice carries the tone of something said the second time. Zane is often so intently focused on his studies that he is unaware of the things going on around him, a trait his parents have gotten used to but still find annoying. Looking up from his book, Zane figures out that it's about noon by noting that the sun's rays from the exactly south-facing window cast light onto the floor tile in a perfect rectangle, taking up equal squares on the tile floor. It is a cool, sunny spring day. The dogwood tree in the front yard is dressed in pink blossoms, and the lawn needs a trim. An ice cream truck in the distance plays "Turkey in the Straw." He thinks he might determine the approximate date by measuring the distance from the wall to the nearest edge of the sunlight. Using that information, he could determine the angle, take the inverse, and, knowing his longitude, look it up in a mariner's table.

His father's surprises are seldom surprising, let alone as engaging as the book he is reading, but Zane realizes that his father requires these father-child bonding moments to feel needed and to feel proud of his parenting skills. Even at five, Zane knows he doesn't really need his father to exhibit any such parenting skills, but Zane wants everyone to be happy, so he does what he can to help.

In the garage, his father stops him by the car. "Do you remember back in February you asked if you could have a bicycle?"

He steps aside so Zane can peer around the Moto-400 and see it. The bike is red with a glittery banana-style seat. The back brake is foot operated, and there is an electric hand brake for the front wheel. At the center of the handlebars it has a display with a GPS, an indicator for low battery, and another labeled Maintenance Required. There are five push-button speed settings, a power-assist dial for when you don't want to pedal so hard, a handlebar-mounted trip-and-calorie meter, a notch for his Wonky phone, and wireless speakers. The bike is obviously secondhand, but it is clean and polished and tilted invitingly on its kickstand. Apparently, it is just what he'd asked for back in February.

His father, obviously pleased at having remembered the details, presents the bike with both hands to the side, spread wide and in front of the bike, like a gameshow model exhibiting a new Moto, or presenting a complete automated kitchen with included grocery-ordering software and self-cleaning refrigerator.

"Happy sixth birthday, Zane. I hope you like it," his father says.

This revelation calls for a show of appreciation, but Zane is *still thinking about the book he was reading. He decides that finite-state machines, defined in a modified Backus-Naur form, could be used as a programming model for quantum algorithms. This would allow coders to think of programming as parsing the input stream, syntax checking it at the same time as form-ing an output stream when doing reductions, just as software compilers did, just as the human mind did—well, at least how his mind did. It shouldn't be too hard to compile the language into a normal form for use in the standard synthesizers, simu-lators, and modeling software. He will write to his computing instructor and ask what she thinks. If she decides it's worthy, she will take the time to investigate, publish a paper, and so on. It might take her grad students a couple years with her guidance, but Zane is sure it will prove an important step in quantum algorithm development.*

Zane understands the gyroscopic effects of the bicycle wheels and their effects on balance. With a smile to his father, he con-fidently mounts the bike and begins pedaling down the gentle slope of the concrete driveway. If regular kids can do this, it can't be difficult. The bike wobbles, at first a little, then wildly. He tries to keep it upright by turning into the fall, but the bike begins to topple anyway. According to what he'd read and seen, the bike isn't supposed to lose balance like this. The curved handlebars interfere with his dismount, and he scrapes his hand trying to stop the fall, then skins his knee and lands on his elbow when his body folds to the concrete. The pain bothers him, but the abra-sions will heal quickly, so there is nothing there to be concerned about. It's the fact that the bike didn't balance that frustrates him. Regular kids ride without difficulty. For a Gifted, this should be child's play. He laughs out loud at his own ironic cliché, then stands, ready to try again.

His father, never one to try to understand why Zane laughs in situations that aren't funny, and also not one to worry about minor injuries, helps him off the ground while saying, "Don't look right in front of you. Focus on the long view and look at your objective in the distance. Remember, be patient and focus on the long view."

Zane knows implicitly that he has all the parameters worked out accurately but that overcorrection and micromanagement are his error vectors. His father's advice will remedy this. Experience can be a better teacher than books and a comprehension of physics.

He gets back on his bike and rides it past the sidewalk to the end of the driveway, then falls again when he tries to turn around at the apron. After he picks himself up, he pedals back up the driveway, turns at the garage door and then coasts back down to the end, then finally turns easily and pedals back.

Zane coasts his new bike into the garage, sliding along the concrete with both feet down, then drops the kickstand as he has seen other kids do. "That was really cool," he says to his beaming father. Seeing the principles he's read about put to the test is pleasing and invigorating. "Thank you for the bike," he says with what he hopes is the right amount of enthusiasm.

His father runs his fingers along the hand grip. "I'm glad you like it."

Zane looks at his father for a moment trying to decide what happens next. Finally, he says, "I do," then picks up the book which explains the development of specialized languages for defining state machines in integrated circuits, thinking that maybe he's had enough of that subject.

His father says, "Why did you stop riding? It's a nice day. Why don't you ride around the neighborhood for a while?"

Zane pauses, wanting to say the right thing. "I don't have any-where specific to go right now. There's no long view, no objective in the distance. But when I do have a destination, now I will have a bike to take me there." He smiles up at his father, liking the idea of having a bike on which to ride to the Gifted school. He will be able to read an extra few minutes before leaving.

CHAPTER 8

I **woke up feeling rested and hungry.**

I drank a cold can of condensed milk, ate three slices of bean-beet bread mushed together with salt, butter, and sugar, then I was back running again, this time at sidewalk level so I could run full-out in stretches and not have to worry about running off the end of a block and slamming into the building across the street. Not all the buildings were marked for running by the RoRuCo E.

While I ran, I thought how nice it would be to have a long view, to see down the road farther than the end of the block. I reminded myself that I should do some grocery shopping because my fridge was almost empty, that I needed to tell my landlord that someone had broken in and my door needed fixing, that I didn't have many Erg pills left in my emergency supply, and that Dart would make a good name for a pet asp, although to Energy, a pet asp might as well be a stick.

Pedal had had a bike. It was a blue-and-green racing bike, but he went too fast, and the car didn't see him.

After running off some energy, I turned toward the Castle Wheel. It was only a mile or so away. I planned to talk to some acquaintances there—see if anyone could identify the man who sapped Bolt. But after a half-mile, I decided I didn't want to be anywhere near the Castle Wheel and changed direction back toward Cagle's office.

It was decision time, and my life depended on it.

The long view, Zip, the long view.

When Cagle gave me the box again, would I take it to Cagle's customer or Damini's preferred destination? Damini's argument was persuasive, but then so was Cagle's. Neither choice offered protection, only death by the other's hand.

If I was going to make the right decision, I needed information. I decided to watch Cagle's building and follow Ratchet or Cagle if either came out. Sticking to that goal would be hard, but getting more information, understanding the situation, was critical. It was the logical, intelligent thing to do. Not like me at all. Still, if I could do it, I might find out who worked on which side of the fence. I was especially curious about Ratchet. Did he actually work only for Cagle? Maybe he reported to Damini too, or possibly someone else.

It began drizzling again just as I climbed onto the third-story roof of the building opposite Cagle's.

I slid the last few feet to the edge of the rubberized surface, tottering there for a moment of imbalance, glad that the builder had put twelve bricks of exterior facade above the silver roofing instead of the usual five. The low wall needed tuckpointing, but the bricks held when I grabbed the aluminum-flashed edge and looked down at the well-lit street below.

The road shone wet and crisp in the rain, lit by bright low-power lighting so police video could catch any night activity. Two cars were parked on Cagle's side of the road; one had been there for several days. Opposite the cars, a bicycle was chained to a transport charger. It had no handlebars, and the front wheel was removed and locked up with the frame. A pothole had opened on the left side of a manhole cover and looked like it intended to swallow the entire road eventually, but a scooter would do as an appetizer until then.

Cagle or Ratchet or both might have already left the premises. Was I watching an empty building? Maybe, but I wasn't going inside to find out.

I would wait.

My watch showed only seconds, so I was wishing I'd brought my TenStop. That watch had an extra hand that swept the dial every second, giving the impression of more time passing. The TenStop was an expensive, impulsive purchase, so I didn't wear it most of the time.

I ran twice around the roof, slipping once and jamming my foot into a PVC scupper.

When I stopped and looked again, nothing had changed.

There was little wind, and the night was mostly quiet except for the distant thump of a cargo truck going over the bridge two blocks past Cagle's building and the murmur of water splashing onto the concrete from the downspouts below. Two streetlights north, a flickering light produced a high-pitched squeal, like a dog not allowed to bark but desperately needing to go out.

The air smelled clean. I looked up into the rain and smiled at the cooling splash of it.

While I paced on the roof, I brooded about my predecessors

in Bangalore. I wished I could have stayed to skim the whole storm article. The aerial view of the city, taken a week after the storm on a beautiful sunny day, showed a huge lake with intermittent stumps of dead buildings and floating debris.

The original E had all probably died in the flood—an astonishing percentage of the residents had. The scientists who had experimented there and created Energy had probably died too, but for them I had less concern.

I played finger games, ran sequences, replayed movies in my head, and danced a little Singing-in-the-Rain on and off the raised edge of the roof.

Six minutes later, a desperate need to run overwhelmed my desire to stay.

If I could have hung around and watched Cagle's place for a while, followed him or Ratchet when one left, maybe seen who they talked to and where they went, perhaps I could have figured out what to do, but I just couldn't fix my attention on it. I couldn't wait. I didn't have it in me.

So, I ran in vague squares around the area, trying to come to some conclusion, but mostly losing track of my objective, my long view. Why was I running, what was I thinking? Oh yes, what to do about the box.

What to do about the box. What to do about the box.

Focus, Zip. Focus.

It seemed my whole life had become attempting and failing to do what were once simple tasks. Not for lack of understanding, not for lack of desire or intelligence, but because I wasn't able to stick to anything for longer than an eagle could play with a balloon. Suddenly my mind would go blank. I'd forget what I was doing, or the world would start coming in strobe shots without meaning or continuity, and I would be thinking of food, or running, or I would find myself doing jacks-and-toes and thinking about cat names.

And what business was I attempting to focus on?

The desperate need to expend energy faster than possible made me want to hit my head against a streetlight pole or race full speed into a concrete wall or an oncoming truck. After a while, the tics and sequences and finger games and mental drills just weren't enough.

I'd made myself sick in six minutes. Getting over the nausea of indecisive anxiety required running, so I took off.

I eventually skidded to a stop near Nicky's candy factory on Clybourn where they'd been loading trucks earlier, but they were closed for the evening. I did find a soggy, mashed-up box of Hoppers that I peeled off the sidewalk and ate. It helped, but I'd made myself desperately hungry running and pacing and thinking. The Hoppers weren't enough.

If I could find Bang, her presence might settle me some. Instead, I climbed up the side of a stone apartment building, went in through an unlocked window, found the kitchen and ate someone's bag of ham slices and a fist full of cheese, and drank from their bottle of wine while dripping water on their bamboo floors and their Turkish rug with a purple stain and worn knotted fringe.

I found a jar of mayonnaise and swallowed three spoonsful before I caught a look at myself in the glass front of the pantry cabinet. Shadows cast from the streetlights obscured my face, but the harsh glare highlighted my stained, wet SkinSuit, my slender E body, with its wide insect-like thighs and forearms, the jar I held, the spoon full of yellow mayonnaise. The image burned me. The ham and cheese I'd eaten felt heavy and uncomfortable in my stomach. I stared at the spoon and felt my eyes well up. The jar slid from my fingers and crashed to the floor.

Some Slugs called us Fleas because we were fast and jumped around a lot, but we are also cockroaches, stealing food in the night then disappearing into the cracks. A seventy-kilogram cockroach.

No one woke up, or at least no one came to investigate.

I slunk back out the window, closed it, and dropped to the ground.

Everything I was, and everything I did, was because I was E. And from society's point of view, we were, each of us, a representation of all E. What's more, they only noticed the newsworthy, the stealing and the damage, so all E were lumped together as malicious. I was not helping our reputation at all.

Not knowing where I was going, or why, only that I needed to move, I raced down the alley and around the corner. The pouring rain distracted me, easing my guilt, but also reminded me that I was in trouble and I didn't know what to do.

Focus. That's what I needed to do. Focus.

I wasn't sure if the Slug woman, Damini, ordered Bolt's sapping, or if the gunman was working for someone else, or if the gunman had even done the sapping in the first place. And why was Damini butting in anyway? Was she just messing with Cagle? Did she want the Velocity vaccine? I'd heard from Jammer that she dealt in those herself.

As soon as I tried to evaluate the problem with any form of logical analysis, I thought about separating eggs in zero gravity or hiding a voice transmission by encoding it on top of another voice to make it appear as interference.

The problem—which destination would give me the best chance of staying alive, Damini's or Cagle's—was always on my mind, but as soon as I tried to focus on a solution or a path forward, it would disappear. Heisenberg would lie back and laugh.

This was the bicycle falling over when I tried to ride one the first time. All I could see was the front wheel, and the more it wobbled, the harder it was to look in the distance, at the long view as my father said. I was just trying to keep the bike upright. I knew that was a mistake.

I decided to visit Bang. When I was released from SlowDown, my parents told me I had three months to find a job before I'd have to start paying for my apartment myself, which sounded like forever, but they underestimated how much food I ate, and my account drained like the stopper had been pulled. Bang had helped me survive those first few weeks. Now, of all the possibilities racing through my mind, finding her was the only one I could concentrate on long enough to maybe complete.

CHAPTER 9

Bang lived in the Nest, an Energy enclave on Fullerton. Her unit was on the south side, third floor, overlooking the roof of a BodMod shop just eight feet below her window.

Because it was raining and I'd had some food, I was able to run all the way. The air was cool and fresh and the road smooth and quiet. By the time I stood on the roof of the BodMod, I felt exhilarated but not anxious. A state similar, I imagined, to a Slug feeling relaxed or at ease.

I jumped up and tapped three times on the window, then trotted around the edge of the roof counting drones, waiting, hoping Bang was home, thinking of her lavender scent, her little nose, and, I'm ashamed to admit, chicken tikka masala.

Only three laps and six pedestrians later, Bang opened the window and motioned me in. Bang's building used to be a factory or a warehouse or something like that, until a Slug got the idea to subdivide it specifically for E-tenants. He constructed each unit as one long, narrow room with a fridge, a quick cooker, and a sink under the one window at one end, and a bathroom with a personal washer-dryer alongside a narrow aisle to the door at the other. He built all the apartments to the same plan. It was the architectural equivalent of a freighter stacked with shipping containers, with an E or two housed in each one. His lease was always with the reliable parent, not with the E who lived there.

There was space for a table, though Bang didn't have one. Energy didn't use beds or chairs the way Slugs do, and very few Energy had Slugs as friends. Energy even slept standing up most of the time. What we needed was a place to take a long walk. The rooms were only three meters wide but over twenty meters end to end, a good pacing and tumbling distance.

I climbed in over the sink and stood dripping on her concrete floor, watching to see if she minded me being there. Bang was as sleek as they came. Energy women weren't uselessly lumpy. They were straight and flat and muscled. This night she was sheathed in cornflower blue slacks and a gray tee that said Allegro Shakers and had their trademark twirling Flea doing a graceful double axel. Her short blond hair was cut so it wouldn't swing in her face and give her away by flashing about in a chase, her smile said she was pleased to see me, but her eyes, at least for that first moment of contact, had the slightly reticent look of a kid whose homework actually was eaten by her dog.

"You got a few?" I asked, while trying to look dapper in my sopping green SkinSuit and soggy E-shoes, with wet hair smeared across my forehead.

She looked me up and down with a slight squint. "You look like something the cat dragged in, then chewed on for a while and spit back out."

If the cat was a metaphor for my problem with the box, then she was only wrong about the last part. "The cat hasn't spit me out yet," I said.

"Sure, Zip, I got time. You want a shower?"

"You don't like cat slobber?" I looked down at myself. I should have washed before I left my own apartment, but I was distracted. For a moment, I considered going back to my apartment as Cagle had asked, but when I glanced up at Bang, I knew I couldn't make myself do it even if I'd wanted to. And I didn't want to. Just being in Bang's apartment felt intimate to me.

Bang ran my SkinSuit through a wash while I showered. I always wore a one-piece olive-green zip-up-the-front when I was out working. It was almost indestructible, had many pockets, and was form fit, so it didn't catch on things. It was wet when I arrived, so it wouldn't be any different putting it back on when I was ready to leave. While I was toweling off, Bang chewed on a pear and bounced off the FibreBlock walls. I wanted to do more than say hello, and I guess I made that obvious.

She set down the half-eaten pear and was in my arms. I massaged her back and she massaged mine, calming, soothing, while we drifted across the floor in a sort of jittery dance. As our anxiety drifted away for the moment, a different sort of urgency developed. Bang slipped out of her clothes and leaned against the wall. I stood between her legs and she wrapped one around me and we had our moment of sweetness.

Then I was looking at that half-eaten pear, and she was too.

"I have a few more in the fridge." Bang smiled, and we raced for the food. We each took a bite, turned and kissed again, mouths full of pear, then we danced around the room swinging each other like square dancers.

Another thing the scientists who developed the Gifted didn't foresee was that Energy were almost all barren. They had only discovered one E who was fertile, and she happened to be the very first Gifted, so they didn't expect the problem. We would be the first and the last generation of Energy. I was ambivalent about that—why bring a new child into the world, only to go through what I'd gone through? Still, there were times I missed the possibility of a legacy. Our biological clocks ticked fast.

We slowed down a little the second time. A table would have been nice, but the sink worked just fine, cool air flowing in over our bodies from the window and gusty bursts of rain spray splashing in on us.

We took another shower together, massaging, teasing, doing hand-slap progressions, and giggling.

When we were back out in the room with our clothes on, pacing the length and dipping into Bang's ice cream, I said, "That was nice."

"Definitely overdue." Bang grinned, spoon turned upside down in her mouth as she dragged it over her tongue to extract all the ice cream.

To this day, I think of that oh-so-brief interlude as the sweetest moment of my life. The whole world was Bang, and I savor that feeling still.

I told her there was a drop of ice cream on the tip of her nose, so she stopped long enough for me to lick it off, then we resumed pacing the room's length. Sometimes the problem of getting easily sidetracked is a benefit, but regrettably, I remembered why I was there. "Remember a couple hours ago when we met by the jewelry store?"

"Sorry, I didn't have time then." She looked sheepish.

"That's OK, business is important, but that's not what I meant. The delivery I had for Cagle was a small refrigerated box with a Velocity in it. The client was sapped before I could give it to her."

Bang stopped. "They killed her?" Her voice was high and tense.

We were near the sink, and she shuddered, then set down the ice cream container. To be turned into a Slug was death to us. I stood there vibrating while her fingers played furiously. She picked up a DesBall and formed it into a dog, then a jet, then a boat. Her eyes darted around while she tried to focus.

I continued. "The delivery didn't go, and he's going to ask me to deliver it again. I'm thinking of keeping it."

She stopped. "Zip, you can't. Cagle will kill you." Then she smacked her boat flat and started on a new dog.

"He will try, but there's another player who will kill me unless I deliver it to a different address when Cagle gives it to me." I didn't tell her it was Damini, but I might as well have—she took a small leap and ran the length of the room.

From the other end of the unit she said, "So, either way, you are dead." She talked to the door, hiding her face.

"Right, so I thought of a third option. I thought I might take it and skeet. I couldn't come out worse than dead."

"Where would you go that they wouldn't follow?"

She was still facing the door. I trotted over to her and wrapped my arms around her waist from behind, but she turned as though I'd cornered her, so we started pacing the distance together. She grabbed her DesBall, and I took a PuzzLit off the hook on the wall and played with it, not really making any attempt to actually solve it, just relishing the feel of the moving parts in my fingers, sliding little clips and rings into slots or over posts with satisfying clicks. It had eight separate clicks, so I was counting to two hundred and fifty-five over and over.

"Maybe I could play mouse under your sink for a while."

"I don't think that's a good idea," Bang said. "How long could you stay here, an hour? I don't think you could last much more. Even a whole day is nothing to Cagle. He'd look for you for weeks. Can you imagine? You would have to leave the city. Go to New York or something."

We were walking in circles and playing E games now. Hold out a hand, palm up. The other person tries to slap it before you turn it over. She kept darting around and slapping my butt instead, then she would set off in a fit of giggles.

Focus, Zip.

Again, I pulled my attention back to my problem. "How would I skeet to New York?" It wasn't like I could stay in a tiny car or airplane or train. There were seatbelts in those things. While trotting the eight hundred miles from Chicago to New York sounded lovely, I doubted I could find enough food along the way. There were a few thousand E in New York. There used to be some in Detroit, but they moved when the area became dangerous due to public resentment and police assumptions.

"You hobo there," she said. "You know, break the lock and hop an empty freight and be prepared. You have room to move in a freight. They're almost as big as this unit."

"I'd go crazy."

"You'd have to have someone along to share the craziness." She slowed and focused those silky gray eyes on me, and I almost melted. "Someone like me," she said. If she'd kissed me then, I would have Wicked Witched—just my SkinSuit, shoes, and thumping heart left on the floor in a pool of goo.

I slowed down too, long enough to kiss her head. Her lavender perfume had been washed off, but my mind filled with the scent anyway. It seemed to me she was being presumptuous in the most pleasing way. Bang and I were close then, but I hadn't realized how close we were until she offered to give up her whole world to be with me.

"No, Bang," I croaked. "Though don't think I don't appreciate the offer; I know what you would be giving up. But we can't do that. If we were captured, cornered in a railcar, say, we would die in jail inside a day. Rail cops aren't going to understand. They would starve us to death by accident, if not on purpose."

"Well, we can't ride the regular trailer. They would catch us as we loaded." There were semi-trailers that ran to other major Energy enclaves around the country. The semi-trailers were air-conditioned, ventilated, and had enough room to move around. They might take ten of us and enough food and toys to make the trip bearable. But they were regularly scheduled and easy to watch.

"In any case, I need to get the thing first. Maybe he won't give it to me, and I won't have to make the decision."

"Can't you just not show up at Cagle's? You could tell him you're sick, and that he should get some other E to deliver it."

"Even Energy don't go from well to sick that fast, and besides, the other player probably wouldn't accept that excuse either." I watched the millisecond LED dot work its way across the time bar on the wall. Running headlong into a truck was sounding better, but Bang was there keeping me out of that kind of trouble.

She did a few flips down the length of her unit. From the other end, she said, "You're screwed."

"Yes, I am. And very well, too."

Her fridge was mostly empty now, and I was feeling like a thief again, so before I could eat any more of her food, I said my good-bye. She gave me a kiss, and I dove out the window, rolling into a splashdown on the BodMod's flat roof.

CHAPTER 10

After my trip to Bang's place, I still didn't know where I would deliver the Velocity vaccine when Cagle gave it to me again. I could just administer it to myself. As it was, some wacko could sap me at any time. Just a quick little stick with a sapper, and I would be a half-dead Slug. I lived with that fear all the time. Having a Velocity would feel like freedom.

As I hit the roof of the Cicada Stop—an "All Insect" restaurant—I remembered that Damini had given me an address. Her card was still in my pocket.

Under a streetlamp, I pulled Damini's card from my pocket. Ratchet's piece of blue paper came out with it.

Damini had given me a tiny map printed on a plasticized business card with the address listed on the flip side. Bang had washed it, but the card was readable, if bent. The company name was India IO.

The writing on Ratchet's paper was still legible, although the note had come apart where he'd folded it. A doctor's office on the northwest corner of North Sheffield and West Wolfram—easy to find.

There was still time before I had to meet Cagle. Plenty of time. I decided to take a look at Cagle's destination.

A small residential enclave with well-separated sloped roofs still lingered in the now mostly industrial area. The first few blocks were quick, running along the streets, then I ran into a group of pedestrians moving like glaciers, taking up the whole sidewalk. They were going home from something fun, discussing in low tones how it made them feel, then breaking out into barely hushed laughter.

Going around them into the street was dangerous at night because of glass, rocks, and other hazards. Then one of the men, wearing a red-and-yellow college letter jacket, saw me bobbing around behind the group and moved slightly aside to give me extra room on the sidewalk. As I darted past, he swung out his arm and clotheslined me flat.

Tittering laughter accompanied my thump to the concrete. He said, "Sorry," like he didn't mean it, then in a theatrically loud whisper he said, "Damn Skeeters are everywhere."

Even though I was good at falling, my backside, the back of my head, and my dignity all smarted from the crash and skid. At least my suit didn't tear, or the laughter would have been more painful. Slugs are always more sadistic in groups.

I wanted to beat him upside the ears and pound him all around the block before he even knew what was happening. Stealing everything he carried and maybe some of his clothes, including his letter jacket, would have satisfied my rage and frustration. Perhaps they had candy or doggy bags with them after a nice dinner. If you were fast and strong, you could rip off a guy's underwear just by grabbing it and pulling hard, although they would scream a lot when that happened.

But what would any of that gain me? No one would be on my side—not anyone in that group anyway. And, when the police eventually became involved, well, jail cells and E don't mix well, and these kids knew that. Slugs relied on our difficulties with the police to keep us in our place. No, reacting to violence with violence wouldn't change anything, and it would only reinforce the stereotype Energy already had. Unless something more than my pride was at stake, running was the better solution.

So, I ran. Always what I did best, and almost always the best option. Was the fall partially my fault? Could I have dodged his arm? I'd been distracted. Should I have run around them on the street? I should have seen it coming. I could have run all the way around the block and avoided the whole situation. But he didn't have to clothesline me either. It was hard not to be angry. I opened my hands flat as I ran, but they balled into fists when I wasn't paying attention.

***

I arrived at North Sheffield, easing to a stop on the roof of a long shopping strip.

The building where Cagle wanted me to deliver his box stood on the corner, diagonally across Sheffield and Wolfram from where I was. It was newer, tan brick, three stories, with a men's clothing store taking up most of the bottom floor. On the right side, facing Sheffield, was an entrance door which I assumed opened to a stair leading to the upstairs offices.

The parking lot, wrapped all the way around the structure, served several buildings and contained a sprinkling of cars. Boxwheels queued up along one side waiting for morning when they would be unloaded. Because of the parking lot and the streets, the building could only be approached at street level, but there were no peds to see me.

I dropped to the pavement, crossed Wolfram, and stood vibrating and watching from the shady doorway of a Candles-N-Crystals store across Sheffield from the building. One security light glowed at the back of the clothing store, vaguely illuminating rows of gray and black pants and coats and a special display of inflatable body-bouncer suits.

A delivery truck with the store's logo painted on the side was parked near the back of the building. Above that was a window.

I crossed North Sheffield, then snaked through the parking lot, sliding quickly among the cars and Boxwheels. A step on the truck's fender, then to the roof and up onto the top of the truck's box. I pulled on my climbing gloves and scanned the side of the building. The brick wall had deep enough tuckpointing, and it was only seventy bricks up to the window. The window might be locked, and the truck roof would emit quite a loud boom if I tumbled back down from that height.

There were still no peds or moving vehicles, so I Spider-Manned carefully to the window. Not only was it not open, but it was designed to never open. Some architect must have thought a lack of fresh air would add to the energy efficiency of the building.

There was another window along the wall to my right. That one might not open either, but I decided to try it anyway. Crabbing over sideways took a while and a great deal of concentration. If Cagle made all his delivery destinations at nice dance clubs like last time, I wouldn't be having this problem.

Bolt lying on the floor. The sapper opening up on her chest.

Focus, Zip.

About halfway across the gap between the windows, I saw that the second window had a screen.

A police Sportster drifted by on Wolfram, traveling so slowly that I thought it had stopped until I noticed that every time I looked at it, it had moved just a little. Hanging there, I couldn't think of anything to do while I waited for the police car to pass. There were seventeen cars and six Boxwheels in the lot. I moved up and down on the wall a few bricks, risking a fall but feeling less anxious.

After the police completed their drive-by, I pulled the screen off the window, then looked around the lot. Seeing no one, I dropped the screen in front of the truck.

This window opened easily, sliding sideways. I crawled in over the ledge, closed the window, slithered onto the floor down to my hands and knees. It had been fairly dark outside, so my eyes adjusted quickly to the darkness inside. In front of me, a gray amorphous lump resolved into a face.

I sprung up, scurried to the window, opened it again. But I couldn't go running off when there was a chance the man on the floor was still alive. A desperate glance around the room told me there wasn't anyone else in the office. The face on the floor didn't move. Peering slowly around the desk, I saw that the body lay flat out and was dressed in dark clothes, making the side of his face stand out bold and white. My instinctive urge was still to flee (dive carefully?) out the window, bounce off the truck, and hit the ground running. I left the window open this time, just in case. Then I remembered that the truck was under the other window.

Ratchet had wanted me to check out the location of Cagle's next delivery. Why did I care where Cagle was going to have me deliver the package? I wasn't even sure if I'd go back to Cagle's office at all. At least I had worn my climbing gloves, so while the police might suspect someone had come in through the window, they couldn't prove it was an E. And in particular, they couldn't prove it was me. The police had every E's prints, retinals, detailed photos, and, of course, DNA. I could only hope the room wasn't on cam. I worried about dropping a few hairs or coughing. When I thought of that, my throat and my scalp both started to itch. Did Ratchet know there was a dead man in that office? Did he want me to find the body? If so, why?

The office was larger than I expected, taking up the whole corner of the building. That it was in an executive's space explained why it appeared to have the only opening windows in the building. The door on the far side of the room was closed. A wooden desk loomed to the right, and behind it was another window on the side wall. The desk held flowers in a vase on the right corner and three photo players arrayed along the left side, presumably showing the family and dog in various poses, playfully moving around throughout the day. A glossy nameplate set in wood and reflecting the light from the window said, *Dr. D. S. Argent.* The name matched Ratchet's note. This office was the specific office in the building where Ratchet had said I was supposed to deliver the package later.

In front of the desk were two wooden chairs, one of which

had apparently been pushed over by a scuffle or perhaps the falling body. The body felt warm, but upon close inspection, there was a broken and bloody hole on the side of his head above his ear that made me think his brains were mixed with bone. Blood still oozed from the wound. He wasn't moving— not his body, not his heart. I could have left then, but I tilted his face away from the dark carpet. He looked familiar, but I couldn't be sure I'd seen him before. People look different when they're dead.

First Bolt and now this guy. That box was hazardous to the health of anyone near it, and I was uncomfortably near it. I snuck over to the door, tried to listen, decided I had listened enough already—a tray of individually wrapped chocolates on a credenza caught my eye. Each time I unwrapped one and ate it, I made a loop around the room trying to decide what to do. There were sixteen chocolates. I pocketed the wrappers.

I'd been in the room no more than fifty seconds.

The body was warm. The victim's blood still flowed out. I hadn't seen or heard anyone leave. The murderer might still be in the building! I dashed for the window again, but hesitated. Whoever it was might have run out the building's back door, but I would have heard the door while I hung outside the window.

A quick glance out the windows showed only parking lot and vehicles, no peds.

If the murderer or murderers hadn't left, they might still be on the same floor.

Did I care who had killed Cagle's client? No. But there might be some advantage in knowing who it was. The information could be useful, maybe worth some folding to keep me going for a while. I jerked open the door and raced into the hall before I'd considered the possible results of that action—lack of impulse control was part of being an E. Although I hadn't closed the office door behind me, and the window I came in through remained open for a quick exit, a bullet would still be faster than I was.

CHAPTER 11

A streetlight shined in through a window at the far end of the hall, and a yellow wash oozed from a dim bulb in an exit sign with a broken red lens. It was shadowy; I was fast. If someone lurked in the hall, I would see them a lot more clearly than they would see me.

I dashed down the length of the hall, observing a recessed set of elevator doors and a stairway door opposite it, centered in the building. No one.

A faint bell told me the murderer had taken the elevator and had just reached the first floor.

I bolted back down the hall, through the office door, bounded over the body, jumped into the window frame, leapt over to the truck, then onto the ground. Using the cars as a shield, I rushed to the distant edge of the lot and circled toward the back of the building until I came across a car which was still warm.

It was a blue Fiola, with a cracked windshield and rust on the quarter panel. The plate said WEASEL. Someone had written "Wash me, weasel" on the trunk lid.

When the back door of the building began to open, I inadvertently backed against the car beside the Fiola and set off its alarm.

I ducked a few cars away, waiting for the Weasel to come out of the now-open door, but he hesitated, looking around because of the alarm. He was a Slug dressed in coveralls. A janitor?

The car alarm screeched out another pulse. I stepped on a gooey wad of gum.

I heard voices from the doorway—an argument, a flash, the thud of a gunshot. As the Slug janitor began to fall, the brown blur of an E raced out the door and over the body still settling itself on the ground. The E headed down North Sheffield. I didn't even get a good look.

After I verified that there was nothing I could do for the Slug—another gunshot to the forehead—I raced down Sheffield after the E, snapping the gum I'd stepped in on the asphalt with each stride.

An E I could follow without going crazy waiting for them to cross the street.

As I ran, it occurred to me that I'd arrived too late to help the first victim, but by setting off the car alarm, I had possibly caused the second man's death. He had hung back in the doorway for several seconds, waiting to see who loitered in the parking lot and thus had blocked the door at a critical moment when the murderer wanted a fast exit. Would the poor guy have been shot anyway? Maybe. But why was I there at all? Just for some information, to make the next trip easier, or did I have a long view I'd already forgotten?

Sometimes I failed to make plans and, as a result, did stupid things or got myself into trouble. Sometimes I decided to do something for no reason other than having no other option come to mind. Other options came to me only after the fact, only after I'd screwed up, or at least wasted a lot of time. Retrospect. I knew a lot of things in retrospect, but those things I knew about myself were overlooked the next time I had to make a decision, when they might have improved my response. Sure, knowing who the killer was might help me with Cagle—he'd paid for good information before, or at least might pay me a little extra for the next delivery—but if I was dead, that would hardly matter, would it?

Distracted, I lost track of the E.

From the middle of the wide intersection where North Sheffield crosses Diversey Avenue, I scanned all directions. A hint of a brown blur caught my eye down Diversey. There wouldn't be many other E running full tilt at that time of night, so I followed.

A poster pasted off-angle around a light pole proclaimed the arrival of Dr. Morose and the Bone Cutters, a Nouveau-Blues/Zydeco band from Italy. They had played at the Velveeta Center almost a year before. It was the Dr. part of Dr. Morose that caught my attention and reminded me who the first dead man might be. He was an E-doctor of some repute. Dr. Argent was too expensive for me, but I'd seen photos of him and his team. I remembered his face. His daughter was E, and he had spent some time in India with the original Gifted Kids and their developers working on medication to mitigate the more adverse symptoms of Energy.

The killer ran up a dumpster and onto a ThinStrip roof. The flat roof was only ten feet deep—I almost stumbled over the opposite edge into a rocky drainage ditch. This wasn't my area, and ThinStrips were new to me. Although the

ThinStrip ran for the whole block along the street, it was shallow shopping. No parking places. Tiny stores. While I recovered my footing, my mark dropped out of sight off the far end of the block.

We ran through the streets and over the roofs toward some unknown objective. The E's hair, like his suit, blended into the night. I counted light poles, giving half credit to burnt-out ones, and wondered why someone would want to kill Dr. Argent. I also wondered if the doctor's killer was lying dead in the doorway, or if, as was more likely, I followed the person who had killed both men.

We finally came all the way around to the Long Ochre Mile. The E ducked in. It was not the gunman who had chased me earlier in the night; this was a woman. Although wearing brown, she wore a SkinSuit with loose pants and a vest over it. What I'd thought was brown hair was actually a shaggy knit hat.

I approached the club only after pausing for a couple seconds down the street, so it wouldn't be obvious that I had followed her.

Cagle had instructed me to stay in my room, but I'd strayed a little. Why should I care about the murders? I should do as I was told and return home. I even began to trot back toward my apartment, but the next moment I decided that if I'd come this far, I should get a clear identification of the murderer. I found myself striding into the Long Ochre Mile having not thought it through at all.

Inside, Ratchet kick-stepped against the bar and slapped the rail to the rhythm; his drink hadn't arrived yet. The E I had been following had disappeared.

It took about fourteen seconds to make a full loop around

the Long Ochre without being too conspicuous. About half-way around on the far side of the main room, I noticed Bang shimmying under a fast strobe with Virago and Six. She held my attention for a long, sweet second, a full strobe. The crowd seemed to part, and the flash froze her in time, framed by dancers, posed like a ballerina, one arm held high above her head and folded inward at the wrist, the other angled across her body, legs together, toes pointed, several centimeters off the floor. Wide, laughing smile.

The strobe died out. I closed my eyes, momentarily calm, and tried to hold that stunning image in my mind—a mental photo, a Degas painting, and I embraced it. But in a moment the image began to disintegrate. When I opened my eyes and the next strobe flashed, she had dissolved into the crowd.

The sweetest moments of my life as an E were always temporary, ephemeral. Problems, on the other hand, stuck solid and could not be dislodged. They latched themselves into my brain like a remora, feeding on my anxiety, growing fat and foreboding. It was as though I went to a memory erasure clinic and had all the pleasant memories erased so I could focus more intensely on the presently painful ones.

Either the killer had blended in, or she was aware of me following and had continued out the other door, or perhaps she had escaped out the upper window to drop her tail. Whichever it was, it had worked. Like a terrier chasing a car, I'm not sure what I would have done if I'd caught her. I hadn't planned that far ahead.

CHAPTER 12

Four minutes remained before Cagle wanted me to pick up the box for the next delivery attempt. I cruised into a secluded corner and tried to decide what to do.

Focus, Zip.

In that dim corner, with my industrious fingers mushing a worn-out, wall-mounted SpaceBall, all I could think about was how great it would be to be safe—to use that Velocity vaccine on myself. The New York City Energy had the reputation of being inhospitable and clannish, hard to approach, but I still harbored this fantasy that I could inject myself with the Velocity, hop a freight or catch a semi, and hide in New York.

Yet going to New York was impossible. If I didn't die on the way, I would probably die when I got there, Velocity vaccine or not. I wouldn't know how to find free food in that unknown environment. In Chicago, I knew which restaurants threw out some food instead of scraping everything into the food-recycling bins for later conversion into food bricks for Russia. Even a half pancake a few hours old could make a difference if it had some syrup on it, or butter.

Pancakes.

And how would I find the E areas? Running around in other parts of town for any length of time, especially while scavenging, could get you arrested, or beaten, or killed, or maybe all three in sequence.

I sure couldn't steal the vaccine, use it, then stick around Chicago. A bullet or a knife would still kill me, although all someone would really need to do was crush my foot or smash my knee—anything that would immobilize me. They could kill me without even committing a felony.

From what I'd seen of the shooter, she was medium height for an E, a little shorter than an average Slug woman; she'd worn loose brown Slug clothes over a SkinSuit and a shaggy brown hat. No, I remembered, shaggy brown hair that looked like a hat. Or was it a hat that looked like hair?

I eyed Ratchet surreptitiously from my secluded corner and tried to decide if he knew who I'd been chasing, if he had directed the murderer out the back door. Had the murderer come to the Long Ochre to inform Ratchet that the job had been done? He seemed too relaxed. But maybe.

Ratchet was always showing up as a maybe.

A space opened up at the bar next to Ratchet. I glided up next to him and punched the ErgBomb button, then palmed the reader.

I turned to Ratchet and said, "Slumming down here with the rest of the Energy?"

Ratchet fumbled a kick and glared at me. He glanced at the clock over the bar and said, "Aren't you supposed to be at Cagle's in a couple? Or are you making the Arkansas trip again?"

OK, so my watch ran a bit slow. I didn't own a synced watch; it didn't seem worth the extra expense since I tended to smash watches on things while running.

"I'm surprised Cagle let you out to play. Aren't you supposed to be there at the door to bark and raise your hackles when someone knocks?"

My ErgBomb rose up through the counter, and I grabbed it. After chugging it down, I remembered that I'd intended to drink it casually, not wanting Ratchet to think I'd just spent my time running around instead of staying at my apartment as Cagle had instructed. My hunger after the chase overrode any conscious planning.

Only after I'd had my energy drink did I realize that by walking up to Ratchet I'd confirmed my choice to take the package again. I'm still not sure that I made that choice ahead of time, or if it was accidental, finalized without thinking about it. I'd like to think I chose to carry the box again on purpose.

Still, once I'd spoken to Ratchet, I had to take it. No feigning illness, no forgetting all about it, no getting lost, no running away.

Damn.

A dancer came spinning off the dance floor toward the bar on Ratchet's other side. A boy perhaps thirteen or fourteen, he would have been one of the youngest E in existence. He wore a beige full-body SkinSuit close to the color of his skin, so he appeared almost nude. He'd mistimed his pirouette, balanced precariously for a moment, then tripped over the step up to the raised bar area. The transition to Energy can be a perilous time. A new E had power and speed but not the experience, not the agility or balance, not the grace.

Ratchet stuck out a foot as though he intended to kick the boy into the rafters for bothering him but instead caught him on his ankle and lowered him to the ground in one smooth flowing gesture, like a tai chi master.

The kid might not have hurt himself even if Ratchet hadn't been there, but any significant damage, especially a broken bone, can drive an E over the edge to insanity, especially a new E.

Ratchet turned back to me. "Don't be late, Zip," he said, then he speed-walked out the open door while someone else was walking in.

The kid lay on the floor, twitching in fright and breathing hard. I pulled him to his feet, confused about Ratchet, not seeing a motive in his apparently altruistic action, but still believing there had to be one.

"That was Ratchet in case you ever want to know," I said to the boy.

He looked like he wanted to know.

CHAPTER 13

Cagle's building was dark except for his fourth-floor office window and a dimly lit foyer. Other than Ratchet crossing the sidewalk, no cars or pedestrians moved on the street. The only parked car was the one that had been there for days; the other two cars were gone. Down the street on the far side of Third, a long black car sat parked in the shadows of a stunted tree.

I caught up to Ratchet just as he entered the front door and followed him in.

He nodded to the uniformed woman wearing Spyders. While Ratchet tapped a rhythm on the elevator button, I slowed enough for the guard to identify me, then entered the stairway. I hopped up the stairs backward swinging my other foot out and singing a jump-rope ditty as I bounced on each step, "Apples, peaches, pears, plums, tell me when your birthday comes," and slapping each course of the concrete walls.

I arrived on the fourth floor ahead of Ratchet, so I darted

up and down the hallway. On the wall next to Cagle's office door hung a copy of that Wyeth painting of a woman looking forlorn, laid out on a sloping field of brown grass. She gazed at some buildings as though they were unattainable, as though she didn't have the strength to walk that far, or maybe she had the strength to but didn't want to. To me, the woman in the painting represented people who were outsiders looking in, even in their own world.

I tumbled to the end of the hall and kick-stepped the wall on the way back.

The cheap by-the-square carpeting so popular in office buildings wore an Aztec pattern colored with magenta and gold with some royal blue mixed in. The four squares in front of the elevator had been replaced, standing out with bold, clean colors. An empty Mountain Dew can balanced precariously on the ogee chair rail above the textured wallpaper wainscot. There were some flakes of beige paint near the window at the end of the hall and a buildup of deposits from water leakage on the chrome sprinkler heads.

The window at the end of the hall was cracked.

The ErgBomb I'd had at Long Ochre was still working, making me feel strong and fast and jazzed.

I did some jacks-and-toes.

Ratchet finally came out of the elevator playing finger games and double stepping, which was kind of like skipping where each time you placed a foot you double-bounce-slid it a little. It used mental and physical energy without really requiring focus, once you knew how to do it.

I figured Ratchet took the elevator to appear even more Sluggish—not trying to pass, no E could do that, but trying to show deference, a willingness to conform to the majority.

Slugs liked that. Ratchet didn't wear Skins: he wore baggy black Slug pants, a black shirt with a collar, and a black net vest with a few canvas pockets. He carried something in his vest pocket. It might have been a gun. It was smaller than the trout.

Waiting for him to open the door, I zigzagged to the end of the hall and back again. When he did open it, I tried to follow him directly in, but he stopped me with a hand on my chest.

"I'll see if Mr. Cagle wants to see you." Then he closed the heavy door smack on my face. Ouch.

With nothing else to do, I idled in the hallway, rubbing my nose and listening at the door, sliding my ear up and down the wood, doing knee bends and waving my hands like a Vaudeville showman with a straw boater hat. I probably should have been thinking about the box, about where I was going to deliver it, about who I would betray—Cagle, Damini, or perhaps both. But even worrying required a concentration I didn't have just then. Like a gas, my anxiety filled all the available space in my otherwise empty head.

Ratchet finished talking to Cagle—something about medicine. I heard my name, so I stepped back, thinking about straw hats, Michigan J. Frog, and high-stepping singers with an array of kicking dancers and sparkly lights.

I also thought that Kaboodle would be a good name for a kitten.

By the time Ratchet opened the door, I was twirling an imaginary hat, bouncing on one foot, and humming "The Michigan Rag." Dignified entry at that point would have been impossible, so I laughed and hopped into the room.

Cagle sat at his desk. His slowly emerging disgust quieted me. I lowered my foot and sagged my shoulders.

"Hello, Mr. Cagle. You told me to return at two?"

"Yes," he said, leaning back in his chair, tapping a red pen against his teeth like water torture, which I guessed meant he was thinking about something, probably me.

Would Kaboodle be a black cat, or would it be multicolor?

There was a smudge on the window behind him, as if someone had thrown a greasy ball against it.

"But I also told you to stay in your apartment for that time, didn't I?"

"OK, I stopped by the Long Ochre for an Erg Bomb. Larder was low. I needed something," I said, not lying.

Cagle grunted.

Four KoolBars lay on Ratchet's tray. I ate one while Cagle gathered his thoughts. I reached for another one, but Ratchet had seen me and swiped them off the table.

He made a show of eating one himself while pocketing the rest. The gun, or whatever he'd had in his vest, was gone.

Cagle asked Ratchet to fetch the package.

Before Ratchet came back, I ran twice around the room, sidestepping stuffed chairs, not caring how disgusted with my behavior Cagle became, venting my energy and my anxiety. Ratchet returned and handed the trout to Cagle. He examined it for a moment, rotating it in his hands before holding it out to me.

"See that it gets delivered this time, Zip. Don't be late. Don't get lost. Don't let anyone take it from you." He paused eons between each short declarative sentence.

Even under the intense lights in Cagle's office, the box still looked like fish skin. It felt cold and moist, probably from condensation, or perhaps I just imagined the moisture based on the box's appearance. There was a V-shaped scratch

I must have caused when I tried to open it, but apparently Cagle hadn't noticed.

While I attached the box to my carrying strap, Ratchet said, "I gave him the address earlier, Mr. Cagle, to make sure he knew where it was."

"Give it to whoever answers the door," Cagle said to me, "and don't stall or detour. Take Ratchet's KoolBars if you need to, but go straight there. They are expecting you."

Ratchet left the room as soon as Cagle mentioned his KoolBars.

By the time Cagle finished talking and ah-humming, Ratchet returned with an Erg pill.

"Here, take this."

The Erg pill was effective and perfect for the situation, but I would have rather had Ratchet's KoolBars. The KoolBar flavor would have been satisfying, and the bulk would have stayed with me even after the hunger came back.

Once I had the package safely strapped to my back, I tried to appear calm and indifferent and asked Cagle how he got his hands on a sapping vaccine, on a Velocity.

Cagle didn't answer for a very long time. Then, so slowly I had trouble connecting the words, he said, "Don't ever ask a question like that again, Zip. I might start to think you want to know. I can hire another E who doesn't want to know. Not just one who doesn't ask, but one who genuinely doesn't want to know."

"No need to hire someone else, Mr. Cagle. I don't want to know either. Just talking. Not thinking."

But I was thinking. I still wondered how Cagle was entangled with Damini. My life might depend on it.

To hide my discomfort, I headed for the door. I could feel

him observing me, watching for a sign that I might run with the package, steal the contents for myself, but I'd already thought that through. There was nothing in that strategy except dead.

Ratchet darted back to the door and opened it for me. In fast E-speech, he said, "Deliver it straight, Zip. It's important. You understand, no detours."

I could have told Cagle that the doctor was dead, I could have told him about Damini and her toughs and what happened at my apartment, but he wouldn't see it in the same light I did. If I had told him that Damini already knew he would give me the package to deliver a second time, he would accuse me of telling her about the second delivery myself. How else could she know? There was no one else except Ratchet, and Ratchet was definitely the more trustworthy of the two of us.

I would become a serious liability if Cagle knew about Damini torturing me for information or her demand that I take the box to a different destination.

I tripped over my own feet on the turn between the third and second floors, pushed off the wall, and twirled into a handstand on the landing.

Cagle's reaction to me asking about where the vaccine came from had unnerved me. I'd expected him to just tell me to mind my own business, but he'd become as cold as the box.

Focus, Zip. Focus.

I had a decision to make. Deliver it as I was asked by Cagle or deliver it as I was asked by Damini. At the moment, both options smelled like dead trout.

CHAPTER 14

Damini's preferred destination was **366 West Superior Street,** the Tagler Building, a big new building on a corner, room 712. I had already been to Cagle's destination, but that was a dead end; if I took the box to that destination, there wouldn't be anyone alive to accept the delivery.

So, I hurried north on Halstead as quickly as I could. That direction would lead me toward both possible destinations for a few blocks, then I needed to turn east across the bridge toward the lake or continue south. Halstead runs under some tracks there, and after I passed them, I sliced into an alley to consider my options.

The stench of urine and moldy rotting cardboard in the alley hit me like a force field and made me turn around almost immediately. When I did, I glimpsed an E cruise by at speed, heading the same direction I had been going. His pace seemed purposeful, determined. I slipped up to the corner and peeked around.

The white-shoed gunman from the Castle Wheel, the

one who I'd thought sapped Bolt, idled at the corner under a streetlight, glancing around. He'd been following me, that much was obvious. My snap-turn into the alley had fooled him. He would backtrack in a moment, so I waited for him to face the other way, then jetted west to Dayton Street.

The whole trip couldn't have taken more than fifty-five seconds.

There had to be a reason why Cagle chose me for the task even though he knew my deficiencies. I was smart enough to admit that I was not actually a very good delivery boy. I tended to get distracted easily, even for an E, and I got lost a lot, preferring to parkour about town, missing road signs and street addresses, rather than just running the sidewalks and following directions. When I was expending energy, I was too happy to concentrate on a destination. It was usually immediately after I ate or when I got very hungry and slowed down that I started to think.

Why didn't Cagle have Ratchet deliver the damn box? That would have made more sense. Ratchet was sensible, trustworthy.

I wanted to think about that some more, but I couldn't let Cagle's possible motives distract me.

Focus.

I slapped myself on the side of the head to emphasize the point.

At speed, I Jackie Channed up the side of a concrete arch that supported an iron garden gate, vaulted over, and landed softly in a small grass patch in some wealthy person's tiny front yard. The yard was lower than the sidewalk by a meter, so there was space to hide.

Copy would be a good name for a cat. My Gifted high

school friend, Winmae, disappeared from school with no comment from the teachers when she was fifteen. I still missed playing chess with her. Did some of the delivery bugs contain surveillance cameras along with their navigation cameras? I'd lost track of everyone I knew in school.

I scanned for the gunman through the spikes in the gate. In a moment, he raced by.

What was Bang doing? I had an Erg pill in my pocket I could share with her.

Blinking, factoring 42,137—who was this white-shoed guy with the gun, why was he following me? How did he know I would be carrying the box again? Was this gunman just insurance hired by Damini? I didn't believe she would think she needed insurance. People generally did what Damini told them to do. Who else could he work for? Did Ratchet send the gunman, or did the gunman work on his own? If he didn't work for Ratchet, how did he know when I'd be leaving?

I held onto the bars of the gate to steady my tremble. Who would want a cat anyway? I could have fallen asleep right there. I wanted to. I probably would have dreamed about school. Maybe about the trip to Los Alamos, or the trip on the *Shepherd* to count whales.

After the gunman trotted by again, apparently giving up and going back toward Cagle's place, I vaulted back over the gate and sprinted off in the opposite direction. Speeding away was the only thing I could decide on. I felt like I was in a baseball rundown between the bases even though there was only one fielder. One fielder and his gun.

Winded and famished, I pulled up a block from my apartment, hid between two Boxwheels, and popped the Erg pill Ratchet had given me. That would last me less than five minutes. After the pill took effect, I focused enough to realize that going back to my apartment was not going to solve any problems.

My Aunt Maria lived in Old Town, about a four-minute run away. She had been one of the few regular people who, after I'd left SlowDown, had tried to like me as Zip, who had tried to talk faster when I was around, who had tried to understand Zip without comparing Zip to Zane. She bought me my first SkinSuit and SpeedShoes. While my parents were distancing themselves, she tried to get closer, and I loved her for that. She even let her kids around me, which made me feel human when every other indication implied that I was not. Not anymore.

In the end, it couldn't last because I was too much of an energy sink for her and even for her kids. I stopped going there, and she didn't contact me. We both knew the distance was necessary.

My aunt's home was not in the direction of either place I'd been told to deliver the package. The trip would be mostly street level, but it was dark, so I thought I could lose the gunman if he caught sight of me under a streetlamp. I ran.

Her building stretched the whole block, one-room-wide townhouses stacked together like so many encyclopedia volumes on a shelf, each attempting to look different in the same consistent way.

I hopped over her little wooden fence and nudged between the sparse bushes to the window. She sat at the dining room table, staring down, nothing in front of her, no book or magazine, no food. From my spot at the window, I longed to be able to sit and think like that. To calmly meditate on my troubles without the disabling anxiety and relentless tension. She seemed so wonderfully blissful.

I hopped her fence again and ran around the block.

When I came back she was still there, but how could I impose on her? How could I go in and ask her to let me destroy her life for hours, perhaps days, running in circles in her basement and eating all her food? Because that's what I'd planned to do, although "plan" might have been too strong a word. I had planned to take one of the few Slug friends I had and abuse her friendship.

And why? For a few hours' reprieve? Just to satisfy my own need for a safe haven? It's not like I'd have even solved any of my problems, just put them off for a while and probably exacerbated them.

What's more, my aunt had children. All asleep at that time of night, of course, but what would they think of having a madman running in circles in the basement? They knew me, but I was only around them when I was at low-anxiety points. At that moment, my anxiety was as high as my fear.

It crossed my mind briefly that it was odd, my aunt being awake at two in the morning, head in her hands, staring at the table. But all I could see then was her peaceful relaxed state, and I couldn't interrupt that. I needed to go somewhere else. I needed to go anywhere else. Why had I gone there in the first place?

Retrospect again. After I made an undirected, random move like going to my aunt's house, I could always see it as undirected and random, but never before the fact. I'd wanted safety, I'd wanted a friend, so I just ran. Without thinking.

Without a plan.

Plan, Zip. Plan.

I went to Lake Shore Park and trotted around the bases on the new Little League baseball field, trying to think.

I couldn't go to my parents' house. They cared about me, I supposed, but even to them, maybe especially to them, I was someone different from Zane, their son. I was a changeling named Zip. I was what their son had turned into, what their son had been replaced by.

My parents sent me money when they could, but I'd used up most of their savings before I'd left home. They would have taken me in, but as soon as I drifted out of earshot, they would have been trying to figure out how to tell me they didn't really want me there.

Back when I turned sixteen and was released from SlowDown, my parents never did succeed in telling me to leave. I got the hint and told them I planned to move out. They didn't try to stop me as I'd hoped they would. Instead, they found a place for me and packed my stuff. They gave me their old green couch from the basement, but I had to get rid of it because it reduced the pacing space in my apartment, and what would I do with a couch? Sit down?

Even at sixteen, I already had considerably more intelligence and education than either of my parents because of my genetic alterations and my constant reading and studying when I was still Zane. I could live alone. And they needed to attend to my younger sister who was having trouble in school and was already pregnant. My parents thought she did it on purpose to get some attention, to get the same level of attention I received. I didn't know. I couldn't talk to my sister anymore. I was an E. She wasn't, which made her mad at first, then mostly grateful, but she still held that grudge that I had been important enough to be enhanced and she wasn't.

I had a few E-friends who would help for an hour—Bang of course, maybe Carrot or Tex. Even Bomb might help for a few hours, but what then? I could ask Bang to help me get out of town, maybe go to New York like she said, but the trip would be dangerous, and I couldn't lead Bang into that.

But Bang could think on her feet. She could come up with possibilities. Without her, I didn't have a chance.

In the end, I couldn't foist my problem on anyone. Peter Drucker had said, "The best way to predict your future is to create it," but that meant you knew what future you aimed at and the basic tools and access to get you there. All I could think of were obstacles.

Clapper Bell would be a bronze cat.

Thirty-seven laps around the bases. Thirty-eight.

Focus.

Damini had instructed me to take the package to an address on Superior Street. The Tagler Building on the corner, room 712. I'd checked out Cagle's preferred destination, so why not take a look at Damini's building? It wasn't like I had anywhere else to go.

There were plenty of RoRuCo-marked warehouse roofs in good condition on the trip down Sedgwick to Superior. Zigzagging around slow-moving wind turbines and solar-power units, swinging on exposed pipes and conduits, leaping over brick firewalls and throwing myself across streets to the next roof in line, I ran full-out.

When I came down from a flip, landing on a clear stretch of warehouse roof, Blinker was approaching from the opposite direction. We were both moving fast, so we stuck out our arms, clasped them as we passed, and checked our forward progress into a circle swing. "Zip! Long time."

Blinker was a kept kid; he received what he needed from his parents and was probably just out for a run, or to visit some friends, or on his way to a dance. His was a different world of Energy, so I said, "On my way to a job. See you at Long Ochre some time."

On the next round, we split, launching each other back to speed again.

Having made a decision, even if only a short-term one, made me feel reckless and wild, like I did when I first got so full of thrust and vinegar that I couldn't stand still. That was before I realized that the extraordinary energy wasn't temporary, like happiness, but would always be with me, like grief or guilt.

I eased back to a trot as I approached Superior, wanting to creep up to the area as cautiously as I was able. Because I hadn't delivered the box on time, I expected there to be some commotion. I wanted to observe the commotion, not become part of it.

The streetlights along Superior lit the tree-lined stretch of road. Shops kept lights on in their doorways to make burglars visible but also to keep the homeless from taking up residence there.

Above the building's door, bold, two-person-high block letters said Tagler. The building was a concrete monolith with the foreboding presence of a prison or a fortress. Black vertical stripes separated regularly spaced windows. In a building like that, none of those windows would open except for one emergency window on each floor which exited onto the fire escape snaking up from the third floor to the roof. Those escape windows would be fully alarmed and very hard to break.

I would have to go through the front door.

From a lower roof diagonally opposite, I watched a Slug pass glacially around the corner. No other peds were in sight.

I backed away a half block, dropped through a ventilator into a furniture factory, went down some stairs, and found a break room with a refrigerator. Someone had left their lunch, and under an aluminum foil tent, I discovered a third of a yellow cake with chocolate frosting which still had the Ha and the Bi left from the "Happy Birthday." There were probably employees dreaming right then about having a piece of that cake for breakfast in the morning, but the Erg pill was already wearing off. I stood with the refrigerator and the freezer doors open to cool off and ate the lunch and all of the cake myself.

I drank some of the soda from the fridge and went to the bathroom.

Feeling fed, safe, comfortable, and worn out, I started thinking about how nice just three minutes of sleep would feel. Already very late for the delivery, knowing full well what a bad idea rest was right then, I felt myself letting go—a microsecond of pause—then sleep.

CHAPTER 15

A seven-year-old Zane stands in the kitchen munching a carrot and imitating Bugs Bunny, making loud chomping noises and doing his best imitation of rabbit teeth. *His mother chops celery for split pea soup. It's Sunday, so it's her turn to cook.*

She is a much better cook than his father, who mostly goes for optimal efficiency and quickest preparation time. He uses frozen, pre-chopped vegetables.

She pauses, holding her knife and staring at the remaining celery core for a moment.

Zane says, "What's up, Doc?"

That his mother is a doctor enhances the humor and makes him laugh at his own joke, which he has made several times before. He thinks it gets more humorous each time he uses it.

She puts down the knife. "Are you ever bothered by the differences between you and your playmates?" She seems about to say more, then waits, still looking at the countertop.

"Sometimes, I guess," Zane says. "It would be nice to be as tall as them. It's a bit annoying always being the littlest, but I

make up for it by being fast." He holds his hand out flat and says, "Shoosh, zoom," as he spins around weaving his hand up and down. He smiles, hoping his egotistical-sounding comment will be taken as humor.

She turns to him, confused. "No, Zane, I didn't mean the older kids you meet up with for pick-up games or at the Gifted school. I meant your playgroup, the one I take you to at the grade school, the regular one."

"Oh, them," he says. "I don't usually play there. I observe mostly, while I read or build stuff. They're pretty immature. They can't focus on an objective, and they are always running around aimlessly, so it's not exactly fun."

Zane pauses here, trying to decide how to best handle the questions. What are his objectives in this discussion? He'd finished a book on managerial techniques the previous day, and he wants to apply what he's learned. Was there anything to be gained by a specific outcome? How can he negotiate in a conversation that's not about negotiation?

"I'm not sure why you take me there," he says at last.

He doesn't want to go to the grade school playgroup anymore, but he knows it makes his parents happy. Still, if he works this right, maybe he can leave playgroup without causing any arguments or disappointment. His parents become upset at the oddest things. "Like on Tuesday," he continues, "they were trying to play soccer, but they didn't understand the rules, let alone strategy. They just swarmed around the ball, everyone at once trying to kick it in the general direction of the other goal, if they could remember which direction that was. So, I just watched."

His mother is still staring at him, so he continues, trying to come up with an example she will understand. "They act a bit like the people Pop talks about in the stock market, where everyone buys the equities that produced a gain the day before, chasing profit around, hoping to catch a rising stock by the coat-tails without ever bothering to do any research or figure out a real strategy, because they don't pay attention to the long-term goal of wealth accrual. They have no long view, they just react. You know what I mean?"

His mother sighs and looks at the celery core again. She shudders, then tosses the core into the organics chute. "You make me so happy and so sad at the same time."

The conversation hasn't gone quite the way he'd hoped. "How do I make you sad?" He thinks he might be able to fix the problem. He doesn't like to see people sad, especially his mother.

"Because sometimes you sound like a wise old man, and I miss the time when you were just a sweet, erratic, nutty little boy."

"I don't remember him," Zane says, hoping to put that kid out of her thoughts, make him unimportant. But she puts her hand over her face and hurries away.

Zane concludes that she needs more Bugs Bunny and less Peter Drucker.

CHAPTER 16

Three minutes is a long time to sleep. In the lunchroom, I'd slept for four and a half.

The delivery should have been completed more than ten minutes ago, so by now they would think I had stolen the Velocity vaccine. Cagle and Damini would be searching for me and the precious package.

Messages would be flying over the network:

"When did he leave?"

"Where would he go?"

"Send someone to watch the semi-trailer transport station."

And recriminations:

"Why didn't you send four people with it?"

"Why didn't you hire someone more trustworthy?"

Those imaginary recriminations made me wonder. How could the gunman follow me so easily? Why was Dr. Argent murdered? And especially, why would Cagle choose me to deliver the box? Twice! He had other options, and he knew I wasn't especially reliable. Before he gave me this assignment, I had thought he wouldn't hire me again even to wash his windows—not that I'd be any good at that either. Cagle must have intended for me to fail—for the box to never be delivered. There was no other explanation. I no longer thought the gunman worked for Damini, at least not directly. He had to have worked for Cagle.

The freezer contained only an ice cream bar with spiky ice growing on it. The fridge held some more soda—mostly diet and so mostly worthless—a half bag of FairPlay donuts, which were useful only to Slugs because, although they tasted great, they held no nutritional value whatsoever, not even calories. No fat, no sugar, no salt. Giving FairPlay stuff to an E was like giving white bread to ducks. We could eat it all day and die of starvation. But Slugs needed that stuff. They wanted to eat like Energy but move like Slugs.

I fingered the last of the cake icing off the tray and decided to skeet.

All the windows and doors had alarms. I could have just opened the front door and run, but I didn't want to attract attention. Police drones weren't all that fast, but if one happened to be in the area, it might at least determine that I was an E, and that identification would add another tick on the list of crimes committed by Energy. There were already enough of those. Whether I liked it or not, each E represented all E in the minds of the Slugs. A demerit for one was a demerit for all.

Exiting back up the ventilator shaft was more difficult than dropping down had been, and it took a few tries, banging around and tumbling back down three times.

From the street, the Tagler Building's seventh floor looked like of all the others—randomly lit, but mostly dark. Security apparently didn't turn off lights for people, and the building obviously hadn't been upgraded to infrared-detecting automatic switches, even though it was fairly new.

Would Damini have henchmen stationed on the roof watching for me now that the delivery was late? Seemed unlikely, but I was in a worrying mood.

Worry: another good name for a cat, or maybe a dog. Dogs worry, cats can't be bothered. I was a dog person, in that respect.

A Boxwheel waited for a green at the intersection. No peds moved on the street.

The building across a narrow delivery alley behind the Tagler Building was one story shorter. I got bored and climbed onto its roof. After a running start, I leapt over the alley to the Tagler fire escape, climbed to the roof, then ducked quickly into the shadow of the brick main stair exit and listened.

If Worry were a cat, it would be a black cat, just like Anxious.

A few seconds later, the need to move outweighed my fear of being shot, so I raced around the roof. Even if someone saw my blur, I could leap back across the alley, down to the other building, and run away before they were able to get up the speed to jump after me.

The roof was deserted.

I found the air conditioning compressor unit, unscrewed the wingnuts, lifted the access plenum, and pushed the insulation aside. There was an empty space in the back of the plenum near where the cold air shunted down into the building. The box fit nicely into it and would stay relatively cool. It made sense not to carry the box around with me. If the gunman, or Ratchet, or one of Damini's torpedoes caught up to me, they would want the box. I would know where it was. I would have a bargaining chip. It could save my life.

I forgot, or perhaps just ignored, how vulnerable I was to simple torture. Just withhold food or tie me down for a few minutes, and I would reveal exactly where the box was. Knowing this, I still left it in the plenum because I couldn't come up with a better idea.

While the cake had helped some, hunger made me consider going back to my room to get some more substantial food. Who would think to look for me at my own apartment? Would anyone think I would be stupid enough to go there?

Yes, regrettably, they might even assume that.

Perhaps I should try Bang's unit or even Long Ochre? Just go dancing. I'd probably never see the bullet coming. A bullet might not be so bad, but then I thought of Bolt and remembered that getting shot isn't necessarily the worst that could happen to me.

One more loop around the roof eased my anxiety, so I went to the stairway thinking I'd go down and check out the seventh floor where Damini had directed me to take the package.

The previously closed stairway door now stood wide open.

With a startled twitch, I spun around looking for whoever had just come out onto the roof. He wasn't hard to find. He stood right there, gun pointing at my knees, then my face, then back at my knees.

"Hands up," he said.

I raised them.

"Where's the package?"

"What package would that be?"

"The one you were delivering, imbecile."

I considered telling the truth. He could have the trout, and I could go home, eat something, maybe go find Carrot, steal his little green hat and go for a chase, or play some dupes and waddles. Or, I could just buy some real donuts and chow down at his place for a while. Go dancing at Long Ochre. Maybe Bang would be there.

The guy with the gun wore brown Slug clothes, loose and easy to run in. His shoes were dusty and marked up, but they were white underneath the grime. He was no more than a year older than me, and his face was soft and round and almost friendly; he appeared open and honest. His gun wasn't friendly at all, though.

"It's gone," I said, not lying, but not telling the truth either, usually my best strategy.

He fired his gun past my ear, shattering a brick on the edge of the stair entry.

I leapt like a gazelle, then sprinted as fast as I could, diving back across the alley and tumbling into a run on the other building.

Instead of asking me where the package was, and trying to scare me a little, he'd fired the stupid gun. What an E thing to do. I'm sure it was intended as intimidation; my reaction surprised him, though. He took a full heartbeat to realize I was gone before he started after me.

Once I started running, I couldn't stop.

I free-ran back the way I came, trying to remember all the

obstacles I had so carefully leapt over earlier, now trying to sabotage his progress, hoping he would jump a firewall and come down on a standpipe or a wireless receptor.

After three full minutes, I was thirsty, seriously over-heated, and desperately hungry. The hunger I could tolerate, albeit temporarily, but the heat I urgently needed to unload, which meant cold water or possibly cold metal. The fridge I'd raided before had had cold drinks. The room had a cool tile floor. I eased a little and veered back toward the factory, knowing I could cool by the fridge, drink the cold soda, even if it was diet. I could hide there.

The gunman hadn't been in sight for a while, and I didn't see anyone when I arrived at the air duct, but when I climbed down, I made enough noise in the thin metal passage to signal anyone on a roof within two blocks. It couldn't be helped, though. I had to chill.

Dropping down onto the top floor, I collapsed in a heap. The floor was cool industrial tile, so I flung out my arms and legs, letting some of my body heat out into the floor.

Someone began investigating the ductwork above me, making noise like they didn't care if I heard them.

Move, Zip. Move. Don't just lie there and die.

I jumped up, handrailed it in the dark down two flights of stairs, darted into the lunchroom, and closed the door.

Fridge. A bottle of cold, sweet soda marked "Denise," hiding behind the diet soda in the back. The lone freezer-burned ice cream bar from the freezer also marked "Denise." I listened, ate, drank, and breathed as quietly as I could. Denise would be very unhappy in the morning.

Unscrewing the bulb in the refrigerator reduced the available light to a muted glow from the small glass block windows high on the wall and an exit sign above the door.

I paced, pausing to cool myself in front of the refrigerator each time I walked by.

He banged down the stairs just after I opened my second soda. It was diet, so I just poured it over my head and pulled out another. This one had sugar without caffeine, just what I needed. Caffeine made me jittery.

A band of light extended into the room as he opened the door. I boosted up onto the table and swung my legs over to the other side. Could I throw the half bottle of soda and dodge past him?

Instead of coming in, he closed the door again, sealing off my one possible exit. I jogged in place for a moment, guzzled the cool drink, waiting. Waiting is hard.

"Hey, Zip. I know you're in there. It's unlikely these good people would leave the refrigerator door open, would they?"

I suddenly had to pee something fierce. There was already soda all over the floor, so I just let go and hoped it would start raining enough outside to wash my suit. That never worked, but when you drank as much as an E and ran around as much as an E, bathrooms weren't always convenient. When the employees showed up in the morning, they wouldn't be happy. I wondered if Denise had cleanup duty the next day. I hoped not. Poor Denise.

"Zip, I know you hid the package," he shouted through the door. "If you tell me where it is, I'll forget I ever saw you. I can even give you a thou to help you get out. You can buy a ride on the semi tomorrow morning. Start over in Cleveland or somewhere. The semis aren't so bad. You get to know people." He paused. "What do you say, Zip? Do we have a deal?"

He was calm, or at least he convinced me he was calm.

Maybe he danced a jig out there, balancing a plate on the end of a stick and making a suspension bridge out of a SpaceBall, but to me he sounded as though he had all night. There was no way I could wait him out.

He knew my name was Zip. How did he know that?

"Why did you sap Bolt at the Castle?" I said. Perhaps I was just stalling, but I really did want to know. He'd looked like a nice guy when we met on the roof.

"Oh, Zip. That wasn't me. I can see where you might think so, but that was Cagle's man, Ratchet. I expected to take the package from her, that's true, but I wasn't going to sap her. Especially not before you gave her the package."

He talked to me as though I were a nine-year-old Slug. Sweet talk, like he was my friend and just wanted to help. He may have been trying to sound like he cared, but instead he sounded like he was offering me candy to get in his unmarked white van.

When I was nine, I could play the piano expertly. At the time I hadn't realized that perfection wasn't perfect in music. Perfection was uninteresting.

Focus, Zip.

I trotted around the table, drank their last soda—another diet, but it was cold. My body temperature had returned to about normal, I had enough sugar from the last non-diet soda for a two-minute burst of energy, but there was only one way out, and there was a gun in it.

Giving the man what he asked for was a viable option. He might even give me the thousand he promised, though I doubted that. "I don't have the package," I yelled at the closed door. Stalling wasn't in my favor. The fridge was out of food, and this guy probably had a whole pocketful of Ergs.

I started going through the few drawers in the cabinet next to the fridge, but they only contained no-calorie sweetener, plastic utensils, and some coffee filters.

"I know you don't have the package. I also know you had it not that long ago. I know you didn't deliver it. That means you hid it somewhere. Where did you stash it, Zip?"

I could hear him pacing back and forth on the other side of the door. He knew I didn't carry a gun. He knew where I was supposed to deliver the package. He knew Ratchet worked for Cagle and claimed he knew that Ratchet sapped Bolt, though I suspected that was a lie. This gunman knew way too much.

"Do you work for Damini?" I asked.

"If I worked for Damini, you'd be dead right now, Zip. She doesn't care if the package is destroyed or never recovered. She just wants to make sure no one else gets it." He paused for a moment, then added, "A thousand for the package. You selling, or am I coming in and shooting you in the leg?"

"You'd do that to another E?"

"Yes. Yes, I would. Because if it's not me, then it's someone else getting that box, and that box means I keep my job."

"But—"

"And I won't even feel bad about it afterwards. Now, I'll count to two. One."

"I'm selling," I said before he could even say "two." He couldn't see me, so he might not know I had lied. My current situation was untenable, and getting out in the open where I might run would improve my chances of escaping him. Just to make sure the charade had a note of authenticity, I added, "Are you so well paid that you carry a thousand around in your pocket all the time?"

"You'll get your thousand. Just lead me to the package."

"That doesn't sound like a very good deal."

"Best you're going to get, and I'm getting tired of holding a finger on this trigger without squeezing it."

"Let's go get the money. Then I'll take you to the package."

It was the standard impasse. I wouldn't show him where the package was until he showed me the thousand, and he wouldn't do that without seeing the package. Still, I felt I had an edge, even if he had a gun.

He stepped in, flicked on the lights, and shot the fridge. The explosion, deafening in that enclosed concrete block room, reverberated in my head and gave me an instant headache. I dropped to the floor in a panic, scuttled under a table, and waited for the next gunshot, the next boom that would take my life, or at least my leg. Why was he always shooting stuff? It seemed to me his gun was threatening enough without him actually firing it.

He walked over and pointed his gun at me. "Get up."

I did, hoping his gun wouldn't go off accidentally.

"Geez, what were you lying in?"

"Diet soda." Lying came easy when the answer didn't really matter—when the person I was lying to already knew the truth.

He pulled nylon hobbles out of his coat pocket and threw them at me. Hobbles again. I was so tired of hobbles. "Put these on."

I stuck a foot through each loop and pulled the tabs.

"Tighter."

I pulled another tab through the slot.

"You run fast, you know that? You're faster than me. Damn near impaled myself on a flagpole trying to keep up with you." He lifted his left foot and wiggled it.

The hobbles allowed a stride of about a meter, which was fine for a fast walk, but I'd land full force on my face if I tried to run.

The gunman latched my wrists together with metal cuffs, then put a Puzzler in my hands so I could bleed off some nervous energy. I had lots of that.

"I'm likely to pass out on you," I said, hoping to nab an Erg pill.

"You won't pass out on me. Not the way you smell. You pass out, you're passing out over the side of a building." He looked me up and down. "Couldn't you at least have unzipped first?"

He stuffed a half Erg pill in my mouth and ate the other half himself.

"I figured you might leave me alone if I smelled like a urinal cake."

"You're close to the truth on that."

"What's your name?" I asked.

"Don't get chummy."

"We're both E."

"That only matters to Slugs. You got something I need. That's all there is."

He led me out the door of the breakroom, down the stairs, and to a side door where I could hear rain coming down outside. "OK, which way do we go?"

I should have thought up a good lie. Retrospect again. I hadn't even decided whether to lie or not. If I gave up the package, it wouldn't be my problem any longer. If Cagle caught up to me, I could tell him truthfully that I'd been waylaid and forced to give up the package. I believed that was what Cagle wanted anyway, to lose the package. Damini might not be in as forgiving a mood, though.

"What's in it? What's in the package?" I asked.

"You don't know? Well, I'm not going to tell you. What would be the point of that? Information is power. You got no power at all. You got nada." He grinned happily, then added, "You got zip."

"I got a thousand, right?"

"Yeah, you got a thousand, but only if you take me to the package without trying to skeet, or trying to attract attention, or trying to fool me. You try to fool me, and I'll make you tell me where the package is, then I'll kill you. You know I can do those things, don't you? You know I can make you tell me just by taking away that Puzzler and tying you to a parking meter."

We stood at the door. It was decision time. Cagle would never hire me again, but I wasn't working for him anymore anyway, and I didn't think he would sap me. Sappers cost too much. Damini might try to find me and kill me, but why? I'd tried to deliver the package and was robbed. Not my fault. I hoped she would need a reason to actually kill me, something beyond me not delivering the package. At least I hadn't delivered it to Cagle's destination.

But this gunman was not some distant threat. He stood right in front of me. "It's on top of the Tagler Building."

He spun me around.

"Right where I caught up to you the first time? We ran all over Chicago . . . ." He smacked me on the side of the head, then unlocked the door and we stepped out. The alarm went off, but he didn't seem concerned. He just kept mumbling about how much work I was and how, just his luck, it was raining.

Jumping from building to building was out of the question with my legs tied, so we trotted by sidewalk all the way. We stopped behind the Tagler Building. He gazed up at the building and then at me.

"It's behind the stairs on the roof," I said.

I waited, playing with my Puzzler. He played with his gun which had a little dial and flick-switch on the side of the butt especially for diddling. It was a bad idea to give an E a gun without something to play with on it. Triggers were the only other thing to play with, and that usually ended badly.

"All right. You're staying here while I go up and collect it."

"Uncuff me then," I said, and stuck my hands out. It was worth a try.

"No, quite the opposite." He grabbed my proffered hands, removed one of the cuffs, and threaded the cable behind the bars on a cast-iron window cage that came to about my waist, then locked the cuffs down tight.

"And if the box isn't where you say it is, I may be hunting for it for a while."

"No! God, don't leave me here in the alley, let me go up with you. I can help you find it faster."

"You say it's behind the stair, right? Should be easy to find."

Fear of abandonment, fear of captivity, fear of starvation, fear of insanity. "It's inside the plenum in the air conditioner housing." The simple truth.

The gunman smiled broadly. A forced admission was so much more satisfying to him than if I'd just told him where it was in the first place. How annoying that it actually turned out that way. He appeared quite pleased with himself.

Damn.

The gunman suddenly frowned and squinted, looking at

me but clearly thinking about something else. I heard a foot sliding over paper to our right. Saw a flash of yellow. His gun went off next to my ear. I yelled, "Shit!" and frantically tried to yank the window cage right out of the concrete wall.

CHAPTER 17

A **whiff of lavender drifted by in the freshening breeze. The** gunman wasn't the only one who had followed me.

The gunman took off after Bang, who I assumed had taken off after the box.

With my level of fear and anxiety, the half Erg pill was already fading.

I waited, fiddling with my Puzzler and wiggling as much as I could while cuffed to the basement window grate.

My watch's hands didn't appear to be moving. The bank's clock down Superior Street didn't even have a second hand. I didn't know how long I would be locked to the grating, but the debilitating milliseconds ticked by. I was desperate for someone to come back before the minute changed on that bank. How could I last until the minute changed?

Logically, I knew I had quite a bit longer than a minute before I began hallucinating or beating myself bloody against the cast-iron bars. Probably ten or more minutes.

Paramahansa Yogananda wrote, "Learn to be calm and

you will always be happy." I believed that was the fundamental truth of humanity, because what you lack is always what you believe to be the most important, and therefore what you desire the most.

My Puzzler kept my fingers busy while I recalled the pear I had shared with Bang an hour ago, eight meals ago.

Hunger. Ice cream. Cheeseburgers. Interference patterns as signal encoding.

I fumbled my Puzzler.

I scrambled to catch it with my feet but only succeeded in kicking it down the alley when the strap holding my legs brought my foot up short.

"Stupid, stupid."

That's all I could say, and I said it over and over again until I was screaming.

I stomped my feet senseless in a puddle, then repeatedly ran the handcuff strap over the metal bar, figuring I could wear out the strap in less than ten minutes. Stupid, stupid.

In ten minutes, I'd be dead.

Well, not really, but it felt that way.

Moose Turd: good name for that bastard gunman who left me there.

Karma gave me a teasing scent of baking donuts. Tortoreo's. I sniffed as though the smell could sustain me, but it only made me cramp up into a ball. It wasn't especially cold, but I began shivering in waves, holding my stomach, rocking, wagging my knees, alternately stomping then just thrashing around. To any watcher it would look like I was in heavy drug withdrawal, cold turkey, or perhaps the early stages of freezing—the stage where you still think you can survive and are trying to stay awake, using random, energy-draining movements to generate heat.

Was it an hour and a half ago that Damini's toughs held me down? I could hardly move at all then. Now, at least I could move my feet.

I did a little kick-stepping as I'd seen Ratchet do at the Long Ochre, back when I'd made the now clearly disastrous decision to accept the second delivery job.

Almost thirty seconds had passed. If I could make a minute, I could make two.

Could I go to sleep to escape my anxiety? Could I shut down and sleep through it? Not likely. I was tired enough, but it was only possible for me to sleep when I felt at least somewhat safe, protected.

If it were just the tether and the cuffs, then some mental work and kick-stepping, maybe some math problems, would have helped considerably. But as soon as that first minute expired, I believed without any doubt that I couldn't make the second minute. My brain told me I could last maybe ten minutes, but my heart had already given up.

Bang must have followed me all night, keeping back or downwind. That had to be extraordinarily difficult. And to what purpose? Why would she do that and not tell me? Was she at that very moment stealing the box and running to Damini or to Cagle with it? I loved Bang, but money was food, and in my current state, the idea of doing absolutely anything for freedom and food was well within my understanding.

I had the urge to bite my finger and suck on the blood. Any real satisfaction from that would require a big bite. I didn't have the courage. If there had been a dying rat on the ground, I would have kicked it up in the air and caught it in my teeth. I could imagine shaking my head to snap its little neck.

More than a minute had gone by, and I wasn't insane yet. At least I didn't think so, although I was aware that people who actually are insane seldom know it. I wanted to stay sane, but that required a level of focus on something other than staying sane—something other than worries, but there were so many things to worry about.

To add to the problems of being handcuffed to a window grating in the middle of the night, there was the box and Damini and Cagle and the gunman and the sapping and the murders and my possible death and my general lack of food and my frustrating lack of any ability to be of use to anyone, even myself; to add to all that, Bang was now in danger of being badly hurt or even killed, and there was no one to blame but myself.

A man with a gun now chased Bang, intent on doing her harm. My fault. Only mine. My fault.

She'd probably been chased by police with guns before, but they most likely would not have shot her because the police were Slugs, so they were slow, and because they didn't want to do the paperwork, and because police were paid on a piecework basis. The police had little incentive to kill anyone, even an E. A dead thief wasn't worth nearly as much as a live convicted one. We tended to stay alive if caught, at least until we were locked up in jail where confinement sometimes killed us.

"What, me worry?" I said aloud, quoting Alfred E. Neuman, but I couldn't raise my hands far enough to bend out my ears. Bending my head down to my hands to accomplish the task didn't even cross my mind.

What if neither the gunman nor Bang came back? What if she grabbed the box, but he returned to me first, and then he threatened to kill me if she didn't give him the box? What would she do?

Or worse, what if he had already shot her, took the box, and now she lay crumpled and dying in a pool of blood on the sidewalk? I pictured her, broken and bloody, laid out on the concrete, legs and arms bent unnaturally, gray eyes open and staring at me.

What if they were fighting and they both plunged from the roof to the street on the far side of the building?

After another minute and ten-point-four seconds of this, I slumped to the ground, crying and twitching. If I could have reached my hair, I would have torn it all out.

The rain squall eased up to just a drizzle. At least I wouldn't smell quite so bad when they found my body.

Bang appeared beside me just then and shoved a whole Erg pill in my mouth. "You're a mess," she said, scolding me as though I was four and had spilled milk on my clean shirt.

I would have given my life for her at that moment. Tears flowed like rain.

A car slammed into the alley, kicking up gravel as the driver hit the brakes and skidded to a stop. The car sat motionless less than ten yards away. It was long, black, and silent-electric, sporting an awe-inspiring silver angel hood ornament with open wings. On either side of the angel were dark dogs with thorny collars, their eyes red LEDs.

I swallowed the pill and waited for it to affect me. Meanwhile, Bang sawed at the bit of cable that linked my handcuffs using a diamond-edged ceramic blade she usually used to saw the bolts and hinges off windows and doors.

The car door opened.

Bang finished cutting the cable and started on the hobbles. The foot hobbles were just plastic, and she cut through them quickly.

A large figure dressed in black stepped out of the car's driver-side door. Someone with a booming male voice shouted, "Please don't move, either of you, or you will be shot. You don't know what you have."

Without hesitation, Bang and I both moved. I knew what we had; we had trouble.

Two shots cracked behind us. I didn't know if the gunman had returned, or if the driver had fired the shots. I hoped they were shooting at each other but doubted the luck of that.

We ran through an alley and out onto Jackson, hung a left, then bounded up onto the roof of a virtual sex parlor, landing inside its giant holographic copulation advertisement.

Bang said, "Meet at the hole in the roof," and dove back to earth, rolling into a run and disappearing around the corner.

Two more gunshots, then I caught a glimpse of someone following us, which was probably the reason Bang wanted to split up. I was too happy with my freedom and had too much built up energy to lose a race to the gunman. I'd outrun him before, and this time I would take him on my own turf.

Using every alleyway and underground and aboveground dodge I knew, I rode the potency of the Erg pill Bang had fed me all the way to Halstead. Heading east, I darted down through Under-the-River, a hive of homeless who had set up a city in the abandoned underground Union Train

Station, before I crossed the river at Jackson—or Hackson; the street signs downtown were all painted over with zapped names—then dropped down to Lower Thwacker. I lost him in the first thirty seconds, but kept going, fueled by Erg and freedom.

Joy is parkour sprinting on a full tank.

CHAPTER 18

Three full minutes later, I dropped down into the condemned building where Bang and I had circled each other only a few hours before. She didn't have time then.

I couldn't smell her perfume, but there she was, coming out of the shadows.

"You cleared him?" she asked.

"Yeah, he's slow."

We began circling.

"I don't smell your lavender," I said.

"I don't use it when I'm hiding or I'm going to be chased. I opened the stick a little to let you know I was there earlier." She smiled. "Did you notice?"

She knew I had noticed.

I wanted to ask her if she had five right then. I wanted to grab her in the worst and best way.

"What about the box?" I said.

"I didn't take it, I just moved it and ran." She trotted a circle around me, keeping her index finger on me as she went. "I figured he would run after me if he thought I had it, which he did. But I only ran for a bit, then I came back for you."

"I'm glad you did."

"It took him a good ten seconds to figure out I went back, and by then I had you free."

She stopped in front of me, grabbed my hands and focused her eyes on my handcuffs while she sawed them off. "Who was in the car anyway?" she asked.

"I have no idea. There are so many people after me, I've lost count. Maybe I have an overdue library book."

"Librarians drive ancient Volvos. Could it have been Cagle?"

"The hood ornament on that car would cost more than Cagle's net worth. I think this guy is much farther up the food chain." I wondered how much farther up. Big fish eating smaller fish eating smaller fish and so on.

"Then not the gov or the police?"

"No, not the gov or the police. Not Cagle, and I don't think it was Damini. She would have just sent one of her E after me. It's a fifth fish. Maybe an ichthyosaurus." That was the biggest, ugliest, most dangerous aquatic animal I could think of. I was beginning to feel paranoid.

Bang and I circled, cooling off, coming down from the adrenaline high of the chase and feeling at least a little safer. She said, "Well, Guppy, what do we do? All we're doing now is killing time and metaphors, and that's not going to get us out of this pond."

As we circled, I tripped over a bottle and fell, more heavily than I normally would. I was usually pretty good at falling—E had to be. Bang rushed over. "You OK? You need to rest, Zip."

"Maybe I do," I said. "I feel a bit woozy. Too many ups and downs and too many Erg pills in too little time."

She said, "Hold on, let me take a quick look around," and she leapt out of the hole onto the roof.

I stood, kicked the bottle into a corner, then paced the length of the room, wondering who the big fish was. Ichthyosauruses had a lot of very long teeth. I imagined coming up with a devious plan to have my antagonists eat each other and forget all about Bang and me. That seemed unlikely—coming up with a plan, that is.

Bang returned. "Go over in the corner where it's darker," she said. "I'll keep watch while you sleep, then you can watch and I'll sleep. Maybe we can come up with a plan after that."

Bang had always settled me, and she did so now. There with Bang, at that moment, success, that is survival, seemed possible. We drifted into the darkest corner. I leaned against the wall knowing Bang would watch out for me, and I switched off.

CHAPTER 19

Zane has spent the last few weeks learning ancient Greek. At eight, he has become fond of the idea of a classical education. He immerses himself in the concepts of translation, trying to translate both the words and the meaning.

On this day, he is reading Aristotle, and he suddenly grasps how music and math are fundamentally related. It astounds him like a sudden view from a mountaintop. His understanding of the world shifts, much as it had when he first learned mathematical limits and derivatives. That was when he started viewing the world in terms of how things changed with respect to each other, rather than just how things changed. He is now convinced that there is a mathematical underpinning to everything.

He goes to his library and downloads Gödel, Escher, Bach: an Eternal Golden Braid, and rereads the music sections, focusing on Bach and the mathematical foundation of fugues.

Zane approaches his father, who is reading in the living room, and tries to describe his newfound understanding. "It's like everything is built out of parts that look and act like the thing that's been built. I get a fractal feel, you know, a recursive feel, out of Bach's music. It seems like there is math in everything."

His father sets his book down, takes a deep breath through his nose, and squints at him. This is what he does when he wants to teach Zane something.

"This is good, that you have this insight, but don't be too quick to apply it to everything. On Friday, I'll show you another way to enjoy music, from its other side. It's not just about math, although you'll see an underlying order, it's more about the emotional side—the human side."

Friday night, Zane and his father go to a dinner club that is featuring a blues band called the Gospel Knockers. The twelve-bar progression of many of the songs seems repetitive on the surface, but for some reason, each song delights Zane. He realizes that his feet move, his hands tap, he has the urge to sing out during the chorus, and to shout out, like some of the other patrons do, at moments of pause. Despite the essential similarity of many of the songs, he is not bored. Each is unique inside the constraining limits of the twelve-bar-blues chord progression.

They play "St. James Infirmary Blues," which is sixteen-bar blues in a minor key—different, yet in many ways the same. It feels like a musical lament. The members of the group clearly put the pain of similar experiences into the song.

Later, Zane notices that people sometimes cheer in recognition of a song when only the opening chord is struck on the electric guitar.

The same chord starts many songs, but it's the way it is struck that tells the audience exactly which song is coming, and they play it in their minds before it really starts, enjoying the song three times—once as a memory, once as anticipation, then again as the current performance.

In the car after the show, his father asks him, "What was mathematical about the blues they played?"

"The twelve-bar progression many of the songs followed was pleasing, even though it was repetitive. The songs also built toward something, like a progression, but never quite got there. It's like the blues is asymptotic to, but never quite reaching, the objective. There's always a longing there."

His father thinks for a while, smiling, humming "Key to the Highway," then says, "What about in the long jams in the middle of many of the songs? What did you like about them?"

"I don't know. They seemed to wander around yet keep to the theme and rhythm of the song. I guess the jams had surprises that seemed just right, as though there was no other way to do it. The lead guitar would do a riff, and the harmonica player would do one back, but just a little modified. The differences were the most interesting part, I guess."

Zane's father takes a breath through his nose, squints, and says, "That's call and response. It's human, it's emotional, it's of the moment. At its best it's not derived, and it's not pre-determined. It's what makes the blues conversational instead of rhetorical. Yes, like a heartfelt conversation."

After three months of regular practice and study, Zane reaches an expert level playing the harmonica. Technically, at least.

He is playing with some other musicians, in the middle of a wild jam, when Dozio, who is the voice and rhythm guitar of the group, stops and looks at Zane. This makes everyone else stop and look at Zane.

Dozio says, "You're not leaving the silences alone, man. Blues *has silences. It's as much about when you leave stuff out as when you put stuff in."*

Zane focuses on what Dozio said. "You mean, time to pause and reflect?"

"Yeah," Dozio says. "If you don't pause, you can't reflect."

CHAPTER 20

When I awoke, Bang was gone.

"Bang?"

She promptly dropped through the hole in the roof and tumbled over to me. "Feeling better?"

"I feel like I fell off a building and landed in a minefield infested with nettles, so yeah, much better."

"My turn?" she said.

"Your turn."

She leaned up against the wall, said, "Thanks for warming a spot for me," and dropped off immediately.

I watched her for a moment, wondering at her ability to be so rational. I just wanted to run most of the time without thinking. But I needed to stay close while she slept for several minutes; I couldn't gambol around the neighborhood.

Trying to stay low, I duck-waddled around the roof, even though it was spongy in places. I played hacky sack with a diminishing chunk of mortar and danced the cha-cha slide combined with a running man shuffle to imaginary music.

Still, I was able to list my problems.

First, there was Cagle, who knew some time ago that I didn't deliver his package to his customer. Did he know the customer was dead? Then there was Damini, who must have been informed that I didn't deliver Cagle's package to her customer. Then there was the guy with the gun who kept chasing me around shooting at me. Then there were the two dead people on North Sheffield, the doctor and the man in the doorway. I still wasn't sure what happened there. Then there was the woman I followed from those murders. Then, out of nowhere, the guy with the deep, loud voice in a big black car.

And then there was Bang.

My rent was due. My SkinSuit had a few holes, was wearing thin, and smelled awful. Gravity was the enemy of all buildings. People too for that matter. Cats, not as much. Cats seem to have some ability to levitate. Levitation. Levity. Cats have no sense of humor.

I dropped back into the building.

Bang still slept. Her hair stuck out in odd directions. Her nose twitched sometimes, and she smiled once in a while. Her fingers wiggled, and she shifted her feet.

I bounce-stepped and skipped around the room, then watched her some more, feeling a bit creepy, but unable to look away.

I couldn't pause, but sometimes I had a moment to reflect, and I wondered how Damini knew I had not delivered the package to Bolt the first time, and how Damini knew that Cagle planned to give it to me again for a second delivery attempt.

Ratchet could have been Damini's information source, but

there would have been no need for the subterfuge; he could have swapped out the contents of the package whenever he wanted to.

The last time Bang and I met below the hole in the roof, when she had business and had to skeet, I told her about missing the delivery and finding Bolt sapped on the dance floor of the Castle Wheel. I told her that Cagle planned to give me the package again. Bang knew where I lived.

Bang was the only person other than Ratchet and me who knew all these things.

I had added up my problems, but I had the disturbing feeling that I didn't have Bang's number right at all.

Bang looked peaceful sleeping against the wall, and that made me feel peaceful too, but my stomach felt hollow, and for once, it wasn't just because I was hungry.

Bang woke with a smile and reached out her hand.

I took it and we swung around in lazy circles.

"Where did you hide the box?" I said, trying to sound calm and detached.

She slowed and studied my face.

"There's a standpipe," she said, "a vent, I guess. It comes out of the roof about three feet, then curves over like a candy cane. It was big enough to set the box up inside on the place where the PVC turns. I don't think it will fall out."

She stopped. "What's wrong?"

"I'm not sure what's wrong." I released her hands and gazed out the hole in the roof without seeing anything. "I've been thinking about how Damini knew I would be given the box for a second time. I've been trying to work out how she knew where I lived, not that she couldn't find out given a little time, but how she knew so fast."

I wanted to search her eyes, hoping to find innocence there, but she looked at the floor. She sagged, then sobbed. Her shoulders shook.

"I need to go get the box," I said. I wasn't sure what was in that damn box, but I knew it was important. It was more important than a Velocity vaccine, certainly. People were willing to kill for it. People had already been killed for it. Having that box might save my life, which at the moment was looking precarious.

Two steps, then I leapt up through the hole and back onto the roof.

I'd been hoping I was wrong, but it was pretty clear I wasn't, and I wasn't about to let Bang know how much that upset me. Or maybe I was running so I wouldn't let myself know how much that upset me.

But Bang was right there beside me when I landed on the roof.

"Wait, Zip. Please?"

Her voice was almost a whisper, soft enough to attract my attention even though I did not want my attention attracted. Even though I wanted more than anything to run, she stopped me with that plaintive, soft voice.

I didn't want to face her either, but I did. Her deep sob pulled at me, made me want to put my arms around her and tell her everything was all right. But everything wasn't all right.

Bang took a deep shuddering breath. "They taped me to the floor. I told her everything I could think of. I couldn't help it." She paused, then louder she said, "They taped me to the floor, Zip. They taped me to the floor."

I ran a full circle around the roof and kicked the low roof wall while Bang sobbed.

"I need to get the box," I said.

I heard Bang yell out my name as I dove to the next roof, but I couldn't go back.

I circled the block a few times, partially to check for tails and partially to travel in a pattern that didn't require thinking. While I ran, I worried that my blurry vision might cause me to run right off a building and smack into a wall.

At least that would solve my problems.

CHAPTER 21

Running on Erg pills for too long without eating real food can cause stomachaches and muscle cramps. A leg cramp while jumping at high speed from roof to roof can be deadly, so I headed for the Kulfi Klatch. The Klatch was a biryani bar with an attached corner market, part bodega and part Indian fast food on the border of the Indian and Jewish communities. It was packed with shelves from floor to ceiling and had small aisles with worn-through tile floors. On my way to grab a KoolBar, which were displayed next to the magazines and newspapers, a news headline in the *Next Day News* caught my eye. "Cure for Gifted Lost in Monsoon."

Halfway out the door, the meaning of the headline sunk in. I pushed a teenager wearing a fluorescent green kippah, an Amish beard, and a sari out of the way, fought my way back to the newspapers, and grabbed a copy.

The cashier, who looked to be over seven feet tall but actually stood on a box, yelled over, "You're going to pay for that, right? I've got you on camera."

In my distracted desperation, I had forgotten to pay for the KoolBar as I went past him the first time. I almost ran off just to make a point, but I wouldn't be making the right point at all and went over and paid him for the KoolBar and the paper.

Outside, I read the first paragraph while walking in circles under a streetlight. The scientists who developed Energy had come up with a serum that would allay some of the symptoms of anxiety and hyperactivity in Energy, using telomerase and a telomerase reuptake inhibitor and a bunch of other formulations I skipped past. The lead biochemist for the project had died in the deluge, and his computers as well as the vaulted backups, which were secured all the way across town, were all destroyed as the buildings and the infrastructure of most of the city collapsed. All known samples of the serum were also destroyed in the flood. The article had a photo of a black vial nestled in a small coffin-like box. A full ten years of work were lost, as well as the driving force behind the research, an Indian billionaire named Butta Nimmala, the article said.

The horrendous and unprecedented monsoon season had been in the news for weeks, but it had seemed so far away, unrelated to me except that it made me feel bad for the people who lost their lives or relatives and friends. Now it felt personal, as though I'd lost a brother or sister.

I understood Nimmala's desire to keep his work close to him and secret, but he had gambled with our future and lost it all in the flood.

My naturally associative mind combined my more immediate concerns with this news story, and I began to wonder if all the samples had actually been destroyed. What if one sample of this cure had survived and somehow ended up in my trout? It would explain a lot. The Velocity vaccine was expensive and hard to come by, but it didn't seem expensive enough to kill for. Maybe the gunman wasn't after a simple vaccine at all.

Could Energy's salvation be sitting in that vent pipe right now?

I suddenly felt responsible for the welfare of my whole people. I didn't want that. The ominous expectations of failure weighed me down, like I was climbing out of water. A frantic worry swept over me—a wave of cold fear mixed with sharp shards of responsibility. Anxiety is caused by pessimistic speculation. Avoiding anxiety starts with avoiding responsibility—responsibility just opens more possible paths to failure.

I needed to retrieve that box and figure out what to do with it. Even if someone waited for me on that roof. Even though the gunman or Ratchet might kill me for it.

I ripped out the article and shoved it in my flat pack, then ran off toward the Tagler Building, running parallel to the route I took last time. The buildings were newer there, so there were more sunlight concentrators and solar collectors on the roofs, more mini wind turbines, network towers, and drone delivery receptacles, but there were maintenance paths through the maze, the roofs were flat and well maintained, and the RoRuCo E had marked the trail well. There were also a few buildings with roof vegetable gardens. Useful information for the future if I survived.

Eventually, I jumped the gap between buildings to the fire escape on the Tagler Building, swung off of a disconcertingly flimsy support bar, and flipped up and over the roof's edge.

Just as I hit the roof, a brick slammed into my thigh.

Ratchet walked out from behind the stairs.

"Arkansas again, Zip? You are fast, I'll give you that. I lost you right out of Cagle's, and I've been looking for you for fifteen minutes. Now, give me the package."

The idea that one E would throw a brick at another was bad enough. First, it prevented my using rule number one, run away, but more importantly, it meant that Ratchet was willing to hurt me. He was willing to break my leg or injure me badly enough to make it difficult or impossible to run. Which indirectly meant he was willing to kill me. He might have considered himself a good throw, and thus not worried about causing such damage, but I wasn't going to rely on that.

"You could have just called out to me. You didn't need to chuck a brick at my leg."

"I meant to hit your head. Where is the box?"

"I already delivered it," I said, holding my leg and miming more pain than I felt. "That was a long time ago."

"No, you didn't. What did you do with the package? You need to give it to me. It's important."

"Why? And why would Cagle give me something that important to deliver anyway?"

"We need that package, you and I. The serum will cure us so we can think straight." Ratchet looked around nervously, paranoid. "The package contains a sample in a little black vial. They should be able to copy it. Give me the package, Zip, before the refrigeration gives out and it's ruined."

My dread sunk deeper. Finding out you were right isn't always a cause for celebration.

I hopped on my good leg. "Who are you going to deliver it to? Cagle's friends? Or Damini's friends? Or that other guy who keeps wanting to shoot me? Or the guy in the big black car who keeps wanting to shoot me? Who?"

Ratchet thought about that for a moment. "What car? Damini talked to you?"

"Yeah, she said I had to deliver the package somewhere else, or she would hunt me down and kill me."

"Where?" Ratchet suddenly seemed nervous. He played with his gun more than I liked.

"She wanted me to deliver it here. Seventh floor," I said, then I spun around once and rubbed my leg some more.

"Did you?"

"Yes."

"No, you didn't, damn it. You suck at lying. Why do you even try? Where is the damn box?"

I paused, not sure if I should tell him, but I decided a little shock would do him good. "I visited the place where you wanted me to deliver it. The doctor's dead."

Ratchet took a step forward. "How do you know he's dead?"

"I saw the body. His head was leaking brains like a dropped jar leaks jam."

"Are you sure it was him?" Ratchet was dancing like a boxer now. Shuffling his feet and jerking his shoulders. More upset than I had ever seen him. I was worried he'd shoot me just talking to me.

"The body was decorating the doctor's office floor, and his blood was leaking onto the doctor's Persian carpet."

I chose not to tell him about the other murder in the doorway. Information was power, the gunman had told me. I was beginning to believe it.

"And anyway," I continued, "even if Cagle decided to give me the box, why didn't you just swap it out for a bonbon? You had plenty of opportunity. Seems like that would have been the easy way, and we wouldn't be having this conversation."

"The vial requires a carefully controlled environment—you can't just put it in the fridge or something. It has to stay in *that* box." Ratchet shook his head as if trying to wake up. "Quit trying to figure things out and tell me where the package is. We don't have time for this."

I stood up and rubbed my leg. "I got time, and I want to know what's really going on. Who was the guy in the car? Who's been chasing after me trying to kill me? Who does he work for? Who sapped Bolt?"

And how does Bang fit into this?

Ratchet stepped forward menacingly. "You're a nice guy. You don't deserve what I'm going to do to you if you don't tell me where the package is. You really don't, and I won't like doing it, but I will. I'll shoot you in the leg, Zip. Don't think our friendship will get in my way."

Friendship? He sounded like he meant it.

"Look, Ratchet, the guy with the gun chased me for a while, and then someone else showed up in a big car and there was shooting, and I don't even know where it is anymore."

There were two vent pipes that Bang could have meant when she said it was at the edge of the building. I wasn't lying, exactly, so I guess to Ratchet it looked like I was telling the truth.

Ratchet's shirt was missing a button, he had something in his left vest pocket that looked heavy, but his gun was in his hand.

My leg hurt.

Where was Bang?

Where was the gunman?

I caught a fleeting eureka moment of a mathematical trick involving magnetism that might lead to the grand unification theory. Then it was gone.

A gun went off. I hit the deck thinking Ratchet had gotten jittery and shot me by accident, but chips from the brick wall sprayed out, and a line of blood appeared across Ratchet's forehead. His gun spun out of his hand. I caught it before it hit the ground, fired a few shots toward where I thought the first shoot had originated, then jumped up and ran.

The gun in my hand went off twice more accidentally, putting holes in the roof disturbingly near my feet before I threw it in a roof drain to get rid of it. I ran like my life depended on it, which I guess it did. I didn't take the time to notice what happened to Ratchet.

The shooter followed. He wore brown. His white shoes flashed when I looked back. Either he moved faster than before, or I was very tired, or perhaps both.

We came to a lumber warehouse that had been converted to a Drone Wars stadium. It had HVAC units, solar panels, and ductwork all over the roof. I extended my lead. On the next jump, I caught a ladder that crawled over the far edge of the roof and swung against the building just below the roof's edge. I flattened myself there until the gunman leapt past me and onto the next roof, running fast even for an E. He appeared to be juiced, which was pretty dangerous.

As I sped back down the street, hoping the gunman hadn't already backtracked looking for me, I remembered that Ratchet might be bleeding out on that roof top. He might be another person to add to the list of deaths that might be my fault. It had only been luck that kept my own name off the list so far.

CHAPTER 22

I ran through a park and circled to be sure I'd lost my pursuer. A blur went by on Sixth. I strobed it with a blink and recognized Go. He was the fourth person who had wanted to be called Flash when he changed over, but the E who'd chosen the name Flash first would have none of it. Go opted for FlashGo, which was annoying, so we just called him Go, which was annoying to him but worked for everyone else. He was not an actor in this drama, however, just a random encounter. I could use his help, at least as a diversion, but having Bang already mixed up in the mess was bad enough.

If the gunman stopped chasing me, he was probably chasing Ratchet around the near north side. Ratchet didn't have a gun anymore—I'd thrown it in a rain gutter. His comment about our friendship still bothered me. Did he really think we were friends? Had he been teasing me rather than berating me all this time? That seemed unlikely, but it made me surprisingly happy to think it might be true.

Only when I considered going back to the Tagler Building

to get the damn box did I wonder what Ratchet and the gunman thought of me returning to that roof. Did they both now deduce that the box had to be there? Why else would I have returned there?

The thought slowed me down. If the box was still hidden, it might not be for long. They would figure out my reason for being on that roof eventually and begin a real search.

I circled back and looked over the Tagler Building roof from a distance. The gunman and Ratchet were both gone. Once on the roof, a closer inspection revealed that the box was gone too. Both standpipes were empty.

Ratchet or the gunman might have found it, but there hadn't been much time to search, and they had each other to contend with.

Bang was the only one who had known exactly where it was.

I ran up the stairs at Cagle's building twenty-eight minutes after I'd left to deliver the box and pounded on the door. Ratchet opened it and stared eyebrows-up at me.

I guess I stared eyebrows-up back at him, neither expecting the other to be there, or perhaps even alive.

Ratchet recovered first. "What? Deliver it already?" He knew better, of course, but he delivered his sarcasm mixed in with barely controlled anger, loudly and slowly, so Cagle could hear and follow.

Then, quickly and quietly, he continued, "What did you do with the box, Zip? What did you do with the damn box?"

He kicked me in the shin.

"I have to see Cagle. Someone took the box," I said loud and slow, not lying exactly.

I heard Cagle shout, "What happened?" He used shortened sentences, so Ratchet wouldn't get bored waiting for the next word, not that Ratchet would ever ignore him anyway.

Ratchet opened the door the rest of the way to admit me. Now he wore a sinister smile, like he wanted to see what was going to happen between me and Cagle, like he was enjoying the possibilities. The slice across his forehead showed bright red, and he squinted a little from the bruise, but that was small consolation to me.

Kicking Ratchet's head for three seconds popped into my mind again. Just three seconds, because we were friends.

I scuttled over to Cagle's desk and slowly said, "Someone took the box." I paused, then walked around the room. I ate two chocolates off Ratchet's tray. "The gunman showed up before I even made it to the bridge, and he was after the box." Still the truth as far as it went. Not wanting to confuse or annoy Cagle, I left out Ratchet and the chase.

Cagle stood and paced.

I grabbed a handful of chocolates before Ratchet snatched the rest away.

"He must have known when I was going to deliver it again," I said. "He followed me right from this building."

I glanced at Ratchet, but he was eating a chocolate and glaring fixedly at a swirly vision pacifier he had attached to the wall by the door.

"Why didn't you outrun him? Why didn't you lose him? You've cost me twenty-five thousand and an important client."

Cagle stared at me. He stared so long I chirped twice to suppress the urge to scream.

The most sure-fire way to look guilty is to try not to look guilty. It works every time. I wanted to look honest. That's always a mistake, trying to look honest.

"Did you steal it and use it on yourself?" Cagle continued to watch me, looking for a sign.

Ratchet grunted and dropped something.

"No," I said.

"Ratchet," Cagle said, still looking at me, "get me a sapper."

I guess I went pale, maybe green, because when Ratchet came back, Cagle waved and said, "Never mind. It's obvious he didn't use it, but you know, Zip, you aren't in the clear yet. At the very least, you're not working for me or anyone else I know anymore, and I may still have you sapped if I find you've been lying to me."

So at least Cagle believed without a doubt that the box contained a Velocity vaccine, not a Cure. But I had to wonder what made Ratchet think it was the one remaining sample of the Cure.

What's more, Cagle didn't seem to be as upset about his twenty-five thousand or his lost client as he ought to be. The Cagle I knew would have sapped me without thinking about it, or at least he'd have slapped me around some.

"I haven't been lying to you, Mr. Cagle," I said, feeling relieved and showing it.

"Get out of here, Zip. Don't come back."

Cagle never wanted or expected the package delivered, that much was clear, which meant that the gunman worked for him. His gunman sapped Bolt, intending to steal the box back after I'd delivered it. I wasn't sure why Cagle would do that, but it was the only answer that made any sense at all.

I zipped to the door, but Ratchet held it closed for just a

moment too long, forcing me to stall and look at him. His expression shouted menacingly at me, but he didn't say anything. He didn't have to.

Earlier, on the way up the stairs to Cagle's office, I had been scared of Cagle, Damini, and the gunman. Now, on the way down the stairs, I was scared for the future of all Energy. What happened to the black vial? Was it ever in my hands?

If Cagle ever figured out that the gunman had failed to take the box from me, he would be after me again, but for now he wasn't my primary concern.

I stutter-stepped down the last stairs, obsessing over Bang. For all my love of Bang, I was still being a hypocritical ass. If she hadn't told Damini everything about me, I would have one less worry. But in Bang's position, taped to the floor, I would have answered any question, exposed any secret, betrayed any confidence. Logically, I knew that, but my heart still yearned for the total, all-out trust I'd had with Bang before she told Damini about the delivery and where I lived.

Still, when the gunman had cuffed me to the window grate, Bang had risked death to help me escape. She could have grabbed the box, run off with it, found a way to sell it. But she didn't. And maybe Bang didn't even have the box now. The gunman may have circled back and found it. If that was what had happened, it would explain why Cagle didn't sap me or kill me.

I trotted back toward the abandoned building with the hole in the roof, imagining that Bang and I were a modern Bonnie and Clyde, the Hole in the Roof Gang, but I'd seen a picture of the shot-up car Bonnie and Clyde were driving when they were finally caught and killed, so I tried not to pursue that line of thought.

CHAPTER 23

When I reached the roof of the Hole in the Roof Gang's hideout, I was thinking about the pair of avatar boxers called Bonnie and Clyde but hesitated to dive in when a man's voice echoed up from the hole. The gunman's voice carried clearly up to the roof. "Typical E, watch the hole in the roof, but ignore the stairs. Don't try to run. I'll shoot you, don't think I won't."

"What do you want?" Bang's voice. She was there, in the room with the gunman.

I circled the hole and caught sight of the gunman and his white shoes. I imagined a novel cover depicting a thin man with wide thighs, stupidly narrow hips and wide bony shoulders, standing on a roof, looking down at a man wearing white shoes who is holding a woman at gunpoint. I should have worn a fedora.

The Hole in the Roof Gang vs. the Man with the White Shoes.

What would the man on the roof do?

Something heroic. He'd do something heroic.

Or stupid. Yes, he'd do something stupid.

I dove through the hole, bounced off the gunman, and tumbled to the floor.

I'd imagined him crashing to the ground and losing his gun in the collision, but he was better than that. I'd imagined him at least losing his balance, but he was better than that, too.

Instead, he batted me aside and still stood, gun in hand, now swinging his aim toward me.

Bang sprung on him like a puma, snarling and slapping. The gunman fell to his knees.

The gun went off. The bullet hit something glass.

I rolled to a stand.

Bang jumped up through the hole in the roof. I followed her, kicking the gunman in the head on the way.

The gunman took another shot, but he was off balance, trying to stand. He missed.

Bang dropped off the edge of the roof, caught a flagpole, and flipped to the ground, with me following close behind. She let me pass her and lead the way. Seeing in the improved light that she had the box in the carrying strap across her back gave me a burst of extra energy and speed.

After a few quick turns, a zigzag dart through a parking lot of Boxwheels, and two through-building shortcuts, we hid in a doorway alcove along a secluded back alley, decorated with convoluted paintings of bandaged thumbs. It was the delivery door for a small medical clinic. There were two Boxwheels parked in the alley, one with its small red light lit on its roof waiting to be unloaded, and the other showing a small green light waiting for another delivery order.

A dim overhead light illuminated cigarette butts and a couple empty Derpal bottles around the doorway. We could see each other, but we could not be seen from the main street.

Still jumpy and nervous, I said, "We should be OK for a minute."

"I'm glad you arrived when you did," Bang said softly, eyes unfocused, listening for pursuit.

"Yeah, me too."

"I hoped you'd find me at the abandoned building, but the gunman got there first."

"Yeah. I'm glad *you* knocked him down. You're pretty good in a fight." I was being noncommittal, still thinking about the Cure. Still acting aloof. Still feeling hypocritical.

She fluttered around, then said, "Yeah, and what the hell was that bit with you diving into the building and missing him completely? With that aim, you could have been a pitcher for the Naperville Burbans."

I had to smile, even though I didn't want to. I pictured an E winding up to pitch, then running in with the ball in his hand all the way to the batter.

Focus, Zip. Focus.

Bang pulled out the box and handed it to me. "I grabbed it when Ratchet and the gunman took off. I thought if I left it there, they might figure out that the only reason you would go back there would be to retrieve the box."

"You think even faster than you run," I said. It had taken me a couple miles of running to realize the same thing.

When our breathing eased, I asked, "So you followed me when I left you to retrieve the box?"

"I knew where you were going, so I didn't need to follow you."

I could feel my muscles tightening and my mental focus deteriorating from standing and talking too long. Bang began running in tight circles on her tiptoes. I kick-stepped against the door. We each played some mind puzzles, not saying anything, just listening for the gunman, trying to avoid the thing that needed to be said.

Bang began to cry.

Finally, I said, "I wish you'd told me about Damini right away."

She played with her fingers and wrung out her hands like washcloths.

"I tried, but there was always something else to do, you know?" She smiled tentatively, apologetically, through her tears. "I wish I'd told you too, but to be honest, the terror of being taped down is just now starting to wear off."

She shook like a wet dog, apparently trying to get rid of the sensation she could still feel.

"I never felt so utterly helpless," she continued. "I completely freaked out. I love you, Zip. I would do anything for you if I could, but Damini, she had her men duct tape me to the floor. They taped me to the floor. They said they would just leave me there. I couldn't, I just couldn't . . . ."

She started high-step jogging in place. Her feet pounded heavily on the asphalt. Her gaze searched the sky like she hoped to find words there, or maybe an answer. The dull light reflected from the tears on her cheeks, and I could sense her replaying the experience.

She let out an agonized keening that penetrated my soul and felt painful in my chest. She grabbed me by my SkinSuit and pulled me back and forth, then she beat me on the shoulders. "I couldn't move, damn it. I could barely breathe. I just couldn't stop talking. They asked me about you and about . . . and I just told them everything that came to my mind." She slapped her hands against her cheeks and sobbed. "I'm so sorry, Zip. I'll do anything to help."

I saw only one way to close the widening chasm in my heart. I grabbed her hands, pulled her close, and hugged her as tightly as I could. I just could not stay angry at Bang. Now that I had a moment to consider, it became clear that I had no right to be. Holding her in my arms, even for that brief moment, softened my ire and helped me focus on the people who had earned my anger: Damini, Cagle, Ratchet, and the gunman with his damn white shoes.

We looked at each other, enjoying a second of calm. I concentrated as much as I could on my enemies and squeezed Bang one more time. "We can't stay here," I said, stressing the "we," and hoping that was enough for now. Hoping that she would understand that by saying, "we," I meant that I was angrier at the situation than I was at her.

Energy were obviously and fundamentally different from normal people. Clear physical differences made us stand out to be carefully ignored or sometimes pitied as pathetic and useless, but we were also despised for being mostly thieves or petty criminals. Fleas had no power, only frustration. We had a desire to be useful but were stymied at every turn because of our anxiety and our hyper life, and because of the Slugs' perceptions of our capabilities and our criminal inclinations. And at the time, there wasn't one of us who could slow down enough to coherently explain, or to represent us to the rest of the world, although a few had tried. We were of such different worlds that maybe the explanations, if they could be formed, wouldn't even make sense. But at a human level, we weren't all that different. Our hearts worked the same way, although I wasn't so sure the Slugs believed that.

I held the box up to the light, and we stared at it. Again, I had the feeling it would explode.

I pressed all eight corners, and the box popped open.

Now that I examined it with Bang by my side, I could see that the top on the inside box slid to the left. There was no trick after all. I opened the inside box, but it didn't hold the little black vial Ratchet had described and that I'd seen a picture of in the newspaper. It wasn't the Cure for Energy. Packed in the chill box was a pressure infuser—used for everything from epinephrine and migraine shots to Happy Pappy euphoria boosts—containing a crystal-blue Velocity vaccine held in the standard Medical Delivery System unit and labeled with a large script V.

Velocity.

Use that vaccine and no more fear of being sapped and then going slowly crazy while the Slugs around you tell you it's OK. You could still die, even with the vaccine, of course, everyone ran that risk, but at least you wouldn't die in that kind of insane agony.

I pulled out the Velocity vaccine and examined it, longing for its protection, for that bit of safety in a world that seemed to be all against me. Just press it to the upper arm and pull the little trigger. It was that easy.

So I did.

Bang tried to jump away, but I held her long enough to make sure the Velocity flowed into her.

Bang, at least, would never be turned into a Slug. It was the least I could do to pay her back for my hypocrisy, or perhaps I was assuaging my own guilt. Either way, I felt oddly euphoric.

She actually stopped, stared at me for the longest moment. Then she threw her arms around my neck and cried. "Now you're dead, Zip. Now you are dead."

"Not yet. Listen, if we get separated . . . ."

She pulled back from me and started slapping her thighs, stomping her feet, and shaking her head. "Why are we separating, Zip? Why would we do that? What are you going to do?"

She could tell I was lying, even though I hadn't said anything untruthful yet. The look in her eyes told me she knew I was going to do something stupid, at least stupid from her point of view. I shuffled around while I tried to come up with something to tell her. I wanted to tell her my plan, hoping that it would sound better out loud than it sounded in my head, but Bang didn't need to know what I actually had planned.

Instead, I lied.

"I'm going back to Cagle's. I'm going to tell him that the gunman caught me and took the box." Bang didn't know I'd already done that.

Bang flapped her arms and jogged in place. "Damini will still be after you. The gunman will still be after you."

We played a quick patty-cake with three turnarounds and a hip bump, but it didn't feel like a game.

"I'll figure something out," I said. "Don't worry."

CHAPTER 24

Bang had become deeply involved in my muddle of packages. If I could have found a way to isolate her from it, I would have. Yet, I was glad she was there, glad that someone would care if I got myself killed. Was that selfish? I guess so. But doesn't everyone, even an E, deserve to believe that someone will mourn their passing?

"I have seven Erg pills and some bars," Bang said. "I have some cash, and we can pick up bulk along the way, if we can figure out what we're going to do after you see Cagle. I want to go with you."

Bang pulled out two QuackenBars and a water bottle.

We ate and drank while we lurched and bumped around in that small alcove under the light. A few mosquitoes buzzed my ears. I caught two between my fingers and squished them, thinking that that feeling of squishing the mosquitoes must be how Damini felt when she was squishing Fleas. Maybe that was how Cagle felt too, or how he wanted to feel—or perhaps how he wanted people to think he felt.

Bang trotted around the empty Boxwheel that was waiting in the alley for its next transport order and came back with an expectant look. "Are we going?"

"I keep trying to think, but nothing happens." Had I already lost the Cure? The possibility of me losing the Cure and messing up the future for all Energy was making me revert to the Stooges. Sometimes the shoe fits.

"The owner of the black car might have been Cagle's boss," I said. "Maybe he's annoyed. Maybe he actually expected me to deliver the package."

When I thought about it, though, the whole setup seemed absurd. Successfully delivering the box was the most remote possibility. It seemed no one, except perhaps the man in the black car, actually wanted the package to reach its destination.

"Didn't Cagle expect it to be delivered?"

"He gave the box to me, Bang. It was worth a good deal more than anything I've ever delivered for him before. He could have given it to Ratchet or to Blink or even delivered it himself with an armed guard. But he gave it to me to deliver. Does that strike you as a man who seriously wanted the package delivered? I was the expendable one."

I knew my limitations.

I didn't tell Bang that the box was supposed to have contained the Cure. If she didn't know, I thought she wouldn't be in as much danger. If I failed to obtain the Cure—if it even existed—or failed deliver it to someone who could use it to save us, then Bang wouldn't be as painfully depressed about it as I already was.

"This is a mess, Zip. We have enough food. Maybe we could lie low for an hour. If all these people are looking for you, maybe they'll start killing each other instead of you."

I smiled because I had thought of that earlier too.

Being a mug was getting old. Always following orders, doing what I was told, being used by Slugs. Sometimes power isn't what you're given, it's how you make use of what you already have.

"If you don't want me to come with you, what should I do?" she asked.

"Hold still," I said.

When she did, I kissed her.

"If we hold still like that, they'll catch us," she whispered.

She circled the alley and returned.

"Or they might see us running around in the middle of the street," I said.

"Sorry."

We listened for the gunman but only heard a motorcycle cough by on an adjacent street. "Damini is probably looking for you too, now. I'd suggest you hide," I said.

"When will we meet up again?"

"Let's try for twenty minutes, here."

Bang tilted her head, quizzical and maybe a little exasperated. Then she spun around once and said, "See you then, Zip. Don't die." She kissed me again and ran off, not looking back.

I hurried back the way we'd come.

I hoped to persuade some of the big fish to eat each other.

CHAPTER 25

Retracing our original path backward from the alcove all the way to the hole in the roof, I didn't see the gunman. Sprinting a zigzag course all the way back to the alcove again, I spotted him under a streetlamp on the main street near the alcove, examining the empty MDS box we'd dropped in the secluded alley.

I slowed just enough for him to glimpse me, then took off down the street and across the river. It was a race I would have lost had it lasted ten seconds longer. He was still juiced, but I knew where I was going, and the gunman didn't. That alone gave me just enough of an advantage.

Although he took a few shots, I'd chosen a route that included a lot of turns and leaps, so he had to slow down to shoot. Some ductwork, walls, and windows got extra ventilation in them, but he didn't ventilate me.

The Tagler Building where Damini had asked me to deliver the vaccine was now mostly dark, with only three lighted rooms visible from the street. One was on the seventh floor where she'd told me to go. No one guarded the front door, and luckily it wasn't locked, because I barged through it barely ahead of the gunman.

I darted across the foyer, heard the front door smack open flat against the wall behind me. I slammed open the stairway door. As I ran up the wooden stairs, a step at my shoulder exploded into bits. A splinter lodged in my neck, but I kept running, rounded onto the next flight, then launched myself up toward seven.

The stairs were two flights per level. I stayed just far enough ahead to avoid giving him a good shot. Barreling onto the seventh floor, I rounded a corner in the hallway and surprised Damini's professional who was standing by a door. I dove to the floor and squeezed my eyes shut, waiting for the impending gunshot. The gunman was left exposed behind me. Damini's pro fired once. No hesitation there. To my surprise, he didn't shoot me. The trip had been a gamble from the start.

The percussive thud of the gunshot still reverberated in my skull when Damini's muscle lifted me up and hauled me toward suite 701.

The Pro strolled over to look at the gunman's body.

Inside 701, the Muscle whispered something to Damini. The room was sparsely furnished. It appeared to be a waiting room, or a room where she held small meetings. A feeble black torchiere lamp cast sinister shadows in the corners. There was a wooden table in the far left corner holding a brass lamp with a white shade, and sailing-ship bookends with no books between them. To the right, Damini sat in a green leather chair with her legs crossed. She was wearing a lime-green pantsuit that clashed with the chair and a dapper black beret that would have been charming and even pretty in other circumstances. She didn't say anything, but her arms and legs were crossed, and her foot bobbed rapidly for a Slug. Where was the poinsettia coat with the duck stain?

The Pro came in and shook his head. The gunman must have dropped the box when he took off after me, or the Pro would have found it.

"Well, Zip," said Damini finally, "where is it?"

I spoke slowly and clearly. "That man followed me from Cagle's place." Stick to the truth.

"Go on," she said.

I shuffled from side to side, worrying, as I usually did, about how guilty I looked and what I could do to look and sound sincere. The big guy pulled out his plastic handcuffs and locked them on me.

I said, "I think Ratchet, Cagle's man, told him when I'd be leaving to make the delivery. That guy with the gun followed me."

"You mean the dead guy on the floor out there?"

"Yes." Don't say more than you have to.

"That was at least a half hour ago, Flea. Have you been hiding all this time?"

"No, I had to go back and tell Cagle what happened."

Damini sighed—an exasperated, disapproving, endless sigh.

"Zip, I told you that if you didn't deliver that Velocity vaccine here, you would regret it, didn't I?"

When Damini spoke to her men, she used short, fast sentences. When she spoke to me, she measured each thought before speaking, lingered on each word, paused to make me nervous and self-conscious. Her speech pattern made me want to rush through the answer to speed her up, like talking quietly hoping that someone who is shouting at you will calm down and talk more quietly too.

"Yes, but I don't have it. I think Ratchet used the Velocity vaccine on himself." I didn't say this particular Velocity, but I did believe that Ratchet had covered himself somewhere along the way. He'd handled the sapper without worry at Cagle's office.

"I spend a lot of time and effort and money to help you Fleas. I provide jobs, bulk food, even medical care. How do you think you all survive around here? Half the Fleas in Chicago work for me, that's how. And most of you are grateful to have a job, because if it weren't for me, no one would hire you spastic buffoons."

Was she offering me a job, or berating me for not doing what she asked even though I didn't actually work for her? She seemed to be getting angrier and more self-righteously indignant as she spoke. The Muscle, who was still holding my wrist straps, relaxed and gave me a little more space to move around, giving himself a little more space to do his dance too. He'd most likely heard the whole thing many times before, so it was probably worse for him. Still, he moved a little more and breathed a little harder every time she said "Flea."

Damini stood and paced to the wall and back. "You, Zip, are not helping your fellow Fleas." She poked me in the chest as she recharged to continue her diatribe. "You are part of the problem. You are the kind of Flea that gives the other Fleas a bad name. I let you live, give you some work, and you, you ungrateful little shit, slough it off like you had other things to do. You are an incompetent, dithering, lying little

Flea who won't do as you're told. I don't suffer Fleas like you. I kill Fleas like you."

She paced the room three more times, forcing me to think about what she said. The problem was that she was right. Even for a Flea, I wasn't useful to anyone. Not to my parents, not to Cagle, not to Bang, not even to my own damn self. I couldn't even hold onto a good friend because I invariably lost track of meeting times and got distracted.

But the Pro, who was standing near the door rolling his washers around on his knuckles, glared intently at Damini. He wasn't grateful either. He was unhappy and alone just like all the other working E's. The Muscle twitched and stomped behind me. I had to concentrate to avoid moving in unison, needing my own bounce to stay focused. Well, as focused as I could be during the agonizingly long and slow conversation.

When she eventually spoke, she startled me into a jerking leap. "Where were you supposed to deliver the Velocity?"

I told her while trying and failing to hold myself reasonably still. The Muscle held me in place, but he only put enough pressure on my wrists to keep me from running around the room.

Damini walked to the door, then turned to the Pro and, with a toss of her head, said, "Sap him."

I was too stunned to move for a moment. "No, don't do that. Please. It wasn't my fault."

Which it wasn't, after all.

The whole thing was Ratchet's fault. Or maybe hers. Or maybe Cagle's. I just knew it wasn't mine. Then I lied. I was so upset, it just came out, smooth as Erg. "The dead guy took it from me. He had a gun. Then he gave the box to Ratchet. I saw the exchange. I got away, but the gunman found me again. He chased me. It wasn't my fault." I'd talked a little too fast for most Slugs, but she understood me. She had a lot of Energy on her payroll.

Damini stopped halfway through the door, her gloved hand on the jamb while the Pro held a sapper poised near my chest. I squirmed and stomped, trying to back away from the sapper, but the Muscle may as well have been a wall. Bang would be lost to me forever if I was sapped. She couldn't stay with me for an hour then, even if she wanted to. She'd had her vaccine. She would never be able to slow down enough to be with a Slug even if I survived.

"You say this Ratchet works for Cagle?" Damini seemed pleased that Cagle's man had stolen from him.

"Yes." I think I was gurgling, but she understood. The Muscle now held me firmly with the wrist straps.

The Pro said, "I've heard of him."

I twiddled my fingers, blinked a lot, and counted eighteen holes by eighteen holes in each of the ceiling tiles, which made three hundred and twenty-four per tile, and twelve and a half tiles in one direction and fifteen in the other made 60,750 holes in the ceiling. That sounded like a lot of holes.

The Muscle danced more violently behind me, yanking painfully on the straps.

Damini considered her options.

"OK, Zip. Perhaps you can redeem yourself." She held out her hand, and the Pro pulled a box out of his pocket and handed it to her. The box looked like another cube of dead trout. She handed it to me, and the Muscle released one hand so I could take it. "Take this to North Sheffield and deliver it as Cagle told you. Can you do that?"

I nodded vigorously. I couldn't talk. The sapper was still

inches from my chest. She'd played me with the sapper, but I felt like she might suddenly decide to sap me after all. She'd said she didn't suffer Fleas like me.

"Let him go," she said with a whimsical head toss, as though I didn't matter anyway. "We got what we wanted. Remind me to offer this Ratchet fellow a job."

Damn.

She left the room, and as she walked down the hall, the big guy released me and said, "No one gets a Velocity from anyone but Damini, got that?" then followed her out the door.

Yeah, I got it. I also got another damn box to deliver.

The Pro gave me a wink as he put the sapper back in his pocket and closed the door behind him, leaving me alone. I wasn't sure what the wink meant, but I had a feeling I'd best stay out of his line of sight.

The dead gunman still lay on the floor, completely still and pale, blood leaking from the hole in his head. I felt sorry for the guy, as I always did for people who had a run of bad luck. He'd seemed like an OK guy, except for the trying-to-kill-me part.

But the gunman was a Flea, and we all had to do what the Slugs told us to do or starve, or get jailed, or get sapped—or shot. He'd been ordered to steal the box, and it had cost him his life. Other than the Energy who had very rich parents, rich parents who still cared, all Energy worked for Slugs. E couldn't be leaders even of other E. Leadership required concentration, planning, having a vision of the future, a long view, objectives.

After Damini and her men left, I ran circles and did a few flips and flailed about for a good thirty seconds shaking off the effects of the cuffs and the slow conversation. My unconscious mind must have been working overtime. As I was performing handstands, a couple facts surfaced. One was that the man Cagle wanted me to deliver this box to was already dead, and that Damini might be intending to frame me for that murder by sending me over there carrying a box that contained something incriminating. Either way, she'd left me un-sapped for a better reason than just that she didn't want to bother, or because she needed me to deliver another box. Sapping me would have been the most logical thing to do—if they didn't want to actually kill me, that is.

The second thing was that there might still be a Cure out there somewhere, and even if I found it, or Bang found it, we wouldn't know who to give it to. The Cure wouldn't be useful unless it was delivered to a research facility while still in its functional climate-controlled box—that is, before the box's power ran out. The Velocity vaccines' refrigeration units only lasted a couple hours after a charge. I didn't know how long the Cure's refrigeration would last.

Jumping over the gunman's body the third time, I wondered what his name was and what would happen to his body. Damini would probably send someone to clean the crime scene. I didn't want to be there when the cleanup crew or the police showed up, so I strapped on Damini's box, ran down the stairs, and set out for North Sheffield Avenue.

One of Damini's torpedoes most likely followed me to make sure I went where I was supposed to go, but I made it difficult for them. Finally pausing atop a Gator Club next to the giant green plastic alligator—which was actually a

Nile crocodile, but Croc Club didn't sound as good as Gator Club—I could see for a block in all directions. I circled, looking for tails, and saw only a few bugs flying their delivery routes.

Who was the man in the black car? How had he found me in that alley where the gunman had banded me to the window grate? Several delivery drones drifted by, skimming the roofs. They were competition, but they got me thinking about exactly what they might be doing other than just deliveries. I had the right to feel paranoid. I had lots of questions, and I had too many people who intended to kill me.

Whatever the outcome would be that night, I was too tired to think at that moment. Tired right down to my eye sockets, and desperate for a rest. I ducked down Carla Alley and sat down to hide behind a dumpster. The spot smelled of rotten food and motor oil, but I didn't care. I still didn't smell all that good myself. I leaned back, counted the bricks in the opposite wall, and snapped to sleep.

CHAPTER 26

Zane finds a book describing the consequences that the switch *from old-growth lumber to second-growth lumber had on furniture and house construction. He reads three and a half pages and gets bored. The writing is good, the story is interesting and well presented, yet he finds himself drifting as he reads, thinking about candy thermometers and lawn-mowing patterns and what a good name for a cat might be. He puts down the book and rides his bike around the block even though he has nowhere to go. Then he drops his bike in the garage and runs as fast as he can around the block. Twice. He had started doing a useless run around the block each day when he had turned thirteen. Now, four months later, he does at least two laps, sometimes four.*

Later, he is playing three-minute chess with Winmae, another Gifted. She sits across the table staring at the board while fiddling with a couple Lego blocks, snapping them in different positions, first forming one style of offset block, then unsnapping them and forming another offset block, over and over. She reaches across, moves her bishop, and slaps the clock, but she's left the right side of the board open for intrusion, giving up the chess game. Although it will take a while to finish it, she's already lost. Zane advances a pawn while she gets some cheese from her fridge.

Zane gets a buzztext from Betsy. "Aarav is going nuts. You should see this."

"Going nuts?"

"He's running in circles and won't stop."

At Betsy's house ten minutes later, Aarav is still running. He's making loops around their in-ground pool.

Winmae says, "He's really fast."

Zane has felt like this a few times lately, like the world has slowed, like he can't gulp information into his head fast enough, and he gets so enthusiastically jittery that he has to run off the excess energy. Running in circles gives the world the appearance of motion he craves at those times. But he always stops after a while, calmed and able to focus again.

Betsy, looking at her watch, says, "He seems to be getting faster. He paused once, while you were on your way over. He said he was hungry, but he didn't stop to eat. He just grinned and started running again."

Ten minutes later, Zane, Betsy, and Winmae are sitting on lawn chairs watching Aarav as though he is giving a show. Betsy stands up. "I can't watch this anymore. He may not stop until dark."

"Should we call someone? Should we tackle him?" Winmae asks.

"I tried standing in front of him, but he got mad and knocked me over."

Zane says, "Call mom," into his Wonky and waits. Aarav continues to run, wearing out the grass and compacting the soil in the circle.

The assistant gets his mother, who is doing rounds at the hospital. Zane explains what is going on. She tells him to hose Aarav down with a mist, so he cools off, and that she will send someone over to help.

CHAPTER 27

When I awoke, I realized Cagle would now never figure out that the gunman hadn't taken the box from me, because the gunman was dead. Cagle would think someone, probably Damini, found the gunman, killed him, and took the box. He'd be right about Damini killing him, but for the wrong reason.

What's more, Damini's pro didn't find the empty box on the gunman, so that meant he probably dropped it when he saw me and chased me.

Back near the streetlight where I had seen the gunman examining the box, I found it open, lying in the gutter.

Food. Bolt. Bang.

I was hungry and distracted, but as I was about to put the new box in my carrying strap with the other box Damini gave me to deliver, I thought to mark it in some way to make sure I could tell them apart. Then I remembered it should already have the distinctive V-shaped scratch that I'd noticed at Cagle's when he gave it to me.

The box I put in the air conditioning plenum had a scratch. The one the gunman had dropped did not have a V-shaped scratch. The box was dirty and a little beat up, but no distinctive scratch. Which meant the box had been switched somewhere along the way. And since I didn't actually remember putting the scratch on the box in the first place, I wondered if Cagle had even given me the same box both times.

The final realization as I searched my memory was that Bang hadn't been surprised by how the box opened. She didn't react at all to me having to press all eight corners at once.

Bang switched boxes on me. No one else had the opportunity.

I sprinted away. Thinking was too painful.

After eating a chunk of clean-looking steak and seven French fries from the Groot dumpster behind Café Filet, then free-running roofs while avoiding obstacles, I could think more clearly. The expenditure of energy, the continuous calculations for path, planning at speed, the immediate course corrections required to avoid air conditioning plenums, vent pipes, solar equipment, stairwells and elevator headers, assorted roof furniture, and puddles all helped muffle the part of my brain that bounced around too much to be anything but distracting. Running allowed me to focus my thoughts, at least as much as it was possible for me to focus.

The box with the Cure was my ultimate objective, but

Damini would be placated if I delivered her new box in the same way as I hoped Cagle was. They should both be satisfied that I'd done as they had asked, or close enough, even if I had no job and no reliable source of food.

It would be nice to think there would be no one specifically after me, although I wasn't sure about the man in the black car. Maybe he was after the gunman rather than me. At least I could hope so.

Because Damini told me to deliver the new box to Cagle's initial destination, I figured it probably wasn't a bomb or any kind of dangerous trick device. More likely it was a note saying, "No one gets a Velocity from anyone but Damini, got that?"

Unless she knew about the murdered guys at the doctor's office. But then I couldn't imagine why she would send me at all. Why incriminate someone who might rat on her if caught?

I stopped on the alley side of the sloped roof on an end-of-the-world-type church and pulled Damini's box out from under my carrying strap. Inside was Damini's business card, nestled in a fine piece of red silk, which I thought was an elegant touch. The card had her name written in script with just a little flourish and printed in raised black lettering on a champagne background. Her Wonky address was listed below in small, crisp type. I guess she figured even crooks should show a little class, and that everyone who mattered already knew who she was and what she did. Her name and how to contact her would be sufficient.

Since I was only dropping off her calling card, I accepted the delivery job. Not that I had a choice, but it was nice to imagine it was my decision.

I trotted to North Sheffield Avenue and hurried around the building, scanning for anything or anybody that might cause me problems. The body in the entrance was gone, although a small rusty-red stain marked the concrete. There were no police or other lurkers about, but I opted to go in through the window I'd used to enter the office earlier anyway. The truck was still there, so after putting on my gloves, I climbed on top and slithered up and across the brick wall to the window. The room was dark except for a dim glow cast from the parking-lot light. I slid open the window and climbed in for the second time that night.

Everything looked the same as I'd left it, except that the body might have been rolled some. As I placed Damini's box on the desk, I noticed a picture of a family. The man's face in the picture didn't match the face on the body. This was the doctor's office, so the dead person was probably not the doctor. Maybe there was still someone to give the Cure to if I ever found a way to convince Bang to give the box back.

By this time, I had accepted that Bang probably had the Cure in her possession. There wasn't any other possibility, was there?

I wanted to blame the switch of the boxes on Ratchet, but I really couldn't. There was no reason for him to have tracked me down and thrown a brick at me for one of Cagle's Velocity vaccines, nor was there a reason for him to have lied to me about me having the Cure. Which meant Bang had swapped it out. She had two opportunities, once when she had moved it from the air conditioning plenum to the standpipe, and once when she removed it from the standpipe and gave it to me at the doorway alcove in the alley.

As I was leaving the building, Damini's pro let me see him in the parking lot, so I slowed. He sauntered over as I dropped down from the truck. "You took your sweet time, Zip. Did you stop for a nap along the way?"

He made it sound ridiculous, but that was the first thing I'd done after slow talking to Damini for so long. I said, "Yes."

"Interesting that you used the window. Most people would have used the door."

"Why didn't you deliver it yourself through the front door?" I asked. "You're here anyway. Too much responsibility?"

"Don't push me, Zip. You don't want to push me. And anyway, why shouldn't Damini use someone who just doesn't matter? She probably thought there might be cameras or cops or something."

"You mean something like the dead guy on the floor?"

"Really? There was a body in there?"

The Pro made a point of moving very little. He had a large washer out, rolling it across his knuckles like he did, and doing small things to keep from dancing around and generally acting like E do. He was very good at being mostly still. The best I'd ever seen.

"Yeah. I'm not sure your delivery will ever be received by the person who is supposed to get it, but I did my job, so I'm leaving."

"OK, go ahead. I was just checking up. We're likely to meet again, Zip. Damini will probably have more jobs for you. Probably the dangerous ones."

"I hope not," I said and took off toward my rendez-vous with Bang. I backtracked and squared around the neighborhood to make sure Damini's pro didn't follow me.

I still had a hope that Bang wasn't putting on an act. I had a hope that she somehow wasn't the one who substituted the Velocity for the Cure. But not much of a hope.

CHAPTER 28

While I waited for Bang at the alcove, I scanned the area, hoping to do a better job of searching for E than I had at the doctor's office when the Pro had suddenly turned up. A small light for the alcove service door cast a dim shadow around the alley. The light bothered me because if anyone happened by, they would see us, but we wouldn't see them. This hadn't occurred to me last time, but I was even more distracted last time.

I jumped up, held onto the door lintel with one hand, and unscrewed the bulb with the other. When I dropped down, I smelled a brief hint of lavender, which made me smile, but just for a moment.

Bang slid up beside me. "You're alive!"

"Yes, I am. Damini came pretty close to changing that, but she decided to let me live."

"I thought you were going to see Cagle."

"He let me live too. What's more, Damini's torpedo took care of that guy with the gun. It's my lucky day."

She thumbed away some blood from my neck. "Seems like one of them had a hard time deciding."

"Where is the other box? Where is the box I carried, that you switched out?"

Bang glanced sideways, then brought her strap around to the front showing me a box I hadn't noticed. It had a *V* scratched in the side. "I'm sorry Zip, but . . . ."

There was a flash, a thud, and a gunshot blast simultaneously. A hole surrounded by slowly falling gray paint flakes bloomed high on the door behind us. We took off in opposite directions. It was an instinctive fight-or-flight reaction. We were E, so really, it was only a flight reaction.

I sped down the alley, then continued two hundred yards on the main street and dropped into a small yard I'd hidden in before. That shot had clearly been a warning. It was too high to be anything other than the shooter just trying to intimidate us into staying in place. An E with a gun is likely to fire it just because it's in his or her hand. The attempt to make us stay put didn't work very well. More importantly, though, the shooter didn't follow me. He or she followed Bang. The shooter followed the Cure.

No pedestrians yet. It was still only 3:30 a.m. I returned to the alcove slowly, at least for me, working my way carefully, staying low and across the street from my previous path when I'd run away from the gunshot. No one loitered in the alcove. The city was surprisingly quiet. Or perhaps my ears were losing their battle with people shooting at me from close range. I continued to work my way north, the way Bang had run.

Almost a minute later, I heard another gunshot, or something that sounded like a gunshot. The sound echoed among the buildings and came at me from all directions. Tension built in my muscles, or, I guess, in my head. I cried while I did jacks-and-toes as fast as I could to ease the anxiety, to settle my mind which was running faster than ever, wildly speculating about what had happened to Bang. I pictured Bang lying on the sidewalk again, only this time there was a bullet hole in her head. What had happened to the Cure?

Why had I run to save myself instead of running to protect Bang? Why had she betrayed me? Twice. Was this another blink? Another spoof designed to keep the Cure and still have me trust her?

I screamed—loud and long.

My throat came out of the scream raw and painful, but the effort settled me. If I assumed that Bang was OK, and that she really had intended to give me the Cure, then what should I do? Because that was the only explanation I liked. The only answer that didn't contribute more to my already stifling anxiety. Any other possibilities just confused and distracted me. Bang trying to make things right was the only idea that gave me any peace. Other disturbing possibilities invaded my thoughts, but I tried to disregard them.

If Bang was able to lose the shooter, she would go to the hole in the roof. That was the only place that made sense. The gunman who knew about that building now lay dead on the seventh floor of the Tagler Building.

I would go to the hole in the roof and wait. And hope.

There are few things more difficult for an E than waiting. I lasted only thirty seconds running circles and juggling two pieces of rotten wood before I leapt back up on the roof and did an outside circuit of the block. I'd hoped to see Bang running toward the hole, but I only saw a few distant drones and another E who I strobed and recognized as Pilfer. Pilfer couldn't be the shooter. He was terrified of almost everything, including his own shadow which chased him all over town in the daylight, so he only came out at night and avoided overhead light as much as possible.

After I dropped back into the hole, it dawned on me that running around the neighborhood, or even just around the roof, was a stupid thing to do. If Bang had eluded the shooter and was headed my way, he might see me, and all would be lost. Just stay down in the hole and trust Bang to lose him. That's what I had to do. I wouldn't have been much help anyway. She seemed more capable in a fight than I was.

Debris from the collapsed roof lay scattered about, so I built a ridiculous replica of a steam engine, tore it down, then stacked the wood lengthwise then sideways. The wood started looking tasty, and I thought wistfully about humans not being able to digest cellulose. That would be a really useful genetic adaptation. Why didn't Energy get the ability to eat wood as we aged, instead of the ability to freak out easily and run away at every noise?

Bang didn't know the gunman was dead! Why would she come to the hole in the roof if she didn't know it was safe? I'd forgotten that. Where would she go instead? Back to her apartment? But I'd told her about the gunman being dead, hadn't I? Yes. I told her that the Pro had killed him. Criminy would be a bad name for a cat. Too many syllables. Crime, perhaps.

I was stacking wood in the darkest corner of the room while trying to figure out where to go, when I heard someone land on the roof. A gunshot boomed above me. I dove for the space below the hole just as Bang came tumbling in. I tried to catch her but only slowed her fall. She hit the floor with a distressing thud, and we tumbled together. Her momentum carried us into a shadowy part of the room, then I held her in my arms. Her suit darkened over her chest.

"Bang, you've been shot!" I pulled her farther into the corner, trying to obscure our location from the shooter.

"I'm so sorry. I thought I'd lost him. I'm so sorry for everything."

The shooter lurked above us. Little dancing footsteps on the roof echoed loud in the small room.

From above, a female voice said, "Just give me the box she stole, and you can both go free."

I slipped the empty box out of my carrying strap.

Bang said quietly, "Oh, Zip, what have I done?"

I yelled, "You've shot her, you asshole. It's too late to allow us to go free."

I didn't know how bad the wound was. Bang wasn't crying in pain, but maybe that meant she was too weak to even moan.

"Just give me the box and we'll call it even."

"Even! You sadistic shit. I should just smash the damn box."

She fired again, this time hitting the floor near us. A burst of dust and wood splinters coated my head and Bang's face. Why were Energy so quick to shoot guns?

"OK, fine. Here's the damn box." I threw the empty box toward the voice. She was E, she could catch it.

"I'd call an ambulance if I were you," the woman said.

Then I heard her sprint off.

"Bang, can you hear me?"

"I'm so sorry," she said, "I should have told you. This is a cure for us, Zip. Maybe Dr. Argent can make more or find people who can. He'll know how to store it. It really is a cure!"

She grabbed me with one hand, then coughed and relaxed some. She wasn't moving, and, although I wanted to jump up and scream, I stayed mostly still. We were talking at E speed, but it still felt slow. She continued, "That man in the black car was Big Easy in his boss's car. When he found out that the last Cure dose was here in Chicago, he wanted it for himself. He wanted to be king of the Energy, the only one who could deal with Slugs on their terms. He sent me to steal it."

I put pressure on the wound, but Bang cried out in pain. I felt like I was killing her, so I stopped.

She laughed a little. It sounded wet. "I told Damini about you to avoid telling her about Big Easy. I'm sorry about that too, but Big E is big and violent. He scares the life out of me."

"You shouldn't talk."

"I should have just given you the right box in the first place, but I was too weak to do what my heart told me. I do love you, Zip."

Bang lifted the box to hand it to me. But the bullet that had hit her had gone through the box before it entered her chest. The whole side of the box was blown apart. When Bang saw the damage, she gasped. "It's ruined."

I pulled the top off, no need to press the corners now. Inside there was another MDS unit, miraculously undamaged. It contained an unbroken black vial.

Bang took the unit and examined it vaguely. She mumbled something I didn't catch, then grabbed me with surprising strength and punched the nose of the MDS unit into my arm. It hissed into me before I could stop her.

"What the hell?"

"It goes bad if it gets warm." She smiled up at me, pixie-like in the shadowy light.

"Bang?"

Her body relaxed in my arms. I kissed her, hoping that the gesture would transcend her final moment. Hoping that she would feel my lips on hers as her last thought rather than a feeling of sadness at having failed me somehow.

"I love you too, Bang."

While holding her for a moment, I felt her chest rise. The bullet had been slowed by its passage through the climate-control unit in the box. Her heart still beat. Even in a regular hospital she had a chance, but only if someone there knew how to treat Energy. If they didn't, she would likely die.

I carried Bang down the stairs to the street and sat her under a streetlamp, then used her Wonky to call a secure intermediary company who patched me to the police. I told them there was a wounded E named Bang and where she could be found. I asked for an ambulance. They started to ask questions, but I couldn't deal with a Slug conversation and canceled the line. One last kiss, then I took her Erg pills, two KoolBars, her money, and her stick of lavender scent. She wouldn't be needing it for a while.

On the other side of the street and up a couple stories, I ate a KoolBar and kept myself busy while I waited for the authorities. I wanted to be with her, but it would probably have killed me to sit and answer questions. Worse, they might have held me for questioning, and I had things to do.

When the ambulance came, I waved my distant goodbye to Bang, then I needed to run again even though I felt tired like I had never felt tired before. I trotted back to my apartment and tried to rest for a while, playing with my Puzzlers and Bobbins, but I couldn't even focus enough for that.

Bang would probably die. There were procedures in place for treating Energy, but few emergency personnel had studied them. Most didn't understand that even twenty minutes under restraint could destroy an E's mind. They might not know that some common drugs made the pain worse. They might not even know that E blood clotted quickly.

Still, she might be OK for a while if they gave her a sedative or put her in a micro-coma. She might be all right even for an hour. But at some point, she would need a patient advocate, and without a doubt, I could not perform that function.

So, I laboriously buzztexted my mother, letter by letter since I couldn't speak slow enough for the voice recognition. She'd lost her job when the Gifted project shut down, but she could still help with Bang. She would make a good patient advocate. But it was the middle of the night, and I had no idea when she might pick up the message. It could be many hours. A lifetime. Still, it was the best I could do for Bang right then.

I already felt tired, and now I also felt ill from worry, or perhaps from the Cure Bang had shot into my arm. I remembered the article I had pocketed and pulled it out. It said the Cure was at an alpha test stage. They had tried the latest version on only four people, two men and two women, and it had worked well on three of them. The fourth had died from complications. Did I even have the latest version? Did the vial contain a full dose or just a test sample, or was it many doses? Was I feeling any complications? What were the complications? The article hadn't said.

When I'd pulled out the article, Bang's lavender stick came out with it and landed on my counter. Now, I stared at it and began to cry. "She will be fine," I repeated aloud as I paced my room, firmly believing that she would not be fine at all.

I opened the stick just for a second, smelled the calming scent, and thought of Bang at her apartment eating a pear. I leaned against the wall and snapped to sleep.

CHAPTER 29

Zane trots at a leisurely pace along a jogging path. It's a sunny afternoon, but an oncoming breeze keeps him cool. He's feeling good just running. A good breakfast and an extra banana and some nuts have given him a sense of ease. He speeds up and feels even better, euphoric even. Then he gets this idea that if he goes fast enough, he should be able to do a flip as he runs when he peaks a small hill.

He speeds up as he approaches, blurs by a man and woman who are out for a morning run too, then just as he tops the hill, he leaps and flips head over heels, lands stumbling but upright, and continues his run downhill. He is charged now and successfully flips again, on flat ground this time. He can't wait to show the running team. They had made him captain, and now he feels like their choice may have been justified.

He runs the measured mile section and times it. Two minutes and forty-two seconds. He'd heard rumors of Gifted running very fast, but he doubted them, even though he'd watched Aarav run himself out doing circles in Betsy's back yard. On TrailMail, a Gifted-only group, the rumors of extraordinary speed were *discredited as unlikely. Side effects were never positive like super speed was. Yet here he is, doing a mile in under three minutes without any significant training.*

Laughing out loud, Zane cruises into a populated area. As he passes a farmer's market, he grabs a couple apples and a squeeze-tube of alfalfa honey and keeps running. He's desperately hungry, and he wants the food to help him keep up his furious energy. He eats as he runs.

After four more miles, he slows and thinks about what he's done. He just stole from those people and didn't even think about it. How did that happen?

Zane turns around. He returns to the farmer's market and finds an officer there. He stops to apologize to the owner and to pay, but he is pointed out and detained.

The policeman pulls out his Wonky.

Zane says, "I was coming back to pay. See, I have my money right here."

"Then why on earth did you steal the food in the first place?" the woman who owns the market stall asks.

"I don't know," says Zane. "I wasn't thinking."

"No," says the police officer. "You weren't thinking."

He asks Zane for a parents' Wonky address. While he's typing it into the record, he points to the owner and says, "Well, pay her. Don't just stand there dancing around. You have to use a restroom or something?"

"No, I'm fine," Zane says, but he can't stop shifting around, and he has to focus to keep himself from running off. He pays the woman. He had plenty of money on him.

The policeman takes Zane back to his parents' house. His mother opens the door. When she sees Zane and the policeman, her whole body droops.

"I guess it had to happen sometime," she says. "Go up to your room."

His mother talks to the policeman. Zane listens in from the top of the stairs while he shifts and wiggles and paces. She makes the standard assurances that mothers and fathers make when the police escort a fifteen-year-old home. "He's never done anything like this before," and "We'll talk to him," and "We'll get some counseling." Anything to get rid of the police.

When the door closes, Zip goes into his room and paces, waiting for his mother. Why did he take the food? He was so hungry, and he just couldn't stop. Running felt wonderful.

His mother opens the door and peers at him. "We need to talk."

Zane sits on the bed, looking at the floor. "I don't know what happened. I just grabbed some food on the way by as though they had put it out just for me. It occurred to me just before I got there that I should stop and buy something. Then I just whizzed by and took what I wanted. It was only a few miles later that I realized I hadn't paid for it. I went back. I tried to pay quietly, but the policeman was already there. It won't happen again."

"No," Zane's mother says, "it won't happen again."

To Zane, this sounds sad and also ominous, a doom-laden prophecy. He stands up and paces from the bookcase to the window. Only four steps. He picks up a chess trophy off the shelf and plays with it as he paces.

"Zane, would you sit?"

Zane sits on the edge of his bed and plays with the trophy. His mother says, "Zane, do you even know why we're here and what we're talking about?"

"Sure," he says, but then he hesitates. What were they talking about? Oh yes. "I took some food and didn't pay for it."

Zane looks to his mother for confirmation. To see if he got it right, but she's staring out the window at the sky.

Zane sees a forgotten granola bar on the desk, picks it up, and tears it open.

"We had hoped . . . ," his mother says, "we had hoped you might not be affected. I guess all parents of Gifted hope."

"Hope for what?" Zane asks.

"Hope for normal things."

Zane finishes his granola bar. "What's not normal?"

"You, Zane, you're not normal. Although, I guess you are normal for a Gifted, in a way. You're just like the rest, regrettably. You're changing into something else. Just like the rest. Something else."

His mother is weeping now, and Zane cries too, although he's not exactly sure what makes him do that. He senses his life is about to become complicated but doesn't know how or when or even why. Something about her demeanor feels final. Terminal. "I'm just me," Zane says.

"But you're not you, Zane. Would Zane have stolen that food? Would the Zane we've known be snapping his fingers and doing leg lifts while I'm trying to have an important conversation with him? A serious conversation. Would he be whistling?"

Zane stares alternately at his own hands and legs as though they don't belong to him. Who was making them move like that? Why was he snapping his fingers? He stops whistling. What was he whistling? The "Pastoral"? Was he whistling Beethoven's "Pastoral"? He knows he's changing; he's felt it coming on for a while, he just doesn't understand why or how.

Zane tries to hold still.

He paces the room again.

His mother tilts her head slightly and sighs. "You know the other *Gifted* have been having problems staying still, focused, learning new things?"

"Have they?" Zane says. "They haven't said anything about it." At least he hasn't heard, although he's become too impatient to use the TrailMail system. Even waiting for his Wonky to start up is painful. He hasn't checked in for a while.

"BetroCo is trying to keep it quiet, but word is out, among the parents at least. The company acts like the change in our *Gifted* is temporary, that you'll go back to being Zane. Back to being our son."

"I'm not your son?" asks Zane.

Zane paces the room and counts the number of objects that have blue in them, then the number of objects that contain green. There are fourteen with blue and only twelve with green. He thought there would be more green.

His mother continues. "We need to send you to Detroit. There's a facility there. They claim they can help."

Later, when he is descending the stairs for dinner, Zane hears his parents talking quietly. His mother says, "I just want my Zane back."

Zane wonders who he is if he's not Zane anymore.

CHAPTER 30

I awoke disoriented, which doesn't usually happen. The kitchen counter was farther away than it should have been. I took a step, felt dizzy. When I reached for the wall to steady myself, I missed and fell. I shivered, but my forehead was wet with sweat. Squeezing my eyes and blinking didn't help my fuzzy vision. I couldn't sit up without feeling like I would fall. The floor tilted, so I lay down to keep from sliding toward the refrigerator.

In a moment, the sensation was gone. The walls became rectangular again, and the floor became level and flat. The room stopped moving. I sat up, then stood up, shaking. What was that? Was I having a reaction to the Cure? Was this reaction the correct one, or was the serum already ruined when Bang injected it into me? I ran around the room a couple times, then climbed up onto the roof. I felt healthy enough, but worried.

If an E could keep a dog, I would definitely name mine Worry. I ran to the park and guzzled from a drinking fountain until I didn't think I could drink any more, then popped one of Bang's Ergs.

While drinking at the fountain, my worry changed to frustration and anger. The only person I was angry at, who I also knew how to find, was Ratchet. I wanted to know what exactly Ratchet had to do with the whole mess. When did he find out about the Cure? Why did Cagle allow the box with the Cure in it to be given to me in the first place? I decided to go find Ratchet and finally kick him in the head for those few seconds I'd promised myself.

The run to Cagle's was uneventful, although I kept checking myself for balance and vision problems. The trip felt normal, if a little weird—like a hypochondriac's nightmare where he can't detect anything wrong. Where everything is just fine.

Running at street level, I smelled smoke. When I turned the corner onto Fifth, I saw Cagle's building burning, or at least the top few floors were burning. The fire trucks' light cannons shined on gray and black smoke flowing out of the upper windows. A few barely dressed E-girls hopped and shimmied near a paramedic truck. I didn't see Cagle or Ratchet.

The three-story apartment building across the street looked like it would provide a better view, so I trotted down Wells a few buildings and swung up via a gutter drain onto a low garage roof, out of sight of the police and fire departments, and worked my way over.

When I landed on the apartment building's roof, Ratchet was calmly watching the conflagration, rocking on a DoubleBar and playing with a metal Puzzler.

I walked right up beside him before I thought out a plan.

He glanced at me and almost fell off the DoubleBar, but he was better than that. "Where the hell have you been?" he said. "And where's that damn box?"

He stepped off the DoubleBar and dropped the Puzzler.

Although it would be satisfying, kicking Ratchet in the head would not help very much, and when we stood together, it was clear that it would be him kicking my head rather than the other way around. What's more, he had given every indication of wanting to save the Cure rather than sell it or use it himself.

"Do you know Bang?" I asked.

"Yes. Well, I know of her. Where is the box?"

"I was in love with Bang," I said. I wanted someone else to know, even if it was just Ratchet. But then I purposefully misled him. I didn't want anyone to know Bang was in the hospital in case someone held a grudge. She was just too vulnerable there, and I would be useless as protection. "A bullet went through the box before it hit her in the chest."

Ratchet balled his fists and turned slightly, like he was going to throw a punch. There was no way I could dodge it. Ratchet was trained in that stuff. I closed my eyes and ducked, but the fist didn't come.

When I looked up, Ratchet was looking at the fire again. He said, "I'm sorry."

"You mean about the box."

"No, damn it, about Bang. That's harsh punishment for any crime."

Watching the fire and swirling smoke while I shuffled my feet and twiddled my thumbs worked like a meditation trick, siphoning away some of my spastic anxiety. It gave me a way to stay and talk rather than run. E talk fast, but it could still be hard to concentrate.

A fireman lurched out carrying a body. "That's Cagle," Ratchet said.

I didn't like Cagle, but that seemed harsh too.

Seeing Cagle's body brought out of the building that way also drove home the point that I would get no more jobs, no more money from him. I had no idea how I was going to live past the few hundred he'd given me a short while before. What horrible crimes might I sink to committing when I got hungry enough? Would I start stealing on spec like Bang? I didn't think I had the abilities. But I could steal random things and try to sell them, I could start fires for profit, or I could hurt people. Unfortunately, I could see myself doing lots of illegal and immoral things for money and food.

Ratchet continued, "Damini stopped by. They tied me to a railing until they got the fire going. They said Cagle wouldn't be coming out. I guess they were right."

"Did she offer you a job?"

Ratchet darted me a look, then smiled. "You know more than you let on, don't you, you little shit?" His smile didn't take all the sting out, but he was right, maybe about both parts of his comment.

"The shooter, the woman who shot Bang, the one who shot the box, she worked for an E named Big Easy. I know that much."

Ratchet picked up his Puzzler and handed it to me, then pulled out a small finger toy I hadn't seen before.

"Big Easy works for Swan. Seems everyone is getting into this melee."

"So, this Swan guy is a Slug? A Damini equivalent?"

"Yeah, they're not friends either."

The EMTs pushed Cagle's body slowly toward an

ambulance. I folded and slid and snapped the toy, but watching the patterns in the smoke and the flicks of fire worked pretty well all by themselves to keep me from embarrassing myself with random jerks and spasms.

"I'm the one who got the Cure into the country," Ratchet said, finally. "I used to run around with a kid named Badger. He was pretty good at focusing, better than me by a bit anyway, so they hired him to do research in India. He helped me smuggle a first sample Cure out as part of a shipment to Cagle. Cagle thought it was one of his Velocity vaccines, but Badger marked the Cure box with a *V* scratch. I thought I was pretty smart until I realized that Cagle wanted to sell the vaccines over and over by using oblivious idiots like you, no offense, to run each delivery and then stealing it back from the mark in public places, in this case Castle Wheel. The scam would let him sell the same Velocity vaccine several times. Stupid, greedy bastard.

"So, when you came back with the delivery, he stomped around for ten minutes shouting, but he had to sell it again, this time delivering it to a private office, so I took my chance. The address I gave you was the doctor. I didn't trust you to actually deliver it with Cagle's gunman on your tail, so I figured to take it from you and deliver it myself, but you both got away, and it all went to hell after that."

I figured that with that admission, I should give him something else. Something that might make him happier. "Dr. Argent is alive."

"What? You said . . . ."

"Yeah, I said his brains were all over his carpet. There is a dead guy in Argent's office all right, but now I don't think it's him."

Ratchet didn't seem any happier. "Maybe he sent his assistant to receive the package. I hope the doc is still alive. He's a good Slug. But it doesn't matter now. We lost this Cure, and the flood took the rest."

"Well . . . ." I got that much said then the roof tilted. I sat down heavily and dropped the Puzzler Ratchet had given me, but it didn't roll away. That didn't make sense. The incline was steep enough that the Puzzler and I both should have slid toward the back of the building. A rhinoceros grunted at me a couple times, but I shut my eyes. I relaxed. I tried to do a meditation trick, and it worked. They never worked before when it actually mattered.

When I opened my eyes again, Ratchet was there shaking me and yelling, "Zip, Zip," over and over again, like he actually cared.

I shook my head to get rid of the vertigo. "I'm OK now."

He smacked me hard on the shoulder. "You took the fucking Cure, didn't you, you selfish little shit."

"No. No, I didn't." I tried to stand, but Ratchet shoved me back down. I tried to look him in the eye. "When Big Easy's torpedo shot the box, the bullet missed the MDS unit, but the refrigeration was shattered. With the Cure out of its climate control, it only had a minute or two of viability. You knew that. I didn't even think about it with Bang lying there, maybe dying, in my arms. But Bang thought about it. Bang knew."

"She gave it to you?"

"Yeah. That was the last thing she did." I started crying. Blubbering, actually. I pictured her strapped down in a gurney in the ambulance, just like Cagle. I could only hope that she would stay unconscious until she was free to move around.

Ratchet didn't say anything. He pulled me up and handed me the Puzzler again. "We need to go see if the doctor is alive," he said. "If he is, maybe he can help us. Maybe they can use your blood to help figure out how the Cure was made and then replicate the process. It'll probably take a few years, but it's got to be a lot faster than starting over from scratch, if they even bother. It took them ten years last time."

"OK, but do you have an Erg or some food?" I had Bang's food and Erg pills, but Ratchet's food would feel better going down.

"Yeah. Eat this, and then we go to Argent's house." He handed me a KoolBar.

CHAPTER 31

The doctor lived in a mostly glass building much taller than the surrounding ones. No access to the roof, even for Energy. There was an arched gate with a small roof at the entrance and a few meters of fence on each side protecting a little garden with those bushes that grow round white snowball blossoms. The gate was closed, and we didn't see a doorman or any security people.

Ratchet said, "They'll have security cameras everywhere. We could hop the fence, but there's no one to let us in. We would need a tenant's key."

"We can wait until morning. At this point, there isn't really any hurry."

Ratchet shook the gate to check that it was really locked. "If I remember correctly, I think the Cure will transform into something else after it's in the body for a while. It's a time-release agent, so it doesn't enter the blood all at once. It's best if he can extract a blood sample right away. And anyway, what if you die before the doc can get the blood sample and refrigerate it in the morning?"

It wasn't clear if he was joking about me being dead by morning, but when I recalled my spells of vertigo and hallucinations, it occurred to me he might have a point. Still, he was being rather glib about it.

"I guess you'd better keep me alive then," I said.

Three E slammed to a halt right behind us. We turned in unison, but by then the three had boxed us up against the gate. The one in the middle was tall and very wide. He wore a newsboy hat and a SkinSuit that was tailored like bib overalls. He wore no shirt, and his muscles glistened under the white streetlights. This had to be Big Easy. I'd never seen an E that big before. He was bigger than Damini's muscle.

Big Easy had tracked me down again. I figured he must have had people all over town watching from hiding places. That or he had a fleet of drones, which also seemed likely.

"Well, if it isn't Ratchet and the Zipper. First, let's have the real box this time, then we'll decide what to do with you."

While calculating the odds of getting in a good kick on Big Easy and running full-out to escape, I said, "Your shooter shot a hole in the Cure when she killed Bang. Your own gun destroyed it."

Knowing that Big E probably had a whole team of people watching us at that moment, I figured the odds of getting away at this point were very, very close to zero. Apparently, Ratchet thought the same thing. He didn't say anything or move other than to fidget, just like I did.

I held my hands away from my body and spun once to show I didn't have the box on me, although I knew that wasn't necessary.

The E on Big Easy's right, a woman, said, "I didn't. I mean, I didn't mean to shoot the box."

He turned sharply on her. "You shot Bang? You killed her? Why would you shoot her?"

"No, I mean, I was just trying to scare them . . . ."

The thing was, Big Easy was upset by the loss of the Cure, but it was clear to me he was more upset about the loss of Bang.

Big Easy shot a punch so fast I couldn't see it. The E's head snapped back. It sounded like a leg being pulled off a baked chicken. The E dropped to the ground, motionless.

Then Big Easy yelled toward several more E who waited behind a parked BuzzCar across the street. "Check the condemned building where Jbird said she found them. Tell me what you find."

He turned to me. "What will they find, Zip?"

"They'll find a shattered box, a lot of blood and, by now, an empty MDS unit." I'd pulled out Ratchet's Puzzler, although I didn't really need it. There was enough wild drama going on to keep me focused.

"Why empty?" He took a step forward.

"Because without the special climate in the box, the serum quickly goes gaseous and fizzes out of the unit." That sounded reasonable to me, but I added, "You know that." I hoped telling him that he already knew might make it sound better.

It would take about three minutes for a fast E to run to the hole in the roof and return with the shattered box. I didn't want Big Easy to start thinking too much, so I asked him, "How did you even know the Cure was in Chicago?"

"Ratchet wasn't the only one who knew people in Bangalore."

Big Easy was surprisingly calm for an E. He hadn't taken

out anything to play with. He bobbed and weaved a bit, but he had remarkable control. As good as Damini's pro. Still, his control wore out, and he stepped over and kicked the obviously dead Jbird several times from different angles.

"Why did you have to kill her?" he asked the body, then he kicked it again hard enough to lift it right off the ground. He ran once around it and stomped on Jbird's leg. The leg cracked loud in the tense atmosphere. We all—Ratchet, the other E who came with Big Easy, and I—stood as still as we possibly could, not wanting his attention to swing our way, but of course he looked at me.

"How do you know Bang? Why were you there when she got shot? Why was she running from me?"

I couldn't answer. How could I when any answer that made any sense at all would probably earn me a punch too? But Big Easy didn't seem to be interested in an answer anyway. Perhaps he didn't actually want to know why Bang had run to me with the Cure rather than him. He turned and looked around, presumably toward his other soldiers hiding in the area.

Ratchet did a little two-step. His fists were bunched. He obviously wanted to start swinging, but the odds weren't in our favor. If it had been just the two remaining E standing in front of us, the odds still wouldn't have been in our favor. In a fight, Big Easy would be worth four other E.

Ratchet said, "You ruined it for everyone. You know that. We could have replicated that vial, and we could have been cured. All of us could have gone back to being able to concentrate, read books, sleep lying down, and have long conversations."

"And have family," I said.

Big Easy turned around slowly. "You want to be a Slug? If you want to be a Slug, I can just sap you. I'd be happy to pay the postage on the sapper." He stomped around in a circle, then continued. "The Cure is about more than being a Slug or being able to exist in a Slug world. It's about being a fucking superhero. It's about being everything an E is but being able to think. I could have focused on problems and solutions. I would have been able to plan something out before I actually committed to it. I wouldn't have to work for Slugs. I could be my own man. Sleep like regular people? Don't be stupid and mundane. I would have ruled Chicago. I would have been King fucking Midas."

Ratchet didn't say anything, but he glanced over at me, and I couldn't help but think he hated me a little then. It wasn't my fault I had been given the Cure, but Ratchet's look made me feel like it was. He made me feel guilty, like I'd betrayed my clan.

An E woman darted up to Big Easy, out of breath, and handed him the smashed box from the place with the hole in the roof. He held it up to the light and traced the *V* with his finger. He looked at Ratchet, then at me, then at the body on the ground.

"Damn it! It wasn't supposed to happen this way. Why did Bang run off with it?" He seemed almost in tears. He threw the box on the ground and stomped on it repeatedly. "Fuck it. Fuck it. Fuck it," he said, and he walked away. Bang was as big a loss to him as the Cure was, which made me jealous for no reason whatsoever.

"You played that well," Ratchet said, once Big Easy and his E had left.

I felt a little woozy and the world wobbled a little, but I

didn't have to lie down this time. I said, "Give me a couple minutes, OK?"

"Not here, Zip. There's a body here we can't explain."

A night security man came out from the entry door and blocked it open then walked toward the gate. We put our backs to the posts that held the gate. When he unlocked it and stepped out past us to see what was going on, we slipped behind him and through the entry door. We ran up the stairs to the fifth floor. At almost four in the morning, no one was around.

Ratchet knocked on Argent's door. We waited, fiddling with our toys and running in place. I leaned against the wall, but Ratchet wouldn't let me sleep yet. I tried to meditate and play number games, but I was too tired. A painfully long time later, the doctor opened the door. "Ratchet? What the hell?"

I fell down.

Ratchet dragged me in and put me on the couch. Argent looked at me like I was some kind of googly-eyed monster.

Ratchet and the doctor conversed slowly while I wiggled on the couch. They came over and took some blood, then disappeared into the other room.

I lay there trying to think, with some success, about Bang being OK. About her still being alive. Ratchet stuck his head into the room and said, "We improvised some refrigeration to hold it till the doc can deliver it to the lab. He says it's good we came to him so fast, because the newer it is, the less it has been affected by being in your body."

I stood up. "I have somewhere to go."

"You're not going anywhere, Zip. You're too dizzy," Ratchet said.

"No, I have to."

Ratchet came back into the room and grabbed me. "What's so damn important now? He drew some blood, but you need to stay alive until the new Cure is fully developed."

"Bang's not dead."

"What the hell, Zip? Do you ever tell the truth? What really happened? And it had better be good, because I feel like breaking your legs right now. You don't have to be sane to give blood, you know, just alive."

"Everything I told you is true. I lied to Big Easy because Bang worked for him, sort of, then betrayed him, and I didn't want him going to the hospital and killing her too." He might get around to that later, though.

"You told me she was dead."

"No, I told you she was shot."

"You let me believe she was dead, and you were all heartbroken about it. That's the same as lying. That's the same as telling me she's dead."

The doctor finally got our attention. He said, "What are you two talking about?" in molasses speech.

Ratchet told him that an E who was important to me was in the hospital with a bullet wound.

The doctor considered this while Ratchet and I jerked and wiggled. "I'll call and check on her on the way, and after I drop off the blood sample at the lab, I will go over and make sure they understand what they need to do for her. Which hospital?"

I told him her name and which hospital while he was finding his car control and his Wonky.

I said, "I need to lie down," to myself, then dropped back onto the couch and fell asleep while recalling the smell of Bang's lavender perfume.

CHAPTER 32

Pacing in front of the screen, watching an anime where people leap from building to building, Zane thinks he could do that. He wants to do that. He races around the room. Zane is at Rallentando, known as SlowDown to the students— or inmates as they prefer to be called. Rallentando is the institution in Detroit where parents send Gifted Kids after they become too much to handle at home.

"Jeez," Carrot says. "Use your Zen, man. Some of us are trying to watch." Carrot and Bomb sit quietly, twitching, watching the subtitled anime while they play hand-slap sequences and listen to music through earbuds. Zane is trying to watch too, but he hasn't mastered "The Zen," as Carrot calls it, the mind games that help make your inner music rallentando, slow down, ease up. Zane is having trouble doing that. Zane wants out of the building, but the students are locked in because if they escaped, no one would be able to catch them.

On the TV, the Naruto character bounds from tree to tree, high up in the limbs. "I want to do that," Zane says. "Why won't they let us do that?"

"You can do what you want after you leave, but until then, you have to do as the Slugs say, even if it makes no sense and helps not at all. That's the rules. Slowdown, dude."

When a teacher sees a new student running around, they say, "Slowdown," as though such a command would result in the corresponding lack of action.

Zane can't stand watching the freeform running on the screen and races out of the room then down to the kitchen where he eats a banana, a few samosas, and a couple VegiBars.

Masika, another inmate, watches him while he eats. Although he knows she's there, he's focused on the food.

Masika is getting thinner each day. She looks pale, even though her natural color is exceedingly dark, as close to absolute black as Zane has ever seen. He picks up a handful of peanuts and offers her some. She takes three and eats them, then she turns to race out of the room but slams into the closed door hard enough to give her a nosebleed and a lump on her forehead. An older Slug, as Zane now thinks of regular people, is also in the kitchen, so Zane lets him deal with Masika's injury. Zane has run into walls and even the ceiling a few times already. As they speed up, his SlowDown cohort is having trouble coordinating their speed and their reactions. They are all becoming clumsier, although the teachers claim that will pass.

After the Slug says Masika will be fine, Zane says, "Are you doing OK, Masika? You don't seem very well." He isn't talking about the door jamb. Everyone does that occasionally.

"I'm OK," she says, but Zane knows she's not.

"You should eat something to replace all that energy you're expending, you know."

"I know that, I'm not an idiot, Zane. Just leave me alone."

"I'm just worried, that's all."

"Worry about yourself. I'm fine."

Later that day, Bomb comes into the long-run room and says, "We lost another one. Masika blocked the stair door open, got up to speed in the hallway, and dove head-first down the gap between the stair levels. Made it a couple floors before she started bouncing around. It's a real mess."

Zane imagines the scene and vomits out his fish burritos on Bomb's legs. Bomb didn't like him much after that.

Zane had liked Masika, but he hadn't known what to do for her. Still, he understands why she did it. He imagines himself diving down between the stairs and goes to look at the stairwell. Someone has cleaned the area already, and now some women are there welding bars into the gap so no one will repeat the stunt. Zane wonders how many of the kids would have tried.

Guilt over Masika's death holds on to him for days. He could have helped. He could have stayed with her. Even if she didn't want him to, he still could have hung around, maybe convinced her to eat more. Or maybe she would have done it anyway. It only took a second to block the door to the hallway, then run and dive.

Zane wonders what he's worth now. He can't even help a friend. He feels like he's worth nothing, nada, zilch, zip.

I'm Zip, he thinks. That's me. The name fits so well that he immediately tells everyone that his E name, his new identity, is Zip.

Overhead, by the exit where Zip and the other inmates will eventually depart, he draws in fat, bold blue letters, "You are no longer the Gifted who came in but the Cursed who will leave."

CHAPTER 33

When I woke, Ratchet was juggling coffee mugs and playing hacky sack with a rolled-up pair of socks. He kicked the socks at me, placed the mugs one at a time onto the table as they fell, then said, "I never knew an E who could sleep for fifteen minutes. I could have gone home and gotten a shower and some eats if I'd known you were going to pass out like that."

"Have you heard anything from the doc?"

"Nah. No time has passed for him. You OK?" Ratchet was acting concerned again, and it confused me until I understood that he was apprehensive because I was the goose and he was worried about the golden egg.

"I feel much better now." I stood. "Gotta go."

"You aren't going anywhere, Zip. We're staying right here until Dr. Argent tells us he's put your blood sample under refrigeration and lock and key." He approached and grabbed my arm. "And even then, I'm sticking to you like . . . ."

"Like white on rice? Like spots on dice?"

Ratchet glared at me. "Not a joking matter. Not a joking matter at all. We all have too much riding on you to let you do anything stupid, and you have a propensity for doing stupid stuff more than anyone I know."

"So, you're my bodyguard? It might be nice having my own bodyguard."

"You remember what I said about you not needing to be sane for research purposes? I could just find some tape and stick you to the wall, put a bucket under your butt, and feed you once in a while."

Taped down? That image was too vivid and raw. Bang. I wanted to go see her. Touch her. Talk to her. Hold her. She was in the hospital though, where even seeing her at a distance would be complicated for an E.

Ratchet trotted around the room, so I followed him, or perhaps he was following me. When I stopped, he kept going. I think I irritated him, and that made him act more E than he usually did.

"I want to go to the hospital and at least see her, at least verify that's she's still alive."

"They don't let Energy into hospitals unless we're hurt. What are you thinking?" He smiled. "I guess I could break your leg. Then they would let us in. Come here, I'll give it a try."

"OK then," I said, "call them. You're used to dealing with Slugs. You call and see if she's all right."

Ratchet produced an exasperated sigh, rather like a parent of a four-year-old might when asked, "Why can't I . . . ," for the nineteenth time. "I don't carry a Wonky and anyway, that would take minutes. We could run over and ask someone to go in and ask for us in that much time."

"OK," I said and headed for the door. I had Bang's Wonky, but running sounded much better to me, too.

"No, and if you open that door, I will knock you down and break your leg."

"OK, if I'm so valuable, you go. I'll wait here. You can ask for just a room number. They should be willing to give out that information."

I could see the acknowledgement just start to dawn on his face, then, like an almost sneeze, his eyes narrowed, and he glared at me. "No." The parent sigh again. It seemed to me that I wouldn't be acting like a petulant little child if he wasn't acting so much like a long-suffering adult.

"What makes you the one that gives the orders?" I asked.

"I'm bigger, stronger, and I'm willing to hurt you if necessary." We stood nose to nose now. We both needed a couple trips around the couch and some jacks-and-toes to settle down.

After some spinning and a headstand, I said, "OK, but you'll have to pee sometime, and I expect it will be soon." I went to the bathroom, then ran the water for a while. I went to the kitchen and poured myself a glass of water and drank it, then poured another and drank that too, making a loud smacking "aaah" sound. "You want a glass?" When he shook his head, I opened the fridge and saw the doctor had some apple juice, so I had a glass of that too. Ratchet looked like he was juggling tarantulas with his eyes, but he didn't hit me.

We did some E meditation and double hacky-sack-patty-cake, ate some pastrami and a half-pound of butter, then found a jar of peanuts from the back of the doctor's cupboard. I figured he wouldn't miss them.

Finally, I said, "We can't stay here, you know that." I opened the bathroom door. "You should never pass up an opportunity use to the bathroom. You never know when you'll get another chance."

When I came out, Ratchet conceded defeat. "All right, we can swing by the hospital, then go to my place and wait. I'll leave the doc a note to call me, but no detours, and no running off by yourself, got it? Do I have your word on it?"

At first, I thought he was joking about having my word, but he seemed to be taking it seriously. It wasn't until then that I understood Ratchet actually thought more of me than I would ever have believed. Running back through our relationship, I could see how maybe he did think of me as a kid brother. He wasn't actually much older than me, but he was a lot more mature; even I knew that. So, when I said, "Yes," it was with some trepidation because I didn't really know if I would run away when the chance came up or not. Running away is what I did. It's who I was. Yet Ratchet didn't think so, and that gave me pause. And pause is hard for an E.

"Wait for me," he said, and he went into the bathroom.

His faith that I wouldn't skeet kept me running in circles, jogging in place and walking around the room on my hands. Also, it was a good idea to have him with me because ultimately Big Easy might decide that losing the Cure was my fault. I had a feeling that with his network, that might not be long. Or he would find out that Bang wasn't dead, and what would happen to Bang then? She had betrayed him, after all. I had the feeling that he considered her more than just an employee, and that made her situation even more tenuous. Sweet compassion can quickly flash to vengeful anger. I resigned myself to dealing with Big Easy in some way. I couldn't leave things as they were and just hope the problem would go away for me or for Bang. Ratchet could take care of himself.

When he came out of the bathroom, I was standing still in front of the doctor's couch, thinking. I'd been still most of the time he'd been in the bathroom. The opening door startled me into a spastic leap, as though I'd been caught staring at a girl's butt or looking at my opponent's cards. Something had changed. I was caught cheating on all the other Energy, and guilt was oozing from me. But Ratchet didn't seem to notice that I hadn't moved. He only showed relief that I was still there, that I hadn't run off.

We ran the boring street-level routes toward the hospital. There were lots of Boxwheels now making early morning deliveries of perishables and a few early buses carrying the people who unlocked the offices or made the donuts. Two to three thirty were the best hours for Energy. After that, the Slugs started messing things up and slowing things down.

As we sped toward the hospital entrance, we spied Big Easy racing toward the entrance from another direction. When he neared the door, he turned and sped back the way he came. He was expending energy while he waited for something. I had a feeling I knew exactly what that was. He wanted to know just what I wanted to know. Was Bang going to live?

Ratchet and I ducked into an alley. It hadn't taken Big Easy long to figure Bang wasn't dead, that she was in the hospital, and which hospital she was in, which showed how good Big Easy's network was. He must have an army of E he had intimidated into watching the whole city for him. "He knows Bang lived through the shooting," I said. "He knows she's here. How could he know already?"

Ratchet glanced around the corner toward Big Easy. "You slept forever, Zip."

"We can't stay here," I said. "His people will see us, and we don't want that." There was no one to blame but myself for the whole mess. I wanted to blame Ratchet. I'd gotten used to a blame-someone-else strategy, but it was clear now that I was always the one screwing up.

Damn.

Perhaps I could sneak past Big Easy himself, but I didn't know who else was watching the street.

That's when Ratchet noticed. He was smacking the PlastiCrete wall and bobbing a little, but I was standing very still, thinking. He poked me. "What's going on, Zip? Are you going to have another fit? Now's not the time. We must go right now." He shoved me down the alley, away from the hospital.

Between Big Easy racing around in the street and hospital security specifically watching for Energy, we weren't going to reach Bang. We couldn't help her now. "Yes," I said, "let's go to your apartment." There was free food there and time to think through the next step. The idea that I might actually be able to do that—think through the next step, that is—startled me into a run.

When we came to an intersection, Ratchet called directions, but he didn't take the lead. He still didn't trust me. I wouldn't have trusted me either, but I actually wanted to go where he wanted me to go, and I needed him to unlock the door.

At the next cross street, he said, "Someone's following us. Go left, then up and over the Forget What building."

When I hit the roof of the forget company, Ratchet landed

at the same time and darted ahead. We leapt across two small alleys, following the single stories, then we dropped down into a playground. I followed him to some kids' crawl-tubes. I was startled to see him slide into one, feet first, but I promptly mimicked him and slid into the one next to him. How were we going to stay still in those little tubes? The claustrophobia disturbed me, but I would also never search inside one for an E. What E would go into such a confined space on purpose? It wasn't four seconds before two E dashed past us and on down the street like they knew where they were going. One said, "Shit," but they were gone before I heard the rest.

Ratchet slid out of his tube, so I did too. We ran on for a couple streets, vaulted up a couple levels, and stopped behind a stair roof-exit. Ratchet pulled out his Puzzler. "Apparently, they know who I am and where I live. Now where do we go?"

"They were expecting us."

"Really?" Ratchet showed mock surprise and put his hand over his chest to demonstrate his shock. While I didn't appreciate his sarcasm, I smiled anyway. He was joking with me. It had been a while since anyone other than Bang had done that.

"Those guys were following us, but I expect they have someone waiting for us at your place and mine."

Ratchet fiddled with his Puzzler. "So where do we go?"

In the past, he'd seemed the smart, calm, thoughtful one, but that only applied in a relative sense. I had a problem and had to think it out myself. The problem was Big Easy. The last time I had a problem like that, Damini shot the gunman for me. Would she do it again? Would I be going back to the same well once too often? I didn't know, but I wasn't used to this thinking gig, and I desperately wanted to latch onto the first option that presented itself and run with it. Decide and run, simple. I didn't want to slow down to think the whole thing through.

Surprisingly though, I had the feeling that if I tried hard enough, I could list possibilities, devise a plan, and I almost had the nerve to do it.

Ratchet grabbed my shoulder and shook it. "You keep spacing out, going dead and stopped, like your brain left on the five o'clock and isn't coming back for a while." He paused and looked at my eyes.

Damini was a neutral in my problem with Big Easy right now, but I might be able to change that.

Ratchet shook me again. "Stop that!"

I just had to show Damini that coming into the war was in her best interests. I abruptly started hopping around and kick-stepping then doing a tap sequence. Apparently, my body hadn't caught up to my now more deliberate mind and decided on its own that I wasn't paying enough attention to the activity scale. I had to agree.

Ratchet said, "Let's go to the doctor's lab. He's probably still there, and they have some security. That's where you should probably be anyway. That's where you would now be if you'd been in any condition to run over there when the doctor left."

"No, Ratchet. That's where I should not be. First because then the blood sample and the source of the blood sample would be in the same place, just like Bangalore. All the eggs in one basket, see? Then there's the fact that Big Easy is looking for us. We don't want him to figure out that he still might have a shot at the Cure. He's too unpredictable. We just don't

know what he'd do with that information. We don't know
how he would react. He might attack the lab."

Ratchet's eyes became erratic. He looked around frantically as I spoke. Even speaking at E speed and playing with
his Puzzler had its limits. He had to run right then, and to
be honest, I did too. I couldn't just dance in place and think
anymore. Something had to happen. I needed a destination.
My old self would have picked the first place that came to
mind and started running. I might have thought a little more
about it after I started running, but probably not. But now
I could consider all the options. I could dither. Thinking
things through took a ridiculous amount of time, and taking
that extra time could be as problematic as picking instantly,
then changing the plan on the go. Damn.

"OK," I said. "Let's go to Bang's place. She's not using it.
She lives on the third floor next to the BodMod shop on
Fullerton."

Ratchet took off as though a bell had rung and he was
chasing a mechanical rabbit. I'd said aloud the first viable
option I'd thought of. Things hadn't changed that much.
Maybe the Cure was all in my head, a placebo that worked.
Lots of them do.

CHAPTER 34

I had a hard time keeping up with Ratchet as we ran to Bang's apartment. I even lost him twice for a few seconds when I glanced back to see if we were being tailed. The drones had mostly completed their night deliveries—they had to clear the air by 4:30—and we didn't pass any other E on the way; I didn't see any at all. It was that quiet time when the night activities died down just before the day's work started. It felt like the juncture between two worlds.

I arrived at the BodMod shop just after Ratchet. "Stand near the window," I said. "We're going in that way."

"What?" said Ratchet, surprised. While using window entrances wasn't all that unusual for us, I think he expected me to have a key. He glared at me, obviously wondering what exactly my relationship with Bang was, but I couldn't help him; I wasn't exactly sure.

"Your palm's not registered?" Ratchet had settled down to be more like himself after the long run. He was thinking again, and wondering, and back to being his suspicious self.

"No, and I don't have a key either. Just stand under the window."

He braced himself under the window. I hopped up onto his shoulders, opened the window, then climbed through. Ratchet followed me in before I even had the sink light on.

It felt eerie to be in Bang's room without her there. The sensation was heightened by Ratchet being there instead. Ratchet picked up a MoldBar and started pacing the twenty meters to the door and back, so I paced too. We both pulled out KoolBars and ate them.

Ratchet glared at my KoolBar. "Where did you get that—out of your ass? You told me you didn't have any food. I gave you a KoolBar, damn it."

"I didn't say I was out of food. What I said was . . . ."

Ratchet slapped me on the back of the head hard enough for me to know he meant it. "You should try telling the truth at least once in a while. It builds trust." He stomped off, mumbling.

Damini was the key. While she clearly wasn't an ally, she wouldn't be Big Easy's ally or his boss Swan's ally either, and that counted for something. We needed her team, her talent, her professionals, because I didn't have any resources other than maybe Ratchet, and he wasn't too keen on doing anything at all that might be dangerous because he wanted my blood.

I laughed out loud when a picture formed in my mind of Ratchet as a vampire. Ratchet paused to stare at me like I might be losing control, maybe because of the Cure, but that made me laugh more, and he returned to pacing with even more energy, skip-stepping, lifting his knees higher, and speeding up to expend more energy while throwing dirty, sidelong looks at me.

The only thing I could think of that would make Damini angry enough to deal with Big E for me, to draw her into the fray, was to convince her that someone else was dealing Velocity on her turf. She seemed to have dealt with Cagle effectively.

Could I convince Damini that the Velocity I had told her I lost to the gunman was actually taken by Big E? That might be a hard sell, since I told her the gunman had given it to Ratchet, but it might work. Still, it was a dangerous game to try to deceive her twice. I was a bad liar, she wasn't stupid, and I was susceptible to bullets and sappers and broken legs.

"Hey Ratchet, did Damini mention a Velocity vaccine to you when she killed Cagle and offered you a job?"

He stopped pacing but continued to manipulate his MoldBar. He gave me his suspicious look. "No. Why should she?"

"Because I told her that the gunman who I now understand was Cagle's gunman stole it from me and gave it to you, or someone who looked a bit like you."

He came at me with his fists balled up. "Why did you tell her that? It's not true." He settled down some then said, "She probably knew you were lying. You suck at lying."

"Yes, I do, that's true, but she didn't know that. Also, I was under duress. She was about to sap me. It was the first thing that popped into my head."

Ratchet started pacing again. Energy generally don't hold onto anything for very long, even anger, although that apparently wasn't the case for Big Easy. He appeared to be angry all the time. Did he acquire his upper body strength from weights and work, or from injections? The injections tend to have strange effects on Energy. And Big E was strange.

"Did you recognize any of the people who worked for Big E?" I asked.

"Yeah. I saw Poker and Snack in the background when they were surrounding us at Doc's place."

"Are they good guys? You like them?"

"Are you kidding? They're both nutcases. Don't go near them. They're on my list of people to avoid."

"You keep lists?"

"You are on my list of people to avoid, too."

"OK, are either of them close to your size? Do either wear Slug clothes like you do?"

"Don't get on me about Slug clothes, Zip. At least mine stay clean and don't smell like a sewer." He took a step back and looked me over.

I looked down and took a sniff. My body suit was covered in grime and sweat from running and crawling through ducts and sitting in slimy alleys. Bang's blood had turned a dull rust color on my left thigh and abdomen, and I remembered my attempt to hide from the gunman in the lunchroom. Ratchet was right. The suit had had a tough night.

"They both wear Slug clothes," he said.

"Could either one be mistaken for you at a distance?"

"Maybe Poker, at a distance, in the dark, if you needed glasses."

"Perfect." By now, we were trotting the length of Bang's room, slapping the walls in a one-two-three-five-eight progression. "Now you just need to get me to Damini."

Ratchet stopped. "What?"

"You said she offered you a job. She must have said where to report or given you a way to contact her."

"Why do you want to contact her, Zip? What are you up to?" He stepped closer, then took a step back. "What haven't you told me?"

"Did she give you a way to contact her or not?"

"I'm not saying."

"Look, Ratchet, I need to know what resources we have at our disposal, so I can come up with ideas on what to do about Big E. He's not going to let this go. He's going to remember us. We hoodwinked him, and he's going to be pissed, which means he's going to kill us unless we find a way to keep that from happening. Remember that woman, Jbird, at the doc's place."

Ratchet winced when I mentioned Jbird. The sound of her neck breaking would be with us for a while. I wiggled my head back and forth feeling the neck bones crack.

Ratchet said, "What do you mean, us?" but he pulled a bent card out of one of his baggy pockets. It looked the same as the card I delivered to the doctor's office.

"That will do fine," I said.

I had a real plan. The first time that had happened in many years. It might not be a good plan, but at least I had an objective, and I had devised a way to achieve it.

It was also a dangerous plan. Anything involving Damini, especially deceiving her a second time, would be dangerous. Any plan also involving Big Easy would be dangerous too, and any single plan including both these people would be suicidal. But Bang was in the hospital, and Big E would be waiting for her when she came out.

Was I doing this to save myself or to save Bang? I decided

both reasons were the same thing to me then. The other possibility, that I was jealous of Big E's perhaps imagined relationship with Bang, meant I wanted some sort of revenge. I didn't like that idea, although I admitted to myself that there was some truth in it. But I was thinking more clearly than I had been in a while, and I didn't think Big E's relationship with Bang, whatever that was, was much of a contributing factor anymore. I just wanted Bang to be safe. That was no lie. I would have known if I was lying. I was bad at lying.

"What the heck, Zip? Are we going to run back and forth all day? What are you thinking?"

"Another minute and I'll have a plan," I said, stopping.

"Ha! A plan? That's good. Well, while you bake a plan, I'm going to go to sleep."

"OK."

"Be here when I wake up." He stared at me, waiting for an answer so he'd know if I was telling the truth.

"I will be here," I said.

He seemed satisfied. He ran down the length of the room, leaned against the wall near the window, believing, I guess, that if I tried to leave it would have to be past him, and he might notice. He promptly snapped off.

I couldn't sleep. I was deliberating, which felt pretty good. It wasn't a new experience, but I'd forgotten how it felt. I also decided to quick-wash my suit for the second time that night and take a shower.

CHAPTER 35

It felt like a new start. I had clean clothes and a plan, which seemed like a win. Ratchet would call Damini and say he wanted to talk about that job. He would bring me along. I would tell her that, since Cagle was dead, I wanted a job too. I would tell her that I had some good information if that would help me get a job. Then I would tell her that the person who ended up with the Velocity was Poker, who I'd seen in person when Big E tried to make us give him the Velocity in front of Doc's place. I figured that would place the seed in Damini's head well enough, and she would deal with Big E quickly. Problem solved.

I still had Bang's Wonky. Few Energy carried a Wonky because they were so laborious and tedious to use, and they tended to mess up the communication. In this case it's all we had, so Ratchet would have to keep the words short and few. Just enough to get an address.

When Ratchet woke, I told him my plan.

You got cleaned up for that. Why? When she shoots us

and throws us in the gutter, you'll be looking like you looked before anyway."

"I think it will work, Ratchet. Think about it. She hates it when someone else is dealing Velocity in her territory. Look what she did to Cagle. She's bound to have Big E offed. They probably have some thieves' pact right now, but she obviously has the Velocity trade. She's going to be very unhappy. That's what we need."

"Why do we need that again?" he said, bouncing off the far wall and running the length of the room once more. "Why don't we just wait it out?"

"He wants to kill us, remember? He's having us followed and is watching our apartments. And because he's trying to get at Bang. We have to deal with him."

Ratchet slowed his run, trying to think. "Yeah, you're right. We have to deal with it. OK, where to?" Ratchet didn't look enthusiastic. He looked resigned, sad, as though he'd accepted death—not at all like he was impressed with my plan or expected success. When I realized that I was feeling optimistic, I shuddered. Optimism was not an E feeling. That was a feeling reserved for Slugs.

"First, you need to call Damini and set up a meeting." I handed him the Wonky and Damini's card.

"OK." He spoke the number. "What do I say?"

Was I that bad at focusing? I knew I was once. "Focus, Ratchet. Say who you are and that you'd like to see her and you're bringing Zip."

"OK." He scrunched up his face like a child trying to tie his shoelaces, then someone answered. Ratchet said nothing for a moment, then said, "Ratchet here. About job. Meet Damini. Bringing Zip." Short words and not very many of them. Still, he was working hard to focus.

There was an astoundingly long wait, then someone spoke, and Ratchet said, "End call." He handed me the Wonky. "Seven minutes, Chen's Chinese, Butler Street."

"I know where that is. Should take us less than three."

"We should go the long way. Let's go now."

At first, I thought he just wanted to get out and run, but I quickly realized he meant that it wouldn't do to have a tail when we arrived. That would be too much of a coincidence even for a Slug to swallow.

So we each popped an Erg and drank some water then dropped out Bang's window and started running. Ratchet led the way while I watched closely for drones suspiciously out past morning curfew, or an E who might report to Big Easy. We ran for about five, then vibrated in an alley and ate KoolBars. When it was time, we darted to Chen's, arriving right on time. I admit Ratchet was better at timing our arrival than I ever would have been.

We slipped up on a woman doing a little soft-shoe out front, but she just thumbed us around to the back. There we were greeted by two Energy, one in a SkinSuit much nicer than mine and the other dressed in a loose Slug jogging outfit with accessory knives strapped to his thigh and arm. I figured he kept his gun in a pocket. A knife would be more than sufficient to deal with us.

"Well, Ratchet," the man in the SkinSuit said, "it's good to see you moving up in the world." His face was narrower and more pointed than any face I'd ever seen, and his bass voice sounded like a sub-woofer.

"Hey, Cricket. It's been a while."

Ratchet's friend, Cricket, said, "Sorry, man. I gotta search you both." The other man just grunted annoyance.

We vibrated with our hands up while Cricket patted us down and took our toys, food, money, and Bang's Wonky then led us in the back door and down a corridor. We entered a dining room from the back just as a group of Slugs left through the restaurant's front door. Damini was seated in a plush chair next to a table with three hard metal chairs. Emptied teacups sat in front of each chair. A speedy waiter in a white shirt and black pants came in with a new cup of tea for Damini, and the other teacups vanished. Damini motioned to Cricket to bring us over.

The room was crimson up to the chair rails, then ivory above that, with paintings of goldfish and boats and women wearing golden clothes. There were twelve four-person tables and one large round one with seven chairs. There was a small bar with bottles and glasses behind it in the corner away from the door. Damini's pro stood by the bar where he could watch the front, the kitchen door, and the windows. He scanned us impassively, swaying and rolling those washers around in his fingers. His gun was out on the bar for easy access. I smiled in recognition. He didn't smile back.

Damini appeared settled in, like she would be doing all her business there during the early morning in that nexus between E night activities and Slug daytime activities. Again holding court, Damini sipped her tea while scrutinizing us with a cold stare.

"I think I know what Ratchet is doing here. I offered him a job. I didn't offer you a job, Zip. As I remember, I only offered you your life. So far, I've kept my part of that bargain." She stressed the "so far," which made the two syllables sound like a hundred to my E ears. She was making a point, and I felt it enter my rib cage.

I spoke before Ratchet could mess things up. "I know you didn't offer me work." I was doing a pretty good job of speaking slowly and clearly. Better than usual. "But I told you something that I now know wasn't true. It wasn't Ratchet who received the Velocity. I mistook an E named Poker for Ratchet when I watched the exchange. I thought it best to tell you." I decided to wait for her reaction before going any further. I wanted to pull her in rather than give her all the information at once. An E would not normally be able to resist blabbing everything they knew. We tended to think in a flurry of fragmented nonsense when confronted with someone like Damini, so she appeared to believe that that was all I would say.

"And how did you determine this, Mr. Zip?"

"Oh, well, when Big Easy attacked Ratchet and me, I saw Poker there and realized my mistake. Ratchet told me who the guy was, so now I'm telling you." Again, I acted like that should be enough information to satisfy her.

"And why did Big attack you?"

"Because he wanted the Velocity. He expected the Velocity to be delivered to him. He had a buyer for it. When he found out that someone had taken it, he got really mad and killed one of his own gang, although it wasn't Poker. He just killed the closest one. Punched her so hard that you could hear her neck crack. It sounded like a chicken . . . ."

Damini held up a hand. "Where was this?"

I told her.

She thought about it for a moment. "Cricket, find out if this is true." Then to me she added, "It had best be true."

Ratchet was trying to stay still, but he was dancing, and his eyes were starting to look like little bobbleheads in his front windows. One of the women standing guard pulled out a couple Puzzlers and gave them to us. We had brought some things, but Cricket had taken them.

Damini tapped at her Wonky, took a sip of tea. She stood, looked out at the street, then came back and sat down.

I fiddled with the Puzzler and shuffled a bit but didn't feel like I had to. It was only then that I understood that what I'd been telling Damini were lies. I was bad at lying, wasn't I? Perhaps I was just bad at standing still long enough to lie. The truth was usually quicker.

Cricket returned. "It checks out," he said. "Big is hopping mad because he lost a box and a girl. Not sure who the girl is, but it sounds like she was E and was one of his better agents."

Damini contemplated that for at least a minute. She stared at me the whole time. Her stare made me jittery. I did my best to look innocent and truthful, although I didn't know exactly what innocent and truthful looked like.

Finally, she said, "OK, Zip. You and Ratchet go kill Big, then I'll give you both jobs. I'll even give you both a fat bonus and a crate of KoolBars."

Ratchet's breathing changed. He sounded like a strangled moose. I didn't look at him, but I could sense his urge to kill me and get it over with. I remembered that punch Big E gave Jbird. I didn't think Ratchet could punch that hard, but he could probably have done a pretty good imitation.

"Neither of us is capable of that. He would just kill us if we tried. We don't know what we're doing on a job like that."

"Either way," she said with a wave of her hand. "You kill him. He kills you. Whatever. If he kills you, then there are two incompetent people I don't hire. If you kill him, then I get two new employees, I get rid of a great annoyance to me, and I get satisfaction. I don't see any downside. I'll give you a few hours." She made a motion to Cricket like she was shooing flies. He pulled us outside, handed us our toys, money clips, food, IDs, Bang's Wonky, and wished us good luck. It sounded like sarcasm.

Ratchet waited until we were well away before he punched me on the shoulder hard enough to knock me down. I tumbled four times, then rolled to a stand and wobbled there.

"What the hell, Zip? Did you actually expect that to work? I would kill you now, but Damini will do a more painful job of it, I'm sure."

"Don't be like that, Ratchet. It's all part of my plan." I felt like I was getting better at the lying thing.

"You're lying."

"But Damini is now on our side. That counts for something, doesn't it?"

He started walking in circles, talking to walls, signposts, and a trashcan. "I screw up once. Not even a big screw-up. Then Zip shows up. Zip, who can apparently turn a bow wave into a tsunami just by opening his mouth." He focused on me and continued, "Well I'm tired of it. I'm going to try to deal with Big Easy, and I'm going to do it on my own."

"But I have a plan," I said.

"You have a plan. You have a plan. Where are you pulling your plans out from, Zip? Your ass? Because if it's from your brain, then you must keep your head up your ass!"

"Listen, I know that last plan didn't turn out quite right, but really we're no worse off than we were before. Big Easy still wants to kill us. But now we have Damini on our side."

Ratchet screamed, "Aaaaagh," and took off running. I couldn't blame him. Talking to Damini for so long took a lot out of me too.

I ran back to Bang's place, climbed in through the window, and paced. I needed a new plan. The last one didn't turn out so well. Just as I realized that Damini had said nothing of Poker, Ratchet climbed in through Bang's window and down off the sink. When he'd brushed himself off, I said, "Is Poker good at killing people, or is he just menacing?"

"Zip . . . ." Ratchet heaved a great exasperated sigh, turned to the sink, and drank three glasses of water, then searched Bang's cabinets for food. He found four BiteSticks and threw one over his shoulder to me. Still facing the window, he said, "He's good at hurting people, then killing them. He's got a grudge against the world for making him an E, and he takes it out on anyone he can. I hadn't thought of it before, but maybe I should go tell him where you are. I might feel bad about it later, but I doubt it."

"My blood, remember. You need my blood." I said, "blood" in an exaggerated, Bela-Lugosi-vampire sort of way, but Ratchet wasn't having any of that.

We chewed on our BiteSticks and our thoughts while we bounced off the walls. Ratchet's pants were torn and wet, his shoes tracked sandy mud on Bang's floor, and he now had a nasty scrape on his chin. "I think we need to get Damini and Big E's people to clash," I said, "or at least have them meet in a confusing situation. Several E with guns? That can't end well, right? If either Damini or Big E get hit, we're off the hook."

Ratchet turned and stepped close, swaying and stomping while clenching his fists then opening his hands wide.

"No, we're not off the hook. If either one of them are hurt or killed, we will be next on the kill list of the one who wins. If someone hadn't run off with my gun"—he whacked me on the back of the head again—"maybe I could get close enough to shoot the bastard."

"That's unlikely, Ratchet," I said. "He keeps an army around him all the time, if our last encounter is anything to judge by. You'd just get killed trying to kill him. Maybe we should go to Big E and see if he wants to hire us? Perhaps tell him that Damini ended up with the Cure. See what happens."

"Since when do you think things through so much, huh? And what makes you think this is really about the Cure? Damini probably doesn't even know about that—at least I don't think so." Ratchet did a couple of jacks, momentarily distracted by his own question. "And anyway, that's your great idea? Just walk up to Big Easy and say, 'Hi, Damini has the Cure.' That's more suicidal than my plan."

I didn't point out that his plan was much more suicidal than mine because he didn't have a gun—someone had thrown it in the rain gutter.

Suddenly, the floor tilted, the window shrunk impossibly far away down the long corridor that had been Bang's apartment, Ratchet's nose was as big as a potato, and his ears shrank to nubs. Bang's orange floor-cleaner smelled strong and pungent. I leaned toward the doorway, trying to put a hand on the wall, missed, and fell. Someone crashed through the door. As I hit the floor, Ratchet darted for the window. He dove out as a bullet hole appeared in the sill, spraying splinters in slow motion across the sink.

Two guys picked me up, put shackles on my feet, but they were moving like Slugs, slow and methodical. I wiggled free.

One of the guys said, "Shit!" and dove for me. Why was he moving so slow? Was it because of the Cure's perceptual change?

I stumbled then tried to run, but the leg shackles caught me up short, and I fell again, this time slamming face-first into the concrete floor. They picked me up again, and I remember thinking that Bang would not be happy about the blood stain from my nose and lips on her floor. She kept her place nice. My left front incisor was loose.

Then the excruciating pain hit me so hard I could actually think. That sounds backward, but that's how it worked. Through the thinning fog, I understood that these guys must be Big Easy's men. Just who I wanted to see! Too bad my face hurt so much I couldn't open my eyes. In fact, although my mind was clear, I couldn't even stay conscious.

CHAPTER 36

Zip is sixteen when he trots out of SlowDown and climbs into the SlowDown extended van. Carrot, Dingo, and Stink (as in, "travels as fast as") all have prearranged apartments that are leased by their parents, so the van will drop Stink off in Detroit and drop Carrot and Dingo off in Chicago, then take Zip home to Glen Ellyn in the Chicago 'burbs. His parents don't have the money necessary to lease an apartment for him in Chicago, and anyway, home is where Zip wants to be right now. As a child, he loved his parents but didn't think he really needed them. In the van, doing the mind tricks they taught him for trips, Zip thinks he does need them now. The van pulls into his driveway while Zip is doing handstands in the aisle.

The spirea in beds on both sides of the garage door look straggly, and some low weeds that look like clover are growing up through the reddish mulch. The lawn needs mowed. The dogwood droops from lack of water. The SlowDown van drives away as soon as Zip has retrieved his duffle from the back.

As Zip approaches the door, his father opens it. His father

wears formal clothes, the style he would wear for company. He says, "Hello, Son," but Zip hears a harsh edge to the word "son," as though his father is using it carefully, considering the implications.

His father steps aside to let him in, then puts a hand on his back and guides him into the living room, a room Zip seldom entered because they have a family room that is more comfortable and doesn't need to stay as perfectly presentable.

"Well, I survived," Zip says, shifting from foot to foot, twirling a sunglasses case into his pocket and pulling it out again over and over while he factors 38,493 into five prime factors and looks around.

His mother perches forward on the green couch, staring at the coffee table where a few pages of official-looking documents lie next to a manila folder labeled ZANE in bold black letters across the tab. His mother finally looks up, meeting Zip's jittery eyes. Her expression is guarded. She has been crying.

Zip tries to stand as still as he can, but it's hard because he is anxious to understand the strange homecoming. "Hi, Mom," he says. She doesn't stand to hug him. Zip hides his desire to run a circle by walking with a stutter-step around the room, looking at the stuff that he's been looking at all his life. The painting of the little girl with a trail of geese, his parents' wedding photo, the brass lamp with the cloth shade that his mother made herself—they all look different now. The room feels like a museum, his parents now caretakers of his previous life as Zane. The photo of Zane when he was six riding his new bike has been removed.

"Zane," his father says, "we'd like you to sign these papers. If you do, we can take you to your new apartment right away. We've paid for the first few months and for a security deposit. That way *if you don't find a job right away, well, you have some time to get used to being on your own—time to make some friends."*

Zip breaks focus and runs once around the room before he controls himself. "I'm not staying here? Why would I go to an apartment? Jeez, I'm only sixteen." Zip races around the room again, trying to understand.

His mother says, "I didn't catch that."

"I did," says his father. "I don't think they prepared him as they said they would. They didn't tell him."

"Tell me what?" Zip says, slowly comprehending that decisions have been made without his knowledge or consent.

"They didn't tell you that you Gifted can't live with regular people. That your, um, special condition makes that pretty much impossible. That's why you need to sign the papers. They will allow you to have your own apartment even though you are only sixteen. It gives the Gifted the rights of a full adult."

He says it like a salesman would say that a car with a broken window has improved ventilation or a house that needs major renovation is an opportunity to remodel it any way you want it.

"I don't want full rights as an adult. I want to come home." Zip races up the stairs and back down, pulls out a PuzzLit, and starts playing with it. He'd planned to use the device only as a last resort, but the situation has turned into a last resort already. Now uncaring of his spastic tics and his frenetic movements, Zip shuffles in place behind his mother, not willing to look her in the eye. "You said if I went to SlowDown, things would get better. You said you'd be waiting when I got out, that everything would be all right. This isn't all right." Zip dashes out the door and runs his old lap around the block, doing a few flips up into the maple at the end of the block, then he runs the course seventeen more times, counting sidewalk cracks and slapping street signs.

All he'd wanted to do when he was in SlowDown was run like this, but now he's embarrassed that he can't stay still long enough to have a conversation.

When he gets back home, he leaps to the roof of the garage and sits on the hot asphalt roofing, pulls his PuzzLit out again. He is quietly mouthing the words from a Fibonacci-based ditty about the number of tigers in the zoo when he hears his parents talking at the front door, waiting for him to return.

His mother says, "I told you we should explain it to him before he left. He would have had the whole three months to get used to the idea."

"They said they would help him through it, counsel him, break it to him gently that he could never live with everyone else. They said . . . ."

His mother interrupts. "Zane is a smart kid. Goodness knows he's smarter than either of us. Once he thinks about it, I'm sure he'll understand." She sounds tentative, but firm, like she's trying to convince herself.

Zane might have understood, but Zip doesn't. Well, maybe he does, but he doesn't want to believe it. He doesn't want to be logical about it. He wants his parents to want him at home. He wants them to be crying about him having to go live somewhere else. He knows his energy level at all hours would deprive them of their sleep and maybe their sanity. He knows they would soon want their regular life back, and, at some point, they would begin to hate him for taking away all that was quiet in their life. Maybe they already do. Still, he would rather be the martyr, the hero, leaving his parents of his own free will to save them from their sleepless, screaming frustration derived from his inability to ever be quiet or even still, from his inability to avoid constant intrusion into their lives.

Perhaps it's better this way, he thinks. At least I won't have to spend all my time trying not to be a burden. Zip hops down from the roof, landing just in front of the door. His abrupt arrival produces a yelp of surprise from both his parents.

"I'll sign your papers," Zip says. "It's for the best, you know. I'd drive you crazy. I really shouldn't stay here."

His father looks confused, but there's a grateful look in his mother's eyes that makes him feel like he's saved her from pain. She doesn't want Zip to leave. Well, she doesn't want Zane to leave, but she knows he must and is trying to show a sensible attitude. Zip knows his father feels the same but is better at hiding his feelings than his mother is.

"It's time I was on my own," Zip announces, surprising himself with that same tentative but firm voice his mother used only a moment ago, then he hops onto his right foot, sticking his left foot and his left hand out behind him and leans over, while presenting an imaginary hat in his right hand. "Ta da."

CHAPTER 37

When I came to, I was lying on a concrete floor but no longer in Bang's apartment. This floor felt greasy, smelled of distillates, and tasted of motor oil. I pulled my bruised lips off the concrete and rolled over.

"There he is! Now can I pull his toes off?"

We were in a car-repair shop. Based on the dust covering the engine block dangling from a hoist in the corner, the shop hadn't been used for repairing anything in a while. I sat up, rubbing my lower lip back to stinging life.

Ratchet was off to the right, attached to a cable that ran between his metal wrist-cuffs and wrapped around the post on a car lift. He scurried circles around the post at high speed, foaming spittle around the mouth. He wouldn't last much longer. How long had it already been?

There were six other people in the garage. Two men shuffled on either side of the closed overhead garage door, a women played with a SlideSnap by the office door to the left, a guy stood on a chair a few feet to my right, and another did knee bends next to a rolling tool cabinet while opening and closing a pair of pliers. Big E paced along a wall stacked full of rotting tires. Someone else sat in a chair in the office. He didn't appear to be moving. He was either dead or a Slug, maybe the boss, Swan. The E standing on the chair was the one who asked about my toes. Like Ratchet and Big E, he was old for an E—probably mid-twenties. The oldest E were only twenty-six back then.

Big E squatted, then leapt into the air like a frog and landed in front of me. He slapped me back to the concrete, and I almost lost consciousness once more. Sitting up again seemed like a bad idea, so I just stayed prone on the floor, swallowing my own blood. Earlier that evening I had considered biting off my own finger for sustenance, but now I knew how bad I tasted. My own blood made me nauseous. I wiggled my loose tooth with my tongue.

"Where is the Cure, asshole? The Cure wouldn't have evaporated just because the cooling broke down. It might go bad, but it wouldn't evaporate. Snatch figured that out. Where is the Cure? Did you take it yourself, asshole?" He kicked me in the thigh, rolling me all the way over so I faced up again. I didn't hear a crack, so I thought he might not have broken any of my bones. Yet.

"Damini." I tried to say more, but I sucked down some blood and started coughing. I tried to cough the blood on Big Easy's blue shoes, but he danced out of the way.

"Bullshit," he said, but the statement didn't have the force of confidence.

I turned my head sideways and coughed out some more blood along with my tooth. Toothless was a good name for an old cat, or maybe a little old dog. Little dogs tend to lose their teeth when they get old, and I wondered why.

Ratchet still ran in circles around the car lift's stand. The other E in the room watched me while each did their own form of twitch. The Valvoline sign hanging above the cluttered workbench had eighteen rusted bullet holes vaguely centered around the *o*. There was a black fifty-gallon drum with a hand pump on top in the corner. It didn't need a sign for me to know it contained grease.

"I wanted the Cure for myself," I said, "but Damini took it. She took it even before Jbird talked to us. She transferred it to some other bigger gadget—a cooling box, probably."

"What was in the empty box you gave Jbird? Before it was empty."

"A Velocity." Then, thinking he might test that by slapping me with a sapper, I said, "I administered the vaccine to Bang." Telling the truth after the lie felt right. He seemed convinced.

He stepped forward and kicked me again. Not as hard this time. "Bang? Why would you give the Velocity to Bang? Why Bang? How do you know Bang?" He said this quietly, emphatically.

In a fit of self-definition and perhaps masochism, I almost told him flat out that I loved her and would do anything for her. I almost told him that she didn't love him, that she was just scared of him, that she loved me—only me. I mostly believed that. Perhaps even I could have sold that as the truth, but I stopped myself. By Big E's tone, I could tell he was hurting about Bang, and even with all he'd done, telling him that Bang was afraid of him would feel like shooting the civilian child to expose the enemy soldier.

Big E didn't knock me back down when I sat up again. He paced, now swinging a four-posted tire iron in one hand

and a pry bar in the other and banging them together in time like he was beating out the strokes for a sculling team. I continued: "Bang stole what she thought was the Cure from me, but that box contained the Velocity vaccine. It wasn't what she was searching for, but she couldn't pass up a Velocity. Who could?"

He glanced repeatedly at the office, barely paying attention to what I was saying. He stopped pacing. "Yeah, yeah, so where is the Cure?"

"Like I said, I delivered it to Damini." He slowed and scrunched his face. I didn't want him to think too much, so I gave him some specificity to distract him. "Tagler Building. I delivered it to 701."

The guy who had been standing on the chair was now twirling it. He said, "She does own the seventh floor, Big. We met with her there with the boss once, remember?"

"Yeah, I remember."

Big threw down his musical tire iron and pry bar then sprang up to the ceiling, grabbed a roof truss, and began swinging around from truss to truss. Finally, he dropped in front of me. He pulled his fist back but didn't hit me. "If you gave Damini the Cure, how did you end up with the box?"

"I picked it up when she was done. She didn't care, and you can sell those fridge boxes for cash, man." We all needed money. Money was food. I thought I sounded believable.

Maybe Damini wasn't after the Cure, or maybe Ratchet underestimated her intelligence network, but Big E was definitely after the Cure. He focused on it with more intensity than any E had the right to focus on anything. Not having the Cure made him furious, but Bang's duplicity made him gloomy. Big E's intentions and feelings danced awkwardly together on his features and showed clearly in his body language. He wouldn't be a very good liar, either.

"Can you give Ratchet some water and a KoolBar or something?" I said. "He's going to die if you don't."

Big glanced at Ratchet and smiled. He said, "No," then kicked my thigh as punctuation. He picked up the tire iron and pry bar and began ringing them together again.

A female E, who looked surprisingly like Bang but with even lighter hair and darker skin, came out of the office just then—someone I hadn't noticed when I first woke—and said, "He says to not kill them and to come in and tell him what you have."

Big hurled the pry bar at the wall of tires. It bounced up into the ceiling, clanged off a truss, then bounced to a stop near Ratchet, who was still running circles around the lift post he'd been chained to.

Ratchet needed help, but I was in no position to offer any. Yet now he eyed the pry bar every time he circled. It was near enough to him to get a foot on it, maybe drag it closer. Not wanting anyone to notice my attention on Ratchet, I watched Big Easy talking to the Slug in the office.

Energy didn't want to work for Slugs, but in the end, it was that, starve, or live off our parents—who were also Slugs. There were no other options. It just wasn't possible for an E to build a business, even an illegal one, deal with hour-to-hour assignments, personnel issues, finance, marketing for new customers, and so on. Working for a Slug was easier and far more likely to pay even if they treated us like trained circus dogs. Would Energy fare better under E-management? It seemed unlikely. No E had the concentration or long-term focus of intent to fill the role of boss.

The last time I remembered being on the floor for more than a few seconds was when I was still in SlowDown. The faculty did teach us some valuable lessons, not the least of which was to trust each other rather than trusting Slugs or teachers. The Slugs would do things, make decisions for us, that they thought were in our best interest, but weren't. And Slugs would never trust us because we weren't reliable in the way they thought of reliability. For us, reliability was more about intent than about actual follow-through. Follow-through was a fickle objective, almost always just out of reach.

OK, the faculty didn't intentionally teach us not to trust Slugs, but that was what we learned while they were teaching us mantras, yoga, Zen meditation, mathematical sequencing, and every other technique known for slowing down, directing, and focusing our brains and bodies. Some of the curriculum helped, but by the time I was enrolled, the teachers already knew we couldn't be cured, that the transition could not be impeded or overcome. They'd seen enough of us over the eight years before I arrived. They had had a success rate of exactly zero.

Big Easy's gang watched me warily while they each did their own thing, but they ignored Ratchet. I wobbled to my feet and began pacing a few steps each way, grunting and moaning and generally playing the wounded E, which I was. My eyes felt sticky, but wiping them just made my hands bloody and sticky too.

Not one of the E in the room looked mean or appeared irritated at me, although they were all hard to read. In other circumstances, we would all be dancing and playing E-games together, rather than each of us acting distrustful, rather than each of us living in our own world doing our own mathematical calming sequences or playing with PuzzLits and MushBalls. I didn't want any of them to get hurt, and I didn't want to get hurt myself, but Damini and the guy Big Easy worked for had fractured our unity, made us into two opposing gangs instead of one team. They made us enemies of each other. We couldn't live that way. We were barely surviving. We weren't thriving, though. We endured second to second, minute to minute, but our Slug masters kept us from optimism, kept us from hope for an improved future, kept us so insecure and dependent that we would steal from and perhaps even kill other E just to cling to that insecure, lonely, paranoid life.

Killing Big Easy was not the solution. That was the problem—too many E killing other E. And yes, maybe Big E was beyond help. He'd obviously taken a lot of enhancement drugs, but maybe he was still E enough to see where the E-world was headed. To see our end if this robbery and killing-for-hire kept up. I didn't know about other cities—New York and Seattle both had large criminal E-populations—but I suspected things were the same everywhere. How could they not be?

The Cure would have made the difference. With that, we would have been prized as scientists and engineers and philosophers and doctors and artists, but that future was on hold, maybe many years off. How many of us would die before then? Probably most of us.

Suddenly, one of the women stood right in front of me yelling, "Zip, what the fuck?" then she slapped me. I had stopped pacing and was standing completely still. Everyone had come a step closer. They all stared.

"What?" I said, then the whole shop tilted toward the garage door. I leaned to keep from falling. Even though I knew that I was still standing upright, I could not avoid leaning into the tilt. I started to fall, but the woman caught me and lowered me to the ground. If there was anything in my stomach at the time, she would have regretted that decision. I dry heaved for maybe ten seconds, then I heard a clang. I rolled over in time to see Ratchet dive through a window and hear the crash of glass.

Big E burst out of the office. "What the hell was that?"

I played dead on the floor, which was an easy part for me to play at the time.

"Stitch, Mocha, go after the stupid bastard. Kill him if you have to, but bring him back."

While I played dead on the floor, I focused on Ratchet's chances. He'd been running circles around the post for a long time, I didn't know exactly how long, but he'd looked worn out far beyond the point of exhaustion. I doubted they'd given him anything to eat or even any water. I figured his chances of escape at about zero. There was a lot of that going around.

Big E kicked me—not hard, but hard enough. "Come on, Zip, the boss wants to talk to you."

CHAPTER 38

S itting up caused a couple more dry heaves. My legs trembled and shuddered as I stood again. When I tried to walk to the boss's office, I only succeeded in wobbling side to side. Big E picked me up by my SkinSuit and carried me into the office away from his body like he might carry a bag of stinky trash.

The office was organized and clean. Not like an automotive shop at all. There was a small table off to the left with three chairs bunched close together so several other people at the table could stand. The walls were lined with shelves of paperwork in open-front boxes, presumably from when the shop was actually used as an automotive garage. The yellowed documents still contributed to the feel of an old-fashioned office, and with that came the sense that important things went on there. There was a large desk, behind which sat a balding, older Slug with a day-old beard, tightly curled, graying hair, and pale white skin. He wore a gray suit and a tie with a white shirt. A Stetson-style cowboy hat hung next to his desk on a wall hook. He had a mole on his left cheek and bushy gray eyebrows.

The Slug continued to look down at his screen while Big placed me in a chair in front of the desk, keeping a hand on my SkinSuit to keep me upright and maybe to keep me from doing anything stupid.

My vertigo dissipated, and my mind cleared.

Big said, "This is Zip, Mr. Swan."

Forever later, the boss, Mr. Swan, finally looked up at me and squinted thoughtfully, trying to intimidate me—which he did, because while he stared at me, he slowly withdrew a gun from under his left arm and placed it with great care on his desk, within easy reach of his right hand. I could have grabbed it before Swan could react, but he apparently trusted Big E to keep me firmly in my chair.

"I don't fool around, Zip," he said quietly. "I don't wait for an E to tell the truth or to answer my questions. An E is of no use to me if they aren't forthcoming and honest. I can always hire another one. Do you understand?"

I nodded.

"Good. Maybe I won't have to use this after all," he said, caressing his gun as though he might call it Mable and clean and polish it lovingly every day. "Tell me about the Cure, Zip. Where did it come from? Where is it now?" His teeth were straight and blazingly white.

Telling the truth sounded like a good idea. I stared at the gun and said, "It was shipped here from India, swapped out with a Velocity. Damini has it now." I tried to believe what I said.

"Hmmm. Damini? How do you know Damini has it? Big here says you gave it to her, but I don't believe that." He leaned forward and placed his hand on Mable. "I'm wondering if you took it yourself and are now trying to get Damini and me into a fight over it."

I swallowed. I couldn't help myself.

The boss leaned back and laughed. "You did! That's what you did." He seemed delighted by my audacity, or perhaps, my stupidity. "You're not a very good liar, are you?"

Not being able to move much because Big's hand was tightening on my SkinSuit, I shuffled my feet and played some finger games. Big E breathed heavily behind me, agitated. "Maybe I did," I said, "but if you kill me, then you lose the Cure completely. All the other sources are gone. They can make more from my blood." Big's grip squashed my shoulder and pinched my skin along with my suit. He would be strangling me with my own SkinSuit soon. It felt like he was already drawing blood.

Swan's triumphant expression told me the whole story. He beamed his victory, and I understood. I said, "You don't want Energy cured, do you? Why would you? Because if Energy were cured, then people like you and Damini wouldn't have us as cheap labor anymore, paying us in food and maybe a place to run. You would lose your workers, your business. You'd lose everything."

Swan brought up his gun and aimed it at me. Big E shouted, "Don't," and dove between us as Swan fired. Big's body carried me to the floor. A huge boom echoed, but it wasn't just the boss's gun—something had exploded inside the garage.

While I struggled to get out from under Big, Swan stepped around the desk. Big groaned as I rolled loose. The frosted door glass broke, Big took a swipe at Swan's legs, and I pulled myself up by the handle on a file cabinet. Swan brought up his gun again to shoot Ratchet, who had reached in the broken window to unlock the door. I dove for the gun, hitting the boss just as he fired. The bullet hit an illustration of an old Dodge Power Wagon next to the door. I pulled the gun free, and as I fell past Swan, I shot him point-blank in the heart. Swan was too slow. A slug for a Slug.

Tumbling to a stand as Ratchet entered the office, I noticed Damini through the big office window, surveying the scene in the garage. She appeared elegant in her bone-colored blouse with frills around the collar, her hair pulled up in a swirl, and earrings displaying a bright blue Ceylon sapphire contrasting beautifully with her brown skin. Her gaze slid slowly to her right until she looked directly at me. I brought up the gun and aimed it at her heart. She was a Slug. I had time to think about killing her. Killing Swan had been retribution for Big, it had been self-defense, it had been instantaneous and without thought. I could rationalize his death. Killing Damini would be premeditated, careful. I would be murdering her. Yes, she most likely planned to have me killed when the dust settled. Yes, she had killed a lot of E over the years. Her gang was killing Swan's E in the garage at that very moment, but there she stood in the garage and she was looking directly at me.

Could I live with killing her? I didn't know. There were a lot of E who would be more likely to live if she wasn't around. Maybe they would be poorer, maybe leaderless, but they would also be independent, still alive. I hesitated, wondering at my own lack of conscience, until I thought about Big Easy. Surprisingly, Big was the hero of the day. I hadn't expected him to save me, but then I guess it wasn't me he was saving when he dove between Swan and me. He was saving the Cure—surprisingly not just for himself, but for all Energy. He already knew he wasn't getting the Cure all to himself. If he could do that, maybe I could live with murdering someone. I believed at that moment that it wasn't about me. I would have known if I were lying.

Just as she started to show fear, I fired. I aimed for her heart, but the bullet shot through the glass and into her right eye. Her eye vanished, and a cloud of blood burst from the back of her head—an image I would be unable to forget, one that would pop into my mind whenever I was feeling altruistic or feeling like I was a good guy in a world of evil, to evoke both humility and resolve. Her face went slack, and her body collapsed slowly to the floor.

I heard four more shots in quick succession, then the garage was suddenly quiet. My heart beat wildly. I lost focus and the room tilted, then straightened. Damini's body was hidden from my view by the wall under the office window, but I knew she was lying there, leaking brains all over her nice bone-colored shirt and those pretty sapphire earrings.

When my focus returned, I understood that Damini would not have simply told Ratchet and me to go kill Big Easy and let it drop. Damini would have had us followed. She probably had her whole E-team and a few drones following us. We weren't important. Big Easy wasn't important. It was Big Easy's boss, Swan, she was after. We were pawns as usual, but this time the pawn had taken the queen and the king.

My plan to have Big Easy and Damini take care of each other had worked, although not the way I'd expected. We got

Damini on our side, and she intended retribution, just as I'd planned, but I hadn't expected to kill anyone myself. I hadn't expected to be a central part of a gang war, part of an invasion.

I kneeled to check on Big Easy. He wasn't dead, but he would be soon. He opened his eyes. "Did you really take the Cure yourself?" he asked.

"Bang injected me when Jbird shot the refrigeration. It was the only way to save it."

"She's such a quick thinker." He sighed long and slow. "Is she OK?"

"Yeah, Big. She's fine." I guess I lied effectively that time, because he smiled as he died. I had hated Big Easy, but now I understood that he was just another E who had been manipulated and coerced into becoming a bully and a killer working for someone else. It wasn't his fault at all. Not really. Energy everywhere were in the same situation. I hadn't been at it long enough to be fully drawn in until now. Now I was a killer too.

Ratchet came and knelt beside me. "Why did you shoot Damini? She was just standing there. She saved you."

"No, she wasn't just standing there, and no, she didn't save me. Big Easy saved me. Damini was intent on killing any E who worked for someone who was in competition with her. She wanted all the E-slaves for herself. What's more, she would have killed both of us because she doesn't want the Cure manufactured any more than this guy here did." I paused for a moment, working out who I was really trying to convince, then added, "And anyway, I didn't kill her; the boss here did, right?" I dropped the gun next to Swan.

"You're getting better at that," Ratchet said, "and I don't mean that as a compliment."

"I know, Ratchet."

Ratchet's face was pale and sagging. He was clearly beyond simply tired, but I was so dizzy I needed him to help me walk. We stepped over the bodies of the boss and Big Easy, then Ratchet helped me into the garage. Four bodies lay bleeding out, dead on the floor. Three E and Damini. All three E were Big Easy's people, including the woman who had kept me from falling when I had the spell of vertigo. The room reeked of guns, blood, and motor oil. I guess I reeked of it too.

Damini's pro was there. He held a gun on me and leaned into the office, considering the scene as Ratchet and I exited. "Who shot Damini?" he asked, staring into my eyes.

"The Slug," I said. "He shot Big Easy too, although he was trying to shoot me at the time."

The Pro continued to stare at me, then at Ratchet, then at Swan and Big Easy lying in a heap by the desk. I think he knew that wasn't quite the truth, but his expression was controlled.

I shook loose of Ratchet. Aware that my face and hands were bloody from my falls and my suit was grimy and torn, aware that I was known as a screw-up and a recently transitioned E, I still stepped into the chaos of the garage and shouted, "Listen! We need to clean this up quickly." I turned to the Pro. "Send someone to get your cleanup crew, I'm sure Damini had one on call." There were three of Big E's people still alive, under guard and lined up along the tire wall. I pointed at them. "Let them go. Damini, Swan, and Big Easy are all dead. It's time Energy quit pointing guns at each other."

Then I turned to the Pro who hadn't moved except to pull out his washers and play with them. "Well?" I said.

He hesitated, thinking, then looked around the garage at the other E there. He glanced back into the office at Big Easy and Swan, then turned back to me. "Yeah, OK." Then he yelled, "Jinx, you know who to get. Go get them."

Jinx hesitated only a moment. He, like everyone else, was wound up by the tense situation and ready to run. Once the Pro shifted, everyone else suddenly felt released, and the garage emptied in a flash.

The Pro studied me carefully before he eased out the door following everyone else.

Ratchet settled me onto the concrete. "You're in bad shape, Zip."

"Help me to the hospital, Ratchet. The one Bang is in."

"Good idea. Dr. Argent is probably still there seeing about Bang, so he can watch them treat you too."

Sure, that's why I wanted to go there. Because of Dr. Argent. I laughed. Ratchet looked at me funny, and I remembered Damini's face when she looked at me through the office window, just before I shot her dead. Every time I remembered her standing there, she became a little prettier, a little softer, and her eyes became a little more pleading. I stopped laughing and I cried. Ratchet tried not to notice.

CHAPTER 39

The hospital put bandages on my hip, knees, and right elbow, inserted a Quick-Gen tooth, pulled a toothpick-sized splinter out of my neck, and stitched up my lips, my nose, and a gouge on the back of my head. In the mirror, I looked like I'd been hit in the face with a chunk of concrete, which was exactly what had happened if you think of Bang's concrete floor as a large chunk of concrete.

Dr. Argent had been at the hospital when we arrived but disappeared before I could ask about Bang. He had taken care to explain to the surgeon that I needed to use up energy while they worked on me, so they'd given me a plastic-coated sheet of mathematical puzzles. That was enough. I didn't feel all that antsy except when they worked on the cut above my eye. Luckily, they didn't have to stitch that one. They just glued it back together and bonded it with UV light.

Still, I was eager the whole time to find out how Bang was.

I had just put my shabby SkinSuit back on when Argent entered my room.

"How is Bang?" I asked.

"What? Oh. She'll be OK. She lost a good bit of blood, broke two ribs, and had some internal bleeding in her lung from the bullet, but she's in an induced temp-coma until she's well enough to move around more." He smiled encouragingly. "You guys heal ridiculously fast. I expect she may be out of here in another couple hours, if they can even keep her that long."

"And Ratchet? He was in almost as bad a shape as me."

"We found him some food and electrolytes, did a little glue-up. He left a while ago."

Examining my face, he said, "You look better, believe it or not. They did a good job."

"Can I go see Bang now?"

Dr. Argent slumped into the guest chair. "You know that's not going to happen, don't you? They don't let any Energy out of their rooms except to leave. You must already know that's the rule. I'm sorry."

I was sorry too, but at least she was alive and in good hands. I'd see her soon. The Hole in the Roof Gang would ride again.

"What about the Cure? Is my blood going to work?"

"Zip, I have no idea. I just drew it and stored it. The real world moves slowly, remember."

"Yeah, slowly." I'd been relatively quiet and still for a while and desperately needed to run. The hospital had fed me two cans of LiquidFood, which were working well, so I bowed to the doctor and darted to the door, but it was locked from the outside.

"You have to wait for an escort, you know that."

This was my first time in a hospital, so I didn't know that, but it made sense. The doctor knocked on the door and said, "Escort needed."

Four long, slow minutes later, I walked out the hospital door, and it felt like I was walking out of prison. Cagle was dead, Big Easy was dead, Damini was dead, even Swan was dead. Bang was OK, Ratchet was OK, I was OK.

And all the damn boxes were gone.

I used up more of the money Cagle had given me for the delivery of that original box on some peanut butter in a squeeze-tube, a SlamGo exercise drink, and a KoolBar, stopped by my apartment, showered, put on my other Skin, then slowly ran the streets of Chicago for the next hour, trying to feel free and easy, trying to feel like everything would be great now that Cagle wasn't directing my life, now that I had autonomy—a very worrisome autonomy. I ran past the smoky ruins of Cagle's building which were still surrounded by police and fire engines flashing blue and red and white, and news vans with intense lights shining on reporters. I ran past the Tagler Building, past my aunt's house—she'd finally gone to bed—past Dr. Argent's office building, then his apartment where police were still puzzling out Jbird's body, past the auto repair garage where the area was sublimely quiet and inky, past Chen's Chinese.

I intended to run past Bang's apartment but instead hopped up on the BodMod building and climbed in. The door was open, and there was a blood smear across the floor where they'd dragged me. I cleaned a little, pushed the door closed, and pulled out Bang's lavender stick. Feeling a little woozy, I suddenly sat, took a sniff of lavender, then let myself sleep.

CHAPTER 40

Zane, now Zip, is just out of SlowDown, just fully transitioned. He runs most of the time because in SlowDown they had tried hard to keep him from running. He is living in his own apartment. No one cares where he is, or what he is doing, or who he is doing it with. No one cares if he comes back covered in bruises and cuts and lumps, because there is no one there to care.

He'd found parkour on the internet before his parents sent him to SlowDown, just as he was figuring out how high and far he could jump, how strong his legs, arms, and back had become. He'd imagined hopping from stairway to roof, then leaping out to a lamppost and swinging to the ground like the people in the vids. While he stayed in SlowDown, he'd had no idea what his full abilities were. The staff limited the kids' activities, but if regular kids could parkour around town, he knew he could too. He had also watched anime and Chinese cinema characters doing amazing acrobatic things, but he decided he needed to work his way up to that level.

Now, a couple days out of SlowDown, he runs just to watch the city go by in a blur. Of course, because Energy vision is attuned to higher speeds (and because even though he feels like he is running faster than his vision, he isn't), the city isn't really a blur, which is disappointing, but running full-out does invigorate him rather than tire him. Motion is the best, most important thing in his life for the few days after SlowDown. He builds stamina and coordination until he is running roofs, then leaping the space between, then running up the side of walls as far as momentum will carry him and flipping or catching railings, flag poles, drain pipes, and electrical conduits to vault up onto another, higher roof.

On the fourth night, because by then he has learned that during the day there are considerably too many people on the street to run long distances, he decides to run for distance and gets lost on Chicago's North Side. The last street name he can remember is Clybourn, but he can't find his way back. He brought some food and a little money, but he went through the last of that twenty minutes earlier. Still, he is having fun, running and vaguely wondering where he is, then he suddenly isn't having fun anymore. A surreal sense of his speed confuses him, and his hunger abruptly becomes debilitating.

Zip leaps across a narrow alley from one flat roof to the next, which is only one story higher, misses, and Wile E. Coyotes himself flat against the metal siding opposite, then plummets into a dumpster. His hand smacks on the open lid. It is a recycling dumpster, mostly full of cardboard, but the fall still hurts.

He lays there thinking how annoyed the recycling people are going to be when they find a batch of their material has been contaminated by a body when he distinctly hears hysterical laughter, the kind of laughter where you laugh so hard you can't breathe and so you hiccough and laugh some more.

In a moment, a girl's face appears over the edge of the bin.

Short blonde hair, big engaging smile, and laughing eyes, about his age. "Comfortable?" she asks, then giggles some more.

"I got tired and decided to lie down for a rest," Zip says, trying to act calm and sensible while lying in a dumpster, legs and arms akimbo.

The smile stops. She hops onto the edge, gripping the corner for support. "You hurt?"

"Just my dignity," Zip says. "And maybe my butt . . . and my knees and elbows . . . and my hand. Otherwise, A-OK."

She steps softly into the dumpster beside him, smiling again. "I'm Bang," she says. "Can you climb out on your own, or do you need help?"

He looks at her for the longest time. Neck to toe, all that is visible are her hands and her face; everything else is covered with a loose blue shirt and pants and some kind of specialty shoe. She isn't the first E he's met on the outside, but she is the first he's been alone with, and the dumpster feels intimate and friendly. She smiles more on the left than the right, and her eyes are a soft and inviting gray. She's apparently been E longer than he has—her shoulders, upper arms, hips, and thighs are muscular and out of standard proportion, but that seems just right to him.

She pats a tune on the metal. "I see another boy has fallen for me."

"If I'd known you were there, I would have been more graceful about it."

She mocks an indignant, "You didn't know I was there? Well, I never . . . ." Then she adds, "You need help to escape, or are you going to continue your nap?"

"Oh," he says, "I think I can get out," but when he tries, he shakes so much he falls in again. Cold chills emanate from his shoulders and chest, then flow to his hands and feet. He might have starved to death here, and no one would have known. He feels his body curling into a ball.

"Have you eaten in the last five or ten?"

"No, I got lost and ate everything I had with me."

Bang takes a KoolBar out of her holster, unwraps it, and gives it to him. He eats it while twitching and wiggling and trying to focus on her face. He doesn't want to forget her face. When he finishes the KoolBar, she helps him climb out of the bin and onto hard, if sticky, ground. They are in an alley between two angled streets.

"It's pretty hard to get lost in Chicago," she says. "All you have to do is head east until you hit LSD or the lake. And by the way, when someone gives you her name, it's customary to give her yours."

"Oh, Zip. I'm Zip."

"Really? Not much of a name, is it." She giggles, pleased with her own joke, although Zip is a little touchy about it.

"Well, it's mine," he says, "even if it isn't worth much."

"Sorry. It just surprised me, that's all. Where to?"

The KoolBar's energy makes him vibrate. He's feeling like himself again. "I live near LaSalle and Ohio."

"You need to get with it, Zip. All the cool kids call those streets LaSally and Obyo now. The old names are for the gov and the parents."

"OK, I live near LaSally and Obyo."

"You're a long way from home."

"Seeing the sights. The view from this dumpster, for instance, was worth the trip all by itself."

Bang pulls her head back slightly, tilts it to the side, raises her left eyebrow, then looks him up and down. She suddenly laughs out loud, a clear, pleasant, genuine laugh. "I think you may have whacked your head. I'd better run you home," she says, and as she takes off like a released rubber band, she adds, "Follow me," over her shoulder. Zip is energized by the KoolBar but has to press himself to keep up, working the pain out of his muscles and bones and flexing his banged-up hand, but he revels in watching her run so smoothly and efficiently—floating evenly along the sidewalk like a glider, like she doesn't have a care. When they get to known ground, he continues to follow her instead of telling her he knows the way.

When she slows at Ohio (Obyo), first jogging at the traffic light, then dodging through the cars when the traffic lightens, she says, "Do you have food at home? Are you stocked?"

"Yeah, I'm stocked pretty well."

She turns as she runs and looks him up and down. "Are you now?"

Zip isn't used to flirting and stumbles, then mumbles something incoherent even to himself.

"You just out of SlowDown?" she asks.

"Yeah." He wants to sound like he's been around, but his newness is apparently obvious.

"Some of the stuff they stock you with at the beginning is pretty good, but most of it is crap. It has the vitamins and minerals and all that, but not nearly enough calories."

When they stop at Obyo, she adds, "Your parents aren't paying for your apartment, are they? This really isn't a good place to be. There aren't any shops down here that carry E-food. There aren't any other E down here, but I suppose the area is cheap."

She trots with him to his apartment, and, when he opens the door, she walks in like they've known each other for years, like they are old friends. Zip thinks it is the sweetest thing anyone has done for him in a long time. She runs once around the room.

"There's nowhere to run here. Come winter this place is going to suck big time." She isn't being mean, just analytical, practical. "Well, try not to get lost, and carry more food and water with you. That's what all those pockets and pouches in that ridiculously old-fashioned SkinSuit you're wearing are for. And remember, go east and you'll always hit the lake eventually."

Zip finally gets up the gumption to talk just as she opens the door to leave. "Would you show me what to buy for food instead of the stuff they gave me to start?"

Her hair flashes when she spins a couple turns. "Sure, somebody has to, or you'll probably starve. Hey, don't be so down about it. Everyone suffers through the learning phase. SlowDown really doesn't do much except make you think you're still kind of normal when you're not. I've only been out for a few months, but I've had some people show me around. I'm just passing it on, just like you'll pass it on in a few months. Clybourn and Division. At 2:47:47. Don't be late and bring some money."

And then she is gone in a flash.

CHAPTER 41

Sniffing the lavender stick again didn't return me to my dream, so I left Bang's apartment, closing the window behind me. The Hole in the Roof Gang's hideout wasn't far, but when I hopped up, part of the roof gave way and I tumbled down to the floor. With the roof almost wide open, it didn't feel like a hideout anymore, which saddened me. Later, in the alley alcove where we'd tried to figure out a plan, I fingered the damage to the wall where Jbird's bullet had scared us into action.

The whole time, I fretted about what I would do now that I had no job or direction, but instead I kept coming back to Bang. She'd betrayed me, then she'd betrayed me again, but she was a victim of Slug manipulations just like everyone else. And she'd paid for it.

I arrived in front of the hospital and spent time trotting circles, feeling anxious, worried, and hopeful at the same time, but mostly feeling dismally alone, which is the way I'd felt for a long time, ever since SlowDown really, but I hadn't had the attention span to dwell on it. Now it seemed I did, and I didn't like it.

Finally, Bang was escorted out. She looked torn up but ready to run. She set off north toward her apartment, so I fell in beside her matching her rapid pace. When she noticed me, her brilliant smile was my reward for being there. She dove into my arms, or perhaps I dove into hers. Concern that she didn't love me, that her previous expressions were just another feint, another lie, vanished in a flash of genuine blissful exuberance as we swung our partner and do-si-doed down the middle of the empty street.

"You're alive!" she said.

"Yeah," I said, and we pulled each other close and kissed. I wanted to stay in that kiss, to remain in the sweet moment, but Bang was off in a joyous flash, spinning and running and laughing toward her apartment. Her happiness at finding me alive made me flush with pleasure. The touch of her kiss and the pressure of her hug lingered as she ran off. She'd been cooped up for a few hours, and I'd been running for a while, but I wondered if she would ever be able to slow down and think about us, slow down enough to tarry in my arms without thinking about pears or ice cream or cheeseburgers. I held the delicious sense of the hug and kiss for a moment before I jetted off after her.

Along the way, I gave her back her Wonky and most of her ErgBombs and money. Her lavender stick remained in my pocket. We stopped by a Q store for food. No checkout, just grab and run if your face is registered. My face wasn't registered—they wouldn't give me credit—but Bang bought ice cream and pears, which evoked a sweet memory. I dumped four ZapCheeseBurgers and two BiteSticks into the bag for the road.

As we trotted toward Bang's room and munched on our BiteSticks, I told Bang what had happened while she was in the hospital, about the standoff with Big Easy in front of Dr. Argent's apartment building, about the doctor taking my blood to work on another vaccine, about Damini's orders and threats, about Big E's toughs breaking down her door—which was still broken—and about the garage, but I couldn't tell her about my spells of vertigo, or that I'd killed Damini, only that she'd died there.

At her apartment, Bang and I used a splinter from the door to wedge the door firmly back into the doorway. She'd have to use the window until she found someone to fix it properly. When we were done, we had some ice cream while stuttering around and bouncing awkwardly off each other like little kids who like each other but can't figure out how to express their feelings. I wanted to ask about Big Easy. Bang's gaze focused everywhere but on me.

Eventually, I stopped by the sink and watched her body as she fast-walked the length of the apartment and back. Bang reached around me to grab a pear, and I grabbed her. We spun around. She bit into the pear and held it in her teeth, and I bit into the pear, and we each took our bite. While we chewed, she set the pear down, slid off her clothes and wiggled up to sit on the sink. Her eyes were wet and a little wild, and I wanted to go slow and savor our moment, savor the intensity. Bang moved with urgency, though, taking hummingbird breaths, and the moment went by in an instant of exuberance and joy and sweetness. I hugged her, but not too tightly, worrying about her ribs.

Bang slid off the sink, picked up the pear, and danced away twirling and giggling. "That was nice," she said.

"Definitely overdue," I said, a reverse echo of our previous encounter. The conversational repetition was a way for the two of us to feel like we were still the people we were before, but we weren't. She was still Bang, but I wasn't really Zip anymore. I was an aware Zip, a partially focused Zip, a Zip who longed for moments to last just a little longer. I was Zip-Zane or Zane-Zip or something. But I was not the Zip I had been.

And I'd killed someone.

We swayed around the room. She tripped over my foot, and as she fell, we twirled into an embrace and rolled to the floor. We made love again, easing into it, rolling over and over down the room to bleed off energy. When we were up and in the shower doing a hand-slap game, Bang hesitated, then said, "The pear is only half gone," then raced, dripping, to the sink and grabbed the pear with two bites taken out. With her bandages off, I could see the stitches that sealed the bullet hole. A little to the left and she would not have made it.

She'd finished the pear by the time I'd dried off and made it to the sink. She looked at the wall, then at my feet. "I have a commission I have to do before morning."

Who did she work for other than Big E?

"Business comes first," I said, and, although I understood that to be the truth, I didn't want to part, not yet, not with my desire for a longer partnership unexpressed, but I dressed and said my goodbyes and climbed out the window.

On the street, I pulled out Bang's lavender stick and flicked it once. I tried to capture the scent, but it moved too fast in the breeze, and then it dissipated.

CHAPTER 42

A half mile from my apartment, Damini's pro appeared suddenly right beside me, fast-walking in sync, like we'd been walking together for a while.

"I see you survived," he said. It was a statement, nothing more.

"Yes."

"You look like shit, like someone took you apart and sewed you back together."

"Thanks. You here to harass me or shoot me?" We continued at street level, crossed another busy street, and turned toward my apartment.

"Tell me why you shot Damini." He said it in a conversational tone, but there was menace in it.

"That Slug, Swan, killed Damini. They were rivals, I guess." I increased speed to a run even though that might imply I was lying. But I had to run.

He grabbed my arm and spun me toward him, making me stumble then stagger to a stop. "No," he said, cold as gunmetal, "you killed her. There was blood on that gun. Swan's hands weren't bloody. Yours were. Don't bullshit me, Zip. I'm not in the mood. There are a whole lot of us without an income because of you. Why did you kill Damini?"

He kept his right hand in his pocket. The Pro had that head tilt that Cagle used to use, but the Pro carried it off. Beyond him, a block away, Ratchet and Damini's muscle appeared vibrating side by side, watching us.

I'd killed her because I'd had time to think about it. I'd killed her because I didn't just drop the gun and run, which is what the old Zip would have done. He would have paid for that lack of decisive action later, but he would have dropped the gun and run, no doubt about it.

To the Pro, I said, "I shot her because she would have killed me. I don't know if you've heard, but Ratchet smuggled a cure for us all the way from Bangalore before the big monsoons destroyed the whole place."

"Yeah, I heard," he said.

I turned and started trotting again. "That Cure should enable us to slow down enough to talk to Slugs when necessary, at least for short periods of time, maybe find honest jobs, maybe see our families, maybe . . . well, maybe lots of things. But one of Big Easy's gang shot the box the Cure was in, and it had to be used or it would be useless. So, Bang gave it to me."

"And that's a reason for me not to kill you? I don't see it that way."

"No. I also killed her because she would have killed the rest of Big Easy's people at the garage, then she would have killed everyone else who worked for him, then all the E who worked for Cagle because even though I think Cagle worked for her, she wasn't the forgiving type. She would have kept the remainder of you in so much debt to her that you'd have no other alternatives, no options but to work for her—to steal and kill for her."

"That's your excuse?"

"It's going to be hard for a while, but it had to be done. Shoot me now, or hold me until the Cure is perfected again, then shoot me, but I would have done the same thing, even if I'd known you would kill me in the end. I still would have shot her to save everybody else."

"You talk a lot."

We ran on for six blocks, me waiting for a bullet while the Pro was either considering letting me go or choosing the best place to shoot me where there were no cameras and the police wouldn't show up too quickly. Ratchet and the Muscle still followed us, keeping their distance.

Finally, the Pro said, "Head for Chen's Chinese. You know where it is."

Yes, I knew where it was, and I didn't find the destination encouraging. "Maybe you could just let me go. I'm not really a threat."

"No, you're not a threat. Chen's, now."

As far as I knew, all the top Slug leadership of the two E-gangs were dead, leaving the Chicago Energy in a tenuous and dangerous situation. And yes, it was my fault. Perhaps I could discover job opportunities for some of us, at least the older ones who had learned to slow down a little. The Pro, Ratchet, Cricket, the people who were used to working directly for the Slugs, but the rest? Who would hire the likes of us? We were only couriers and thieves to them. There weren't all that many courier jobs and even fewer open to Energy. We were fast but not reliable, and reliability is the main reason someone might use a private courier instead of a drone company.

Maybe half of the E in Chicago received what they needed to live from their parents. They could dance and eat and run without worry. But the rest of us—the ones whose parents had either rejected us because we were no longer the kids they brought up or because they just couldn't afford our food and rent—the rest of us had to support ourselves, preferably doing something that contributed to the world in a way that made us more welcome in the Slug world.

As we ran up to Chen's, Carrot, Quake, Quip, and others watched us from across the street. When we entered the restaurant, it felt like an execution scene from the old movies I'd seen when I was Zane. Everyone gathered to watch the hanging.

Inside, there were four other E: Jinx, who had gone to get the cleanup crew at the garage; the man who stood next to Big Easy when he killed Jbird; the woman who had called Big Easy into Swan's office and looked a bit like Bang; and Cricket. Ratchet and Damini's muscle followed us into the restaurant.

Cricket said, "Glad it worked out, Gato. Expected you to show up alone."

The Pro, whose name was apparently Gato, grunted and walked me over to the table where Damini had held court. Damini's muscle moved behind him. Big Easy's man came up to the table, and the woman from Swan's office stood behind him. Ratchet looked uncomfortable for a moment, then stood behind me. It felt like a gang summit of three main players and their seconds. Why was I at the table? And why did Ratchet stand behind me?

Damini's pro, Gato, said, "What's the plan?"

I looked back at Ratchet in confusion. He whacked my shoulder. "You're the one with the plans, Zip. We need one now."

Gato, who seemed to be the most respected person in the room, had chosen me of all people as the leader, at least for now. I'd passed the test apparently, and the responsibility was mine because the problem was of my making. They expected me to clean it up.

How had it come to this? Was it Ratchet's doing? Was it due to my actions after the garage deaths—my focused response to the incident? Or was it my willingness to kill Damini, showing I could think about a future farther away than the next meal? Responsibility was the one thing I had carefully avoided since I'd become Zip. Now they placed me in the position of leadership because I was the most deliberate thinker. They twitched, jerked, and shuddered. No one wanted to be there. They wanted to be running, eating, but they stayed, waiting for me to say something.

It would be me, or it would be some Slug underlings of Swan and Damini who would decide to take over their boss's business. The E in that room, the E outside, the E all over the city didn't want Slugs to always be in charge if there was any other choice.

"First," I said, "we stop killing each other. Are we agreed that all feuds and divisions among us are ended?"

Every E in the room jerked his or her head up and down,

urgently wanting to speed up the meeting, to run, but forcing themselves to focus long enough to see what would happen.

I wanted to say more—that we needed to stop stealing from and disturbing the Slugs, that we needed to find ways of showing our worth, that we had to find ways to work together. If we didn't, new laws would slowly suffocate us, the police would jail us, and the Slugs would hate us more and more. That disassociation wasn't the future I envisioned. I wanted to say that we just had to keep up a good effort long enough for Dr. Argent and his people to recreate the Cure, then we could break loose of our bonds and become the people we were destined to be.

But I couldn't say that. The E standing around were already twitchy. Their whole future was anxiety inducing. They were already hungry and ready to run, and I was too.

So instead, I said, "Damini and Swan must have had networks of Slugs who worked for them. Some of their business dealings had to be legitimate so they could hide the money they made off us. Who were the seconds-in-command to Damini and Swan? Get that information to me, and we'll go from there. Also, make me a list of all the E who currently have jobs that aren't illegal, like Quip the bartender over at the Long Ochre. Meet back here in half an hour."

The room emptied almost as quickly as the garage had. I did some knee bends, waved my hands around, and jogged once around the room to relieve some anxiety. A feeling of dread thudded through my veins.

Sleep. Ratchet was there, so I felt safe enough, but I didn't want to talk about it, I just wanted to sleep, so I leaned up against the bar and snapped off.

For the first time since I became E, I dreamed about the

future. I dreamed of a time when the Cure was perfected. I dreamed of spooning with Bang on a bed. I dreamed of talking to my aunt about some new movie I'd seen, and I dreamed of a jerky, spastic line of Energy waiting for their shot at freedom.

When I woke, Ratchet handed me a VegieTofuCube and a handful of almond cookies. "You going to stick this out, or were you just talking to get away from Gato?"

I danced out of the dining room and into the foyer, twirled an imaginary hat, bounced on one foot, and hummed a quick chorus of "The Michigan Rag." "No, Ratchet," I said. "I have a plan."

Ratchet stared at me for a few heartbeats, which seemed like ages for an E who had already been focused for a long time. He said, "You're not lying to me, are you?"

"No," I said, "you'd know if I was lying."

But I wasn't so sure of that. Not anymore.

In physics, the definition for velocity isn't the same as the definition for speed. Speed is distance over a period of time, like kilometers per second. But velocity is speed with a specific direction, like kilometers per second, northeast. Energy had all the speed we could handle. What we needed was a course, an objective to aim at to make progress. We needed not just speed, but velocity.

Velocity would make a good name for a cat.

CPSIA information can be obtained
at www.ICGtesting.com
Printed in the USA
LVHW010714090621
689682LV00013B/489